# MURDER IN THE MIX

A Shilpa Solanki Mystery Book 3

MARISSA DE LUNA

BLOODHOUND
— BOOKS —

First published in 2022 by Bloodhound Books.

www.bloodhoundbooks.com

Print ISBN: 978-1-5040-8244-0

# Also by Marissa De Luna

*For Neha, Subrina and Jigna*

# Chapter One

S hilpa heard a scream and ran to the window. It was pitch black outside. The lamp, which had functioned intermittently since their arrival, chose this moment to fail. She opened the door and shouted to her friend, but no reply came. Robin should have been back by now. And where was her best friend Tanvi and her boyfriend Brijesh? The scream was high-pitched and shrill. Definitely female.

'Murder's beginning to follow you around,' Tanvi had joked with her earlier in the evening, and Shilpa had laughed away her comments, but inside something had stirred. It played on her mind now with that blood-curdling scream coming from somewhere on the island.

There was something eerie about Dreamcatcher Island, and Shilpa had sensed it as soon as she had stepped ashore. The immaculate mansion and gardens in the dead of winter felt false, like they were masking a dark secret.

Shilpa grabbed her coat from the stand, and flashlight and mobile phone from the console table and stepped out of the cottage, shutting the door firmly behind her. She pushed away the uneasy feeling. The scream came again. This time longer and louder.

She tried to place where it was coming from. Using her torch, she carefully opened the old wooden gate that led from the walled garden of Rose Cottage into the grounds of Dreamcatcher Mansion.

She raced towards the infinity pool and the lower terrace, its large grey porcelain tiles illuminated by the yellow light emanating from carefully placed orbs. She heard a noise from the vicinity of the house and looked towards it. A couple of the upstairs windows were open. Surely someone else had heard the screams.

'Is anyone there?' she called.

Silence.

Shilpa shone the flashlight towards the boathouse and bay. She couldn't see anything, but she could hear distant voices. She crept down the stone steps, straining to hear the muffled tones. She stopped on the first step and pulled out her phone from her coat pocket. There was no reception on the island unless she was huddled over the wifi in the cottage. She sent Tanvi a quick text message and stared at her phone, waiting for the progress bar to reach the end, but it failed. As she slipped her phone back into her pocket she noticed that her hands were trembling.

Shilpa made her way down to the bay. She lost her balance once, nearly slipping on the wet stone. Whoever had designed this house hadn't thought of late-night revellers wanting to explore in the dead of night. But then Shilpa supposed that's what the guests liked about the place. The feeling that they were free, not being wrapped in cotton wool like they would be in a five-star hotel.

Although everything else about Dreamcatcher Mansion was five star: the luxurious bedrooms and bathrooms, the cinema room and the exquisite food – if last night's meal was anything to go by. Shilpa turned and looked behind her. She didn't feel free on Dreamcatcher Island. She felt like she was being watched.

Shilpa reached the bottom of the steps and followed the path towards the beach. It was then that she heard giggling. She followed the noise, the torch by her side. In the distance she saw three people. She raised her light. They were standing around a body.

## Chapter Two

S hilpa walked over the small pebbles towards the group. As she neared, she held up her flashlight towards the body. She instantly recognised the dress. 'What's happened here?' she asked.

'Shilpa,' said one of the people standing around the body.

She lifted her light towards the voice. 'Robin?' Shilpa's heart skipped a beat. The last time they were together they had been walking off the apple brandy that they had consumed after dinner. Shilpa had wanted a clear head for the morning when she was due to teach a class and put the finishing touches on the birthday cake she had been commissioned to make.

But as they had headed back to the cottage, Felicity Grave had called to him. 'Excuse me,' she had shouted in a friendly but shrill voice that went through Shilpa. 'Do you mind giving me a hand with this?' She had pointed to a large metal case.

'Sure,' Robin had called back. He had given Shilpa's hand a squeeze and had leapt up the steps towards the patio where Felicity stood in a twenties' red-and-black Charleston dress, her blonde curls kept in place by an exquisite black flapper headpiece studded with crystals.

Robin had lifted up the heavy case, and Shilpa had walked back to Rose Cottage alone.

Half an hour later, Shilpa had heard that blood-chilling scream.

Her friends were standing over Felicity's lifeless body. Shilpa tried to examine the woman's face, but it was twisted away.

'What do you think?' Tanvi said.

'What do you mean?'

Felicity's face turned. Her mascara had run and her lipstick was smeared. She opened one eye. 'Convincing enough?' she asked with a grin.

Shilpa took a breath, her heartbeat beginning to slow. 'What are you doing?' she asked, irritated by Felicity's performance.

The woman sat up. 'Am-dram at school,' she said, her eyes sparkling. 'Was I credible? We're doing a murder-mystery thingy tomorrow night. I'm playing the victim.'

Shilpa forced a smile to her lips and nodded.

An hour later they were back at Rose Cottage. Tanvi and Brijesh had walked Felicity back to Dreamcatcher Mansion and had returned with a bottle of champagne. A thank you from Felicity for their efforts.

'Bit of a drama queen,' Shilpa said as Tanvi opened the bottle.

'She just wants everyone to have a good time,' Robin said.

Shilpa gave Robin a look. 'What was in the case?' she asked. She took a glass from Tanvi and leaned back into the sofa.

'She wanted it in the boathouse. Mumbled something about her birthday tomorrow.'

'They gave us strict instructions not to fraternise with the family,' Shilpa said.

'Maybe she's got a secret stash of weed or whisky. The annual Dreamcatcher Island firework show is on tomorrow for New Year's. It's a big thing. Something paying guests come back for year after year,' Tanvi said. 'She probably wants some supplies on the beach.' Tanvi took a sip of her drink. 'This whole set-up is a bit bizarre though, don't you think? A millionaire, his wife and ex-wife all on the island together with their kids.'

'It's all for Felicity,' Brijesh said. 'Her big thirtieth. I overheard her telling Gina that this has been a dream of hers.'

'Her stepsister?' Tanvi asked.

'Rashmi's daughter. Rashmi is Alan Grave's second and current wife. Sounded like Gina and Felicity are close though,' Brijesh said. 'They were huddled on the boat together and then walked from the ferry to the house arm in arm.'

'They would have grown up together on weekends and the like,' Shilpa said.

'And the two wives just get on? Not possible, if you ask me,' said Tanvi.

'You think some kind of polygamy is going on?' Robin asked.

'Don't even think about it,' Shilpa said. 'The journalist stays at home this weekend. You promised.' Robin leaned over and kissed her on the cheek. She stood up.

'Don't go,' Tanvi said. 'You've barely touched your glass.'

'I've got a big day tomorrow,' Shilpa said.

'I'm right behind you,' said Robin.

## Chapter Three

Just yesterday, before the Grave family had arrived with their amateur dramatics, Shilpa had watched from the kitchen window of the cottage as Robin attempted to navigate the bay. Her boyfriend had been making light work of rowing the little wooden vessel towards the boathouse. After a moment Shilpa had lost him behind the thick magnolia tree. He was returning with groceries for their New Year's Eve dinner. Shilpa hadn't wanted him to leave. The vessel didn't look seaworthy and she didn't like being alone in the cottage.

Grey clouds hovered above and threatened rain. This was a far cry from the brilliant blue skies she had been lying under just a fortnight ago, on a beach lounger in Goa.

Goa. It had been everything she imagined, from the locals' warm welcome to the fresh seafood and spicy curries. Her best friend Tanvi had taken to the beach parties that were once infamous, but Shilpa preferred to spend her time exploring the historic churches of Old Goa, and reading on a beach lounger, drinking *nimbu pani* – fresh lime soda – and Kingfisher beer and eating poppadoms stuffed with delicately spiced prawns. Shilpa closed her eyes and recalled the warm sea breeze that invigorated her senses every time she stepped onto Palolem Beach.

Tanvi and Brijesh, Robin and she had had the perfect holiday, and they had returned with a bad case of the post-holiday blues. It was then that Tanvi had suggested they did something different for New Year's Eve.

Shilpa was ever ready. She still had a steady stream of her regular orders supplying bakeries in Otter's Reach, Mermaid Point and Dartmouth, but the orders for her occasion cakes had slowed, and she could afford to take a few days off. She and Tanvi had looked in earnest for places to stay, but everything from a converted monastery near Smuggler's Cove to the luxury resort on Burgh Island was fully booked.

'Why is everything so booked up?' Tanvi had complained. 'It's not like you can spend the day at the beach at this time of year.' At the time, the wind had been whipping up Otter's Reach Estuary below Shilpa's house in the way that she loved. There was something about the South Devon coast in winter. It was raw. It was real.

The two of them had eventually given up their search. Brijesh, Tanvi's doting other half, had mocked them. 'Quitters,' he had said, noting their large glasses of Gavi and forlorn faces.

'Shilpa's going to host,' Tanvi said. 'We're going to have an exquisite banquet here with champagne and cocktails.'

'Am I?' Shilpa had asked. 'I'm not sure I like the sound of that.'

'You've got Robin to help,' Tanvi had said with a smirk.

Shilpa and Robin had barely been dating a couple of months when they went to Goa together.

'First trip,' Tanvi had said, 'is make or break.'

Shilpa couldn't have asked for a better travel companion, and so when they returned home and the owner of Robin's rental in Saltmarsh Creek gave him notice, Shilpa impulsively asked him if he wanted to move in.

Robin's nature and seascape photographs were beginning to appear on her walls, and her home was slowly turning into their home. She didn't mind too much. She supposed she was still in that honeymoon phase because when Tanvi said his name, she had to refrain from blushing.

Shilpa had eventually accepted the task of catering for New Year's Eve. She couldn't be angry with Tanvi for long. They had been best friends for too long, suffering each other's broken hearts and dramas.

Just last month her best friend had moved from London to Devon, the same move Shilpa had made not too long ago.

Shilpa had been making a list of things she needed for her last-minute party when she received a call. It was someone who identified herself as the house manager at Dreamcatcher Mansion.

'Have you heard of us?' Millie had enquired.

Of course Shilpa had. Everyone knew about the once infamous Dreamcatcher Island, which was home to Dreamcatcher Mansion. Built in the fifties and painted a striking shade of yellow, it stood proud on the highest part of the isle. Flanked by chusan palms and agaves, it boasted fifteen bedrooms, a cinema room and a twenty metre infinity pool overlooking the Devon coastline. The house and island had been bought by millionaire Tobias Grave in the nineties to host his son Alan's thirtieth birthday party and to celebrate that Alan had been on the cover of *The Greats Magazine*, a who's who journal that had been a must-read for executives thirty years ago but had since died a death with the rise of social media.

Rumour had it, Alan Grave had never returned to the island after his party. Instead he rented it out, fully staffed, and made a fortune. Celebrities hosted parties at Dreamcatcher

Island, or so the magazines said, and it was often featured in glossy magazines as *the* wedding venue in the South Hams.

Tanvi and Shilpa hadn't bothered to call when they had been making their enquiries. They knew it would be booked up, it always was, not that they could have afforded it. 'And besides,' Tanvi had said, 'I'm not sure I know fifteen people I would like to spend New Year's Eve with.'

'I've heard of it,' Shilpa had said to Millie, which was the right thing to say because ten minutes later she was being offered a stay at one of the smaller properties on the island. It came with the condition to make an exquisite passion fruit and chocolate birthday cake and to run a baking lesson for the guests.

'He's asked for you, personally,' Millie had said.

'Who?' Shilpa had to ask.

'The owner,' said Millie, which had shocked Shilpa into silence.

'It's over New Year though,' Shilpa found herself saying when she found her voice again. 'My partner and I and a couple of close friends...' she started.

'Rose Cottage has capacity for four people. Two couples,' Millie said, cutting her off. 'You can bring your friends, provided that they stay out of the way of the guests. It isn't hard to do. Rose Cottage has its own grounds.'

As soon as Millie told her how much they could pay Shilpa for the long weekend, she agreed. In one weekend she would make what she usually did in six months. She almost laughed out loud over the phone. She wasn't sure what the Graves were expecting, but she would certainly be ordering in some gold leaf.

A ferry ran to and from the island twice a day, morning and night, and there was a small wooden craft that the guests could use if they needed to get to the mainland at any other time. Shilpa wasn't sure why they called it a ferry. It was more like a water taxi paid for by the resort, but she supposed it enhanced the romantic idea of the place. Robin had decided to give the little rowing boat a try. Parrot Bay was only fifty metres or so away. Shilpa had tried to dissuade him given the weather, but Robin had shrugged away her comments.

Shilpa turned away from the thunderous sky towards the interior of the cottage. She noted that unlike the exterior of the stone building, the house was modern, recently renovated and boasting the latest gadgets. Voice-controlled curtains and lights, paper-thin television screens and a gorgeous wood burner. Perfect for this time of year. She wasn't surprised; the property had to be well equipped. But despite the luxury, she couldn't shake the feeling that there was something a little off about the island. A strange aura to the place which unsettled her. She had even started to have doubts about Robin. One minute she was irrationally cross with him, the next she didn't know what she would do without him.

'Maybe it's the ghost,' Robin had said when she brought up the peculiar feeling. 'Haven't you heard about the local legend? Prior to the Graves purchasing the place and turning it into a resort, the first owner of the isle fell to his death here and has haunted the place ever since.'

Shilpa had made a face at him.

But moments later, she was practically screaming, 'Who's that?'

'Who?' Robin had asked, staring out of the window into the pitch-black night.

'I could have sworn I saw someone out there,' she had said.

'It's dark. Even if someone was out there, you wouldn't have been able to see them, unless they were holding a torch to their face.' Robin had put his arm around her and laughed, and Shilpa softened as she relaxed into his embrace. But later that night she couldn't help but think of the silhouette in the walled garden of Rose Cottage.

It certainly gave credibility to the feeling of being watched whilst on the island. That first night at the cottage, after their meal with Duncan and Millie, she had slept fitfully.

~

The night before Tanvi, Brijesh and the other house guests arrived on the island, Millie and Duncan had invited Robin and Shilpa over for dinner at the exclusive Dreamcatcher Mansion and had filled them in on the island's inhabitants. Excluding Rose Cottage and the main house, there were three other houses on the island. These houses were set back from the main house. Two of the three houses still served their original purpose as staff quarters. Duncan and Millie lived in one; the on-call chef Andreas lived in another.

Millie had described the chef as the temperamental sort, but his food was too good to let him go. 'He's what the guests want,' Millie had said, and after Shilpa tasted the fresh crab starter, she could vouch for that. The crab had been delicately paired with yuzu and samphire and was simply delicious. 'Andreas likes it here on the island,' Millie had said. 'And living here isn't for everyone.'

'What about the third house?' Shilpa had asked. Millie said it was occupied.

Shilpa pressed for more information about its inhabitant, to which Millie replied, 'A cantankerous old man,' and said no more on the subject. Shilpa observed as the house manager, with her mousey brown hair and aquiline nose, sipped her white wine carefully after this statement, giving her husband Duncan a sideways glance.

'Stay away from the old man if you can,' Duncan had said as he cut into his rare steak. 'He never has anything nice to say.'

'What's he doing on the island?' Robin had asked, unable to help himself.

'He was here when Mr Grave bought the place,' Millie had said.

'For the birthday party?' Robin asked, knowing full well that Tobias and Alan Grave had bought the place on a whim, used it for a party and never returned. They had Googled Alan, the retail mogul, verifying the various rumours after Shilpa had been offered the job.

Millie had nodded and said nothing more, so of course Robin had probed her in that subtle reporter way of his. 'You'll see Alan Grave soon enough for yourself,' Duncan had said. 'He arrives with his family in a couple of days.'

# Chapter Four

And what a family the Graves were. They arrived in their fancy coats and dark sunglasses the day before the party. Their luggage came on a separate boat. Large metal Rimowa cases and Louis Vuitton holdalls were carted off by the handyman and gardener who came to the island every morning by the ferry along with a handful of cleaners. Even Tanvi had gawped before questioning whether she had brought the right number of shoes with her.

'We're not going to be invited to their luxury dinners,' Brijesh said, relieved.

Tanvi made a face. 'We might be.'

'You don't need shoes,' Robin said to Tanvi. 'You'll be in the kitchen mostly, with me.' With Shilpa running a baking class in the morning and then icing the four-tiered passion fruit and chocolate ganache cake, complete with gold leaf, in the afternoon, there was no time to cater for her friends as well. So Robin had volunteered to cook.

Robin's cooking was yet to be sampled, but he seemed determined to prove himself to Shilpa and her friends, and Shilpa had to admire him for his determination.

But as the day grew closer, Robin seemed to get cold feet, and he had somehow dragged Tanvi into being his sous chef. 'I have all the ingredients,' he had announced after his trip to Parrot Bay, looking delighted with himself.

∼

Millie had watched as the Graves arrived. She had the perfect viewing spot from Felicity's bedroom. She hadn't specifically walked up to the bedroom to spy on them. No, she had been up there to check that everything was as it should be, that everything was in place.

Felicity always used the blue room when she stayed at Dreamcatcher. She expected her exclusive lavender shower gels and bath oils from Provence to be ready and waiting for her, her Frette robe hanging behind the bathroom door and her Penelope Chilvers monogrammed velvet slippers to be by her bed. Felicity wouldn't think to thank Millie if everything was just so, but she knew just who to call if anything was not to her liking. Felicity wouldn't be disappointed this time; everything was as it should be. Everything.

Millie had adjusted her pastel pink cashmere jumper before standing at the window, waiting for the ferry to unload its passengers. She had just spritzed the room with a personalised calming fragrance containing geranium, cedarwood and eucalyptus and held on to the bottle as she crossed her arms over her chest and told herself to get over it.

The Graves were the owners of Dreamcatcher Island. They were her employers. She had to bow and scrape and do anything they asked of her while they were here. That was what her employers expected. They would be the worst of the worst, and that was saying something. During her time in Dreamcatcher Mansion she had experienced it all, from children peeing on the carpet to adults drunkenly doing the same. It made her skin crawl sometimes the way the super-rich behaved and let their children behave. What the next generation were going to be like, she couldn't imagine.

Millie was a first-class student in obeying orders when it came to paying guests, although she found that the worse the behaviour, the smaller the tip. It was the decent ones that tipped the most. Guests would ask her to do all manner of things, from sourcing rare glass figurines for a spontaneous birthday present to chartering a yacht for the following day.

Millie took it all in her stride. She did draw the line at some requests though. Anything sexual was a complete no-no, and she was grateful to have Duncan around, which prevented some invitations, but not all. Drugs were a bit of a taboo as well. Well, sort of. What she sourced depended on who was asking and what they were asking for.

Millie couldn't complain though. She had years of experience heading up a team at an exclusive hotel in central London. London life had got to her though, and after Duncan was caught with his pants down with one of the housekeeping staff, she knew it was time for a change. They had been lucky that the positions at Dreamcatcher Island had come up when they did, otherwise she couldn't tell what she might have done to Duncan or his lady friend.

Her husband, even though he was more social than she was, agreed to the move easily. He didn't say it, but she knew that he didn't want things to get ugly, and they could easily have done, like they did many moons ago in Leicester.

Duncan had assured Millie that his philandering would stop, and for a time it did. She was naive to think that rich guests staying at Dreamcatcher Mansion wouldn't try it on with her man. They had with her, so what would make Duncan any different?

As far as she could tell though, Duncan had kept to his word. He had stayed away from the young heiresses and bored wives. On more than one occasion she saw Duncan from the corner of her eye reject the drunken advances of male and female guests. With each rejection her heart sang, but sometimes late at night when she reached out to him and his side of the bed was cold, she wondered if it had all been an act.

She never followed him on his late-night escapades and allowed herself to believe that he was often working on his manuscript at his desk in the study. Millie wasn't stupid enough to believe that Duncan was never tempted. She knew the type of woman to garner his attention, and that type of woman was heading up the path.

Millie observed from her prime position in Felicity Grave's room. Standing by the heavy curtain to the balcony, she had a perfect view of the owners as they made their way towards the house. It surprised her that Felicity Grave hadn't asked someone to lift her out of the boat. Of course, Andreas, the gardener and a porter hired for the occasion, had been quick to help the guests with their bags. The owners, not the other riff-raff that had been allowed to stay at Rose Cottage.

That Alan Grave had allowed such nonsense suggested the man was losing his marbles. Millie couldn't believe it when she was instructed to invite a nobody to the island to give a cooking class – of all things – and make a cake.

It must have been some banana bread he had tasted to have Alan Grave singing Shilpa Solanki's praises. As soon as she had received the instruction from Yvonne, Alan's PA, she had sent for a loaf of the cake and had tried it along with Duncan and Andreas. They had all been silent as they swallowed the first mouthful. None of them knew what to say until Andreas said that the cake was good. It was. It was excellent, in fact. But it was beyond her why Alan was so taken by it that he had allowed Shilpa Solanki to stay at the cottage with all her friends. Friends that Millie had to do background checks on before they arrived. It was all part of her job at Dreamcatcher Mansion. She had detailed her findings to Yvonne, and she had to chase up as to whether Alan had any reservations.

It seemed that the millionaire had none. She certainly would have if a journalist and amateur detective were staying alongside the family on the island. The last thing they wanted was any kind of family drama to get out. Millie had raised this but was immediately shot down by Yvonne. So she had taken it upon herself to invite the couple to the main house for dinner to decide whether they would be trouble. By the end of the dinner, she was still unsure. Millie had been clear in her warnings: they were not to make a nuisance of themselves in front of the Grave family.

Millie took a breath. Felicity sauntered down the path in her silk coat, completely inappropriate for the ghastly weather. Gina was walking with her, hand in hand, looking very pleased with herself. From what Millie knew, Gina had always been desperate to step out of Felicity's shadow, and judging by the diamond that was shimmering in the morning sun, Gina was about to do it. Much to Felicity's annoyance, no doubt. The spoiled little rich girl always wanted to be the first to do anything out of those two.

Andreas, the chef, had delivered the bags to the front of the house and was now having a cigarette by Rose Cottage, hidden from the view of the guests by the large magnolia tree. He was watching Felicity as he took a drag on his roll-up. Of course he was. He claimed it was unrequited love when Millie teased him about it, but she had noticed the way Felicity had glanced over at the chef now and again. Of course, it was only when Felicity was bored or was desperately seeking attention.

Millie had also noticed a dark look cross Duncan's face every time she provoked Andreas about the owner's daughter, and so Millie did it as often as she could, each time waiting for a reaction. She was always rewarded, but as much as she liked to win, it didn't feel like winning, not at all.

Andreas was free to have his feelings; he didn't have a barren wife at home to look after. So what if Felicity chewed him up and spat him out time and time again. It wasn't anything to do with Millie, and she didn't give a jot if his feelings got hurt. On more than one occasion, she heard some of the cleaning staff say that Andreas had fallen into a depression after Felicity had been to the house.

Millie had often thought about going to visit the chef in his cottage to see if he was all right, but she never got around to it, and it seemed that his excellent cooking got even better when he was in one of those volatile moods, so who was she to say anything?

Millie had been about to step away from the window when something to the right of the house caught her attention. Behind the bushes her husband was watching the group arrive. Duncan stood in his dark suit and crisp white shirt with his feet apart, staring at one of the guests like a lovelorn teenager.

Millie felt something inside her stir.

'Ow,' she said, her gaze going to her hand. A drop of blood fell onto the carpet. 'Blast it,' she said. She opened her fist and saw the shards of glass from the delicate room fragrance bottle she had been holding. She cursed again.

'You okay?' said a tall, balding man in uniform. The hired porter was bringing in Felicity's bags.

'Perfectly fine,' she said through the pain. 'I'll just clear this up. You carry on. I'll have these unpacked in no time.'

## Chapter Five

S hilpa stepped out of the cottage in her cosy grey cashmere cardigan, carrying her book and hot drink with her. From a sliver of a window in the walled garden of their cottage, she had the perfect viewing spot of the lower terrace of Dreamcatcher Mansion that led to the infinity pool. She glanced at her watch. She had an hour before she had to get ready for the class.

Shilpa sat in one of the wrought-iron chairs and put her book on the garden table. Warming her hands on her mug of coffee, she stared though the stone window of the walled garden of Rose Cottage. Despite the winter chill the family were assembling for breakfast. She was surprised the family were outside. It was December. It was cold, not terribly so, but cold enough. Then she spotted the large patio heaters and thick blankets on the chairs that would keep the family warm while they ate.

She was glad she could people-watch for her morning's entertainment. She had never given a baking class before, and getting to know some of her students would put her nerves at ease, or so she told herself.

Rashmi, wearing a bright pink knitted poncho over orange flared trousers, was certainly trying to coax the sun out. It was a bright morning, and Shilpa could understand why Felicity, seated opposite Rashmi, needed gold-rimmed sunglasses.

Rashmi was seated next to her daughter Gina, and Jane, Alan Grave's ex-wife. Shilpa was grateful to Brijesh, who, after a thorough internet search, had given her the lowdown on the family complete with screenshots of each member.

Felicity's gaze was directed towards the bay as she stirred her yoghurt. Hungover, Shilpa assumed. Felicity called over one of the waiting staff and said something. The man returned minutes later with a pot of something, tea, Shilpa thought, and a plate of sliced lemon.

There wasn't much chatter amongst the party, not what you'd expect for a close family. Shilpa thought back to her own clan. When they were together, they were loud, animated and opinionated. They discussed anything and everything, and they always had something to say. Mrs Solanki at the helm usually guided their conversation subtly enough so that no one ever suspected her of doing so.

Shilpa turned to her book. 'We could have gone anywhere,' Rashmi said. Shilpa started. It sounded like Rashmi was sitting next to her. But the guests were still in their seats. Their voices carried well from the lower terrace. 'Barbados or even India's great this time of year,' she said.

Shilpa put her book down and lifted her mug to her lips.

'We've done all that,' Felicity said. 'We do it every year.' She paused, turning to Rashmi. 'I've done it every year,' she said. 'This year I wanted a bit of home.'

'It's hardly home,' Rashmi said. 'Suffolk is home.'

'But we used to come here as children all the time. I've fond memories playing by the boathouse with Julian.' Her mother, Jane, smiled.

'Speak of the devil,' Rashmi said. She turned towards the

French doors. A man was coming out of the house, dressed in navy chinos and a striped shirt.

'We used to spend a month here every summer when the kids were young,' Jane said. Shilpa stretched her neck to get a better look at Julian. He was tall and slim and walked with his hands in his pockets. His movements were slow as he walked to the table, his head slightly stooped.

'Without Alan?' Rashmi said.

'Naturally,' replied Jane. 'We never came here when we were married, and after…'

'You met here, didn't you?' Rashmi asked.

'Alan's thirtieth, yes. I suppose that's why Flick wanted her party here.'

Felicity appeared to ignore her mother. She turned to Gina. 'What time are Albie and Richard getting here?'

'Interesting book?' Shilpa heard Robin ask before he bent down and kissed her neck.

'Shhh,' she whispered.

'Did the body on the beach last night whet your appetite? You're sleuthing, aren't you? I don't think there's much to investigate. There'll be a body on the beach, but it isn't going to be a real one.'

Shilpa turned back to her book and refrained from saying something to Robin that she would regret later. She took one last glimpse through the window. With the arrival of Julian, Felicity's younger brother, the mood appeared strained, even more so than before. She noted the time and then stood up.

'Why did Felicity Grave scream last night?' she turned and asked Robin. 'If she was just faking it, why was the scream necessary?'

'She wanted to know if anyone would come,' Robin said.

'And did they?'

'Only you. Didn't you hear or see anyone else in the house stir?'

Shilpa shook her head. She remembered glancing up at the house. Some of the windows had been open, yet no one had bothered to investigate. She told Robin as much.

'They must have had music on and didn't hear,' Robin said.

Shilpa nodded as they headed towards the cottage even though she was certain that no music had been playing. Apart from Felicity's scream, the night had been eerily silent.

After Millie had cleaned up herself and Felicity's room, she had started to unpack the young woman's belongings. She did it methodically, only stopping to admire a dress or two and the woman's impressive collection of lingerie.

She unpacked with as little malice as possible despite imagining her husband ripping off Felicity Grave's underwear but eventually Millie lost her cool. Her blood boiled. She saw red.

Had the Graves not been paying her salary, she would have a good mind to… A good mind to what? She couldn't afford a repetition of Leicester. Second chances were one thing, but third and fourth were something else. Millie closed her eyes and steadied her nerves. She told herself that this was all in her head. The words Duncan had told her a thousand times. If only Duncan wasn't such a liar.

She heard a voice, a familiar voice. 'Need any help in here?'

'No, Duncan,' she said quietly.

'Are you okay? Your hand…'

Millie took in the neat bandage she had only just applied. 'Small accident with a glass bottle. I'll be fine. I just need to get this done and the others and then I'll be downstairs.'

'I've asked Hannah to do the others. This isn't your job. You shouldn't be doing this.'

Was there something in Felicity's luggage that Duncan didn't want her to see? Millie peered in the case and saw a red silk bag containing a pair of heels. She took the bag and slipped out one of the shoes and held it up.

'That's quite something,' Duncan said.

'You always did have a thing for shoes,' Millie said.

'Millie,' he said in a low voice.

'You could kill someone with a heel like that,' Millie said, ignoring him. She eyed him suspiciously and pulled the other shoe out of the silk pouch. Holding the pair, she stepped towards the shoe cupboard and placed them on the top shelf.

'It's rather cosy in here,' a voice said.

Millie turned around. Felicity was standing in the doorway only inches from her husband. Duncan shifted his weight from one foot to the other then he took another step into the room.

'I'm just finishing in here. If you want me to leave and come back, I can,' Millie said, professional as ever.

'No, you carry on. It's Duncan I need.' Felicity winked at him. He gave her a smile reserved for paying guests. It did little to calm Millie's nerves. 'Come on then,' Felicity said. 'It's downstairs.'

Duncan followed the heiress like a dog, whilst Millie's heart hammered in her chest. She opened the balcony door as soon as she heard movement outside, confirming that it was Duncan and Felicity standing by the rear entrance to the pool.

'Please,' Felicity was saying in that annoying whine of hers.

Millie strained her ears but couldn't hear Duncan's response.

Jane closed the door behind her and sat at the dressing table. She picked up the silver brush and held it to her auburn hair. One hundred and fifty strokes and she would feel much calmer.

As she started to drag the brush through her hair, she realised what a task she had set herself. It wouldn't be easy saying to Alan what she needed to say, nor Felicity, but if the rumours were true then she didn't have much time left.

It had been a difficult decision for Jane when Felicity had declared she wanted to celebrate her thirtieth with her close family and a couple of friends on Dreamcatcher Island. Seeing Rashmi and Gina with Alan would be hard on Jane, but she couldn't let Felicity down, and then there was the other matter. The dark secret she had kept hidden for so long. How much longer could she hide it from her daughter? From Alan?

Jane's marriage to Alan had been one of convenience. It suited both their families. It worked for her circumstance, because not long after she and Alan tied the knot they announced that she was pregnant, and not quite nine months later Felicity was born. Alan had said he loved her and she had reciprocated the comment, but was it true love? Hardly.

The marriage didn't last long. Alan had lost interest in her long before Julian arrived. She foolishly thought another baby would fix things. It didn't. As soon as Julian arrived, Alan upped his imports from India. He was there most months. Sometimes for a week or two, sometimes longer. She wondered if the baby had actually pushed him further away.

Jane shook her head as she lifted the brush once more. Even now she didn't understand. It wasn't as if Alan had been expected to do anything for the baby. They had installed a live-in nanny at their Suffolk house soon after Julian's arrival. She fed, cleaned and cared for Julian, making sure that Alan's sleep wasn't interrupted.

Jane often felt a pang of guilt when she thought about this. She had sacrificed time with her son for her husband, and it had been fruitless. When Alan was away she had tried to make up for leaving Julian with the nanny. At night, she let him sleep in her bed, and she made sure that only she fed and cleaned him. Jane devoted her time to her only son. Of course, the moment Alan was back, she turned her back on Julian again, leaving the nanny to deal with the fallout. Now Jane wondered if her hot and cold attitude towards her son had made Julian the way he was.

She couldn't dwell on that.

In some respects Julian was better behaved than Felicity. Felicity grew up with everything she ever wanted, so naturally she was spoilt. The firstborn of Alan Grave was never going to be anything other than indulged. A princess room and a pony were just some of the gifts he showered on the apple of his eye.

Felicity barely had tantrums because she got whatever she asked for, and this poor parenting showed in her behaviour now. She sulked when she didn't get her way, and although Felicity loved Gina, she envied her to the point of concern. The only thing that kept Gina safe, in Jane's eyes, was that Gina wasn't Alan's biological daughter. Felicity never said anything to her best friend and stepsister, but silently she had the upper hand.

*No one is a perfect parent,* Jane reminded herself as she pulled the brush once more through her hair. Jane had tried not giving in to her daughter's demands once or twice. The emotional game she played with Julian didn't last long because before Julian was a year old, Alan had asked her for a divorce. She had tried to fight it, but Alan told her that he no longer loved her and offered her a settlement she couldn't turn down. Jane tried to make him love her again. She spent a small fortune in Agent Provocateur and lost a stone, but it was no use. When she saw Rashmi, she knew she could never compete.

Rashmi had swanned into their lives as a rich heiress to a garment-dyeing company in Mumbai. She had the wealth to match Alan's, and she was young and beautiful. Too young in Jane's eyes. She had only been twenty-one when they had married. Jane quickly did the maths. It meant Rashmi's fiftieth was approaching. She smiled at that and hoped Rashmi feared the milestone. But who was she kidding? Rashmi was forever youthful. Whether it was her genes or Botox, Jane didn't know. She didn't want to know. There was no use dwelling on Rashmi's smooth skin and radiant glow.

Alan had met her at one of the many parties he attended in India. Alan waited for the decree absolute to come through, married Rashmi and swiftly adopted her daughter Gina who had been born out of wedlock. It was all done so quickly and Gina was so small that no one ever remembered that the child wasn't his, biologically.

Jane put the hairbrush down. 'There,' she said to herself. 'One hundred and fifty strokes.' She was feeling better already. She pinched the tired skin on her cheek and opened a pot of cream. Applying it to her face, she waited for it to sink in before adding some blusher. She dabbed some perfume behind her ears and on her wrists and took one last look in the mirror.

*Time to bake some cake,* she thought. She wasn't the least bit interested in baking banana bread, or whatever it was that they were making, but it was a better way to pass the time than staring at her wrinkles in the mirror; another pointless occupation of hers.

## Chapter Six

'Shilpa Solanki,' a man said as Shilpa opened the door to Rose Cottage.

'You must be Andreas, the chef,' she said, observing the man's checked trousers and double-breasted white jacket. 'We ate up at the house the other day with Duncan and Millie, and the food was exceptional. I had meant to seek you out, but by the time we'd finished it was late and you had already retreated to your cottage.'

Shilpa had wanted to speak to the chef after their meal, but Millie had insisted on giving her a tour of the house, and it had taken longer than anticipated. The house had been everything Shilpa had imagined. High moulded ceilings, chandeliers, fancy paintings and installations, and bathrooms with dark-veined marble floors, slipper baths and double sinks. She was sure her entire living room could fit inside the master en suite.

'Thought I'd show you around the kitchen before your class,' Andreas said, ignoring her compliment. He didn't smile, just folded his arms across his chest and looked at her.

'Thank you,' Shilpa said. 'Let me just grab my things.' She left Andreas with Robin while she collected her customised

Sweet Treats apron. She walked with the chef the long way around to the rear of the house instead of walking towards the French doors that opened out towards the pool and Rose Cottage.

'Tradesman's entrance,' Andreas said as if reading her mind, his voice monotone. Well, Millie had told them not to fraternise with the guests.

The back kitchen was the location for the class. It was already set up as she had planned. She had emailed over some brief instructions to Millie before her arrival, setting out what ingredients were needed and the quantities required.

Millie had in turn responded, asking for the recipe. 'We want everything just so,' she said. 'As you can imagine, no one will want to measure sugar and flour on the day. It needs to be set out.'

Well, there's the fun gone, Shilpa had wanted to say, but refrained. With that in mind, she had another recipe in addition to the banana bread up her sleeve, because by the looks of it the cooking class was going to be short.

Andreas showed her around the kitchen, explained how the industrial-catering-sized ovens worked and left her to it. Shilpa had tasted the choux pastry that Andreas had offered up when she had dined at the house, and it was excellent. She couldn't help but wonder why the chef hadn't been asked to run this cooking class. No wonder he had been so abrupt with her earlier.

Shilpa had been taken aback when Millie had called. She knew her grandmother's banana bread recipe was world class, especially with the touch of ginger and cardamom syrup, but she never thought it would be requested by a millionaire. The thought had crossed her mind that her closely guarded recipe was now no longer a secret, but the opportunity was too good to pass up, and she doubted anyone staying on Dreamcatcher Island would exploit her so blatantly.

Shilpa started checking her station. The ingredients, like at the other seven stations, had been set out carefully. She located a set of digital scales and checked the amount of flour the recipe required. It was spot on. With her mind at ease, she walked around each island to ensure little vials of cardamom and ginger syrup sat on each table along with the rest of the ingredients. 'Perfect,' she said under her breath, impressed with whoever had been tasked with all this work.

As she adjusted the oil and butter at her station, her first student walked in. Alan Grave's Wikipedia profile, if it were to be believed, said he was sixty. He appeared closer to seventy. She had found pictures of the millionaire online, and his features matched. He had a chiselled jaw, and his navy suit was immaculate. He was five minutes early. This was her chance. If she could impress him, who knew where her banana bread could end up.

Shilpa introduced herself to Alan, who was a man of few words. Her mind flitted as she tried to cope with the awkward silence, and she realised that this class had probably been forced upon the guests and was most likely the last thing they wanted to do. Her ego wounded, she busied herself by measuring out her flour again when Alan spoke.

'I was in Dartmouth sometime in November visiting a friend, and they served me a slice of your banana bread.' The millionaire spoke slowly, and Shilpa wondered if Alan had finished his sentence or if he had just paused. She took a breath, ready to say something, but he saved her by continuing. 'It was quite something,' he said. 'The cake had been purchased from a local deli, and you were the baker, I understand.'

Shilpa smiled. 'Thank you,' she said. 'It means a lot that customers like my bakes.'

'When Felicity was young, she loved banana bread, so I thought this would be a nice surprise for her, especially as she wanted to be here for her birthday.' Alan's eyes wandered around the kitchen. He wrinkled his nose. 'A curious choice for a young woman, but that's Felicity for you. All her choices are somewhat…' He trailed off, staring into the distance. 'She's my firstborn, my blood, and it's important to me that this weekend goes well for her. You see…' Alan said, 'The kids are busy with their own lives, and soon they'll be married with children of their own. One of my biggest regrets was that I never spent enough time with them when they were growing up. And now, being here, I suppose I am trying to make up for that. At my age, you realise what is important and maybe it has come a little late.'

Shilpa nodded. 'You had a business to run,' she said, trying to justify his actions for him.

Alan seemed not to notice Shilpa's words. He studied the little bottle of syrup at one of the stations. Then he spoke again. 'Lately, I've spent more time with my brood, and it's made me realise that my children are not what they appear. My children are sad and lonely. Their friendships are hollow. What is most concerning though is their greed. I never saw it before. I thought I gave them everything, but maybe that was the problem. Now I see them and the craving that seeps out of their pores. They're desperate, and I can't underestimate what they will do to get at my wealth.' Alan rubbed his neck and took a breath. He turned to Shilpa and, as if just realising he had an audience, he smiled. 'This is great,' he said, as if these were the first words he had spoken to her.

Shilpa tried to ignore the sense of foreboding creeping up on her.

A group of five youngsters walked in. Shilpa could smell the alcohol on their breath as they greeted her and giggled as they took their stations. Alan bristled beside her before walking away.

'Just the mums now,' Julian said.

To Shilpa's surprise he picked up each ingredient and sniffed it. He was younger than Felicity, maybe by a few years, and Gina appeared to be similar in age. She put Gina and Julian at around twenty-five, which meant that there wasn't much of an age gap between the three children. She wondered if Alan had been having an affair with Rashmi while he was married to Jane. It was highly probable, and Tanvi was right in that it was a bizarre set-up. Jane and Rashmi must be extraordinary people to agree to be in the same house together for a family celebration. Surely there must have been some bad blood between them.

Several minutes later, Jane entered the kitchen with a genuine smile. She was closer to Alan's age than Rashmi. Alan's current wife was a vivacious woman who liked to wear bright colours, speak her mind and make assumptions. Shilpa had got this impression when Rashmi mistook Brijesh for the gardener and failed to listen to his protests, so much so that he ended up moving the living Christmas tree away from the terrace as she had requested. Indians were not quick to age, but still, Shilpa would hazard a guess that Rashmi was in her forties.

'Couldn't find it,' Rashmi declared as she floated into the kitchen ten minutes late. Her statement fell on deaf ears.

'Let's get started then,' her daughter Gina said. Shilpa smiled, but Gina didn't reciprocate.

'Right,' Shilpa said. 'Let's get started.'

## Chapter Seven

Shilpa walked back to the cottage, her head pounding. It had been a mistake coming to Dreamcatcher Island.

'So?' said Tanvi, opening the door before Shilpa had put her hand on the handle.

'Failure,' Shilpa said. 'None of them were interested in making banana bread. We got three loaves out of nine of us.'

'Did they taste good?'

'It would have been hard to get it wrong. The way everything was measured out, it was more of an assembly than cooking. They would have been better off with a packet of Betty Crocker.'

Tanvi laughed and patted her friend on the back. 'You did it,' she said. 'You ran a cookery class. The guests loved the cake. Done. That's another string to your bow.'

'Hardly,' Shilpa said, pushing past her friend and slumping onto the oversized grey sofa. She had done little to impress Alan Grave. He had left halfway through the class, claiming he had a headache. She assumed he was just bored. The other guests had shown little willing. Rashmi was more interested in observing her daughter and her friends from the corner of her eye than mixing the butter with the flour.

Shilpa had to admit that this young group of friends, not far off from her in age, were an interesting bunch. The atmosphere had lifted with the arrival of Albie and Richard, and it didn't take her long to figure out that Rashmi's daughter Gina was engaged to Albie, the taller and better looking of the two. Although the way Gina had been flirting with Richard, you wouldn't have thought it.

Shilpa had watched the charade over the duration of the class, and although she was initially taken aback, she soon realised that the flirting was innocent. She had got the distinct impression that this friendship group had an over-familiar way with one another which could be misconstrued by a casual witness. What was odd was that at one point Rashmi had made her way over to the station where Gina and Albie were cooking. Rashmi had shared a look with Albie while her daughter was concentrating on her mobile phone. The minute her daughter turned back to her, Rashmi had busied herself with something.

'What, Mother?' Gina had said, staring at Rashmi.

'Just checking how you're getting on,' she had replied.

Her daughter turned away again, but not before putting a protective arm around Albie.

'I'm sure she wants to give my mother a full report when we return,' Albie said. He had turned his eyes towards Rashmi, but she had simply walked away.

Shilpa had been about to turn away when Albie caught her eye. He winked at her, and she bristled. Later, when she had been walking around the cooking stations talking to her students, Albie had tried to strike up a conversation when Gina was at her mother's table. 'Don't believe everything you hear,' he had said.

'Hear?' she asked.

'Oh, there'll be talk this weekend about this and that. And you seem the sort to want to know.'

Shilpa felt her cheeks flush. She was about to make her excuses and walk away when Albie leaned towards her and said in a serious tone, 'Be careful.'

His words made the hairs on her arms stand on end. She wanted to ask what he meant by it when he started muttering something else. Shilpa strained to hear what he was saying. 'Sorry,' she said. 'I didn't hear you.' As the words left her mouth, that ominous feeling that she increasingly felt on the island hit her.

'Murder,' Albie said. 'Someone is going to get hurt.'

Shilpa took a breath.

Albie laughed. 'The murder mystery,' he said, and Shilpa realised how foolish she had been to think otherwise. But now she thought about it, it had been a strange choice of words that Albie had used. He didn't say that someone was going to die. He said that someone was going to get hurt, and for some reason it sounded a touch more sinister.

Felicity had been sullen for the duration of the cookery event. Whether it was Gina's five-carat diamond ring that had put her in a mood or that her stepsister was flirting with Richard, who appeared to be Felicity's boyfriend, Shilpa wasn't sure, but the usually bright-eyed Felicity Grave was solemn. The young woman's mood only picked up halfway through when her father left the kitchen and Richard moved over to share her station. Shilpa noticed that he affectionately put an arm around Felicity's waist and drew her in as she mixed the mashed banana with the eggs.

'You're being too hard on yourself,' Tanvi said, drawing Shilpa away from her thoughts. 'That's the main task done. You can kick back now. We came here to bring in the new year and relax a little. That's exactly what you need to do. Wine?'

'And who's going to finish the cake if I start drinking now?' she asked.

Tanvi waved away her comment. 'Don't worry, Robin and I took care of it while you were out.'

Shilpa removed herself from the sofa and leapt to the kitchen. 'You what?' she said, eyeing the tiered passion fruit and chocolate cake.

'Thought we'd help out a bit,' Tanvi said a little uncertainly. 'It's unfair that you've had to do all the work around here and we get to enjoy all this.'

Shilpa walked around the cake, carefully inspecting what her boyfriend and best friend had done. It wasn't bad. They knew her work well. She took the spatula lying next to the cake and superficially adjusted some of the icing. It would taste good; she had mixed the icing herself this morning. She made a face.

'Well, don't just stand there,' Tanvi said. 'What do you think?'

'It'll do,' Shilpa said, not wanting to give her friend too much credit.

'Great,' Tanvi said. 'I'll get the boys to deliver it to the house. You take a shower and get ready. This is our New Year's Eve party, and we are going to celebrate our way.'

Shilpa smiled as she left Tanvi in the kitchen with the cake. Her headache was already starting to ease.

Rashmi hurried back to her room. She opened the door and stepped inside. Alan was lying on the bed, his eyes closed, his arms by his sides. He was so peaceful. Strands of his grey hair were stuck to his forehead with perspiration. She walked over to the bed and pulled back the covers. She followed the rise and fall of his chest, mesmerised for a moment. Then she covered him up again and stepped back.

She settled into the maroon velvet occasional chair that was placed in prime viewing position out over the infinity pool and over Dreamcatcher Bay.

Rashmi's gaze moved from the bay back to her husband. How many people knew his secret? She doubted Alan would have told anyone. It would have shown a weakness in his character, but surely now he had to come clean, now that his time was almost up. Every time she broached the subject though, Alan changed it. Perhaps he had told Felicity and that was why she wanted this family break together under the guise of her thirtieth birthday.

That girl was greedy. It wouldn't surprise Rashmi if Felicity Grave was plotting something. And her mother was after something too. Why would Jane so readily accept an invite to come here otherwise? Wasn't it enough that she had holidayed here with Julian and Felicity on Alan's coin for a good decade if not more? Fair enough, this occasion was different – after all, it was her daughter's milestone birthday – but honestly, they could have celebrated elsewhere, another time.

Rashmi took in her surroundings. It was luxurious. Duncan and Millie had earned their money, but it was so remote, and Devon wasn't her scene. The English seaside never was. She had to admit that Dreamcatcher Bay was more upmarket than Bognor Regis, which she had made a fleeting visit to once in her youth, but still, it was hardly exotic.

Had they been in Mumbai they could have celebrated in style at the Taj. She had fond memories of the hotel from her wedding to Alan, so many years ago now. Gina was only little and had been the sweetest flower girl. She recalled her daughter clutching a basket of rose petals as her mother led her to the front of the room where the ceremony was being held. She missed India, and she missed her mother despite her prejudice.

It had taken Rashmi some time to convince her parents to accept Alan as her husband. Firstly, he wasn't the right age, almost fifteen years older than her, and secondly, he wasn't the right colour. Her parents were the traditional sort. They had wanted their children to marry into the same religion and caste, but her brother had ignored them and so had she.

'He's just not right for you,' her mother had said of Alan. 'We'll find you a better match.'

Rashmi let them get on with it. She didn't have a choice, but she knew there was no better match, so she had taken some solace from that. Her parents eventually conceded defeat. 'With the baby...' her mother had started.

'Nobody wants me.' Rashmi had finished her mother's sentence for her. 'I'm what they call damaged goods.'

Her mother looked away. Her father shook his head. 'Where did we go wrong?' he asked. Her parents never liked talking about Gina, and so the conversation ended there. The next time she broached the subject of marrying Alan Grave, her father smiled. 'I think it'll be a great match,' he said, giving her a fake smile that he usually reserved for distant relatives.

Rashmi accepted their false blessings and married Alan. After the marriage, her parents seemed to soften. Alan wasn't this evil white man who was taking away their only daughter, making her wear western clothes and eat bland food. Alan was the opposite. He embraced the Indian culture and even learnt a little Hindi. It wasn't long before he had charmed her parents, and they convinced themselves that they'd never had a problem with him. She let them believe that.

She and Alan had been happy to begin with. When they weren't abroad, they were either in their Marylebone mews or in Suffolk on Alan's estate. Rashmi loved it there. They entertained, they spent time together, but then Alan started travelling alone for work. The gaps between trips were shorter, and the duration of his trips longer. Her heart broke.

She imagined Jane must have felt the same way when her marriage to Alan deteriorated. Jane didn't want to live a lie. It was this that annoyed Rashmi most about Jane. Rashmi rarely admitted to herself that Jane was the stronger person, but she was. Rashmi had to be grateful to Jane in some ways though, because had Jane not confronted Alan, he may never have left her.

Rashmi wasn't going to turn into Jane. She despised her grey life. Her clothes were drab, and her holidays were only decent when she travelled with her daughter, because Alan couldn't bear Felicity to have less than the best. It was a life half lived.

Rashmi lived life to the full, in multicolour. Her life was good, and it was easy. She didn't want to give up the limitless black credit card, the chauffeur or the lunch parties at Nobu. No, she wasn't willing to give up any part of it, and so she continued with the charade.

'You're young,' one of her friends had said to her a while ago now. Lorrie had popped over when she had been at a low point and Rashmi found she just couldn't keep Alan's cheating to herself any longer.

'He's the old one,' Lorrie had said. 'You could start again.'

Rashmi considered this. It was true, of course it was, but a divorce would drag on, and she had been worried a settlement wouldn't be enough, because she was certain she was never going to work again.

She hadn't voiced these thoughts out loud, but Lorrie knew her well enough. 'You'll meet someone else,' she had said with a wink. 'I can make some introductions.'

And she did. Her friend had kept her word. Rashmi looked back out over the bay and smiled. She allowed herself a moment, then she shook off her dreamy gaze. A storm was coming. She could smell it in the air. Devon was a million miles from India and the monsoons, but she still recognised the smell of an approaching rainstorm.

Alan began to stir. Something inside her tightened. She had loved him, she had, but now... now it was different. She wouldn't quite call him a nuisance, but he was close to becoming one.

She had wanted to leave him, but by the time she got around to it, his affair, his wild ways, whatever he was going through, had come to an end. He expected their relationship to go back to what it was, and to some extent it did. But she didn't love him, not like she had done. She had moved on. Only she hadn't moved quick enough. Rashmi stalled. She had it easy with Alan.

She told her lover a pack of lies to buy her some time, but by the time she made her final decision, it was too late. Alan broke his news to her, and any chance of happiness she had in the near future slipped away.

'Rash,' he called out.

Her eyes shifted to the soft white pillow next to him. How easy it would be.

She stood up and walked to his bed. She held his outstretched hand and gave it a light squeeze. He smiled at her, and she forced a smile to her lips to reciprocate.

## Chapter Eight

'New Year's Eve,' Robin said as his eyes opened. He scanned the room for his girlfriend and found her standing by the large Crittall window which provided views over the bay.

'This room's so gorgeous with a window each side,' Shilpa said. 'You can look out over the bay in the morning and towards the house in the evening. The Graves could sell this property for a small fortune if they were ever short of cash.'

Shilpa had woken from her afternoon siesta thinking about the island and its select inhabitants. From the online booking calendar, Dreamcatcher Island was fully booked, which would keep most of its residents busy. Duncan and Millie, the house managers in charge with running the place, had each other, and she imagined Andreas would be on call most evenings. Paying clients wanted food delivered hot and freshly prepared.

But what about the lone man in the cottage that Millie and Duncan had told them to avoid? It was hard to believe that someone unrelated to the Graves would choose to live here. She imagined that the inhabitant's tenure on the island was a condition of the sale and that was why the Graves were stuck with him. Although she found it difficult to believe that someone as charming and powerful as Alan couldn't move the man on.

This bead of curiosity had spiralled. Shilpa had even gone to the trouble of checking the Land Registry website to find out who the Graves had bought the island from. She found out that for a few pounds she could download the title of the land, but she refrained. It was unlikely to tell her something she didn't already know.

The Graves owned the island, purchased from an eccentric earl. Whether or not he was the one whose ghost still stalked the island she didn't know, but he was dead. It had been reported in countless online articles.

Shilpa told herself to turn her attention to the new cakes she could try in the new year. She was acutely aware that in order to keep her clients happy and coming back for more, she had to be innovative with her flavours, she had to keep her offerings fresh. Shilpa had been toying with the idea of a rasmalai cake sweetened with condensed milk and saffron.

Dreamcatcher Mansion was so dominant and close to the bay, but the island had more to offer. She didn't have much time. Once Tanvi was ready, they would be busy preparing for their dinner.

'Come back to bed,' said Robin.

'I'm going for a walk,' she responded. 'Want to come with?'

'Aren't we on holiday?' Robin said. 'Holidays are for afternoon naps.'

'There must be some beautiful bays on the other side of the island. Don't you want to know what the other cottages on the island look like?'

'Not really. I'd like to stay in bed where it's warm.'

'Suit yourself.'

Robin groaned. 'Okay then,' he said, pulling back the covers. 'Do I get coffee first?'

Half an hour later, the couple had zipped up their puffer jackets and ambled along the path past the house and the large greenhouses that grew orchids for the mansion, and peaches and kumquats amongst other things used in the kitchens. Behind the mansion's manicured lawns and the area used for growing produce, the land was uneven and barren in parts. The Graves could have put in a few more holiday cottages or a glamping site if they had wanted to, but Shilpa supposed that would detract from what the rich paid for, the exclusivity. She voiced her opinions to Robin.

'Rose Cottage is pretty close to the mansion,' he said.

'For the entourage of those staying at the main house,' Shilpa replied.

'Mr Grave doesn't need the extra cash,' Robin said and then muttered something about possible planning restrictions. 'It's not that dissimilar to Greenway,' he added, changing the topic. Shilpa had dragged him to Agatha Christie's famous holiday home last year. He had been reluctant to go at first, but even Robin had been charmed by the place and the quaint pub in Dittisham from where they had taken the ferry to the National Trust house.

'The boathouse and jetty are similar,' Shilpa said. 'Dreamcatcher Mansion is more majestic though, more opulent. It exudes wealth and something else that I can't put my finger on. And unlike Greenway, so much of the island has been left to ruin. It hasn't been landscaped like you'd expect. It's such a contrast to the main house.' She stopped and surveyed the land in front of her.

'Maybe that's what gives it its charm. Keeps the punters coming back,' Robin said.

'Maybe,' she said, although Shilpa didn't believe it. She waited a moment before speaking again. 'There's an uneasy feeling about the place. There's an atmosphere here. Our dinner with Duncan and Millie, it felt like… like something was unsaid.'

Robin was silent, which meant that he didn't entirely disagree. She smiled as they passed the first cottage behind the house. It was a similar size to Rose Cottage and had a once white picket fence around it. The lights were on, and voices could be heard.

'Shh,' Shilpa said. 'It's Duncan and Millie. Are they arguing?'

'They must get a little stir crazy out here. Catering to the demands of their rich guests while they live here.'

'There are worse places to live,' Shilpa said.

'What do they do for entertainment?'

Shilpa laughed. 'They argue. Anyway, it's not like they can't leave the island. This isn't like *The Beach*. They're free to leave.'

'Are they?'

Shilpa playfully hit Robin's shoulder. 'Slow down,' she said. 'You're practically running.'

'That must be Andreas's house,' Robin said, pointing to a house just past Duncan and Millie's to the left. 'And that,' Robin said, motioning beyond that, 'must be the old man's.'

The houses were all similar in size. Dreamcatcher Island was a beautiful place to live if you didn't like people much. She wondered if the old man was a recluse or if he had little choice. They had all assumed that the man had options to relocate, but maybe he didn't. Maybe he didn't have anywhere else and the island was everything he knew.

'You okay?' Robin asked.

Shilpa nodded. It was blustery towards the coast. The cold wind made her eyes water, and a tear slid down her cheek. Robin wiped away the tear with his gloved hand and took her hand in his. 'So you want to find another bay? Come with me.'

Ten minutes later, to the east of the island, behind the old man's house, they had found a sheltered stretch of beach. Robin pulled out a thermos from his backpack and two mugs. 'Coffee?' he asked.

Shilpa gratefully accepted a cup. The bay was beautiful, despite the wintery weather, with its jagged jet-black rocks and rough coastline, but it wasn't a patch on Dreamcatcher Bay with its sweeping wineglass-curved inlet. They drank their coffee in silence until Robin suggested they headed back. Shilpa noticed she felt calmer this side of the island, away from the mansion, but she had to admit they did need to get back.

# Chapter Nine

'Come on,' said Robin, leading the way back over the craggy landscape.

Shilpa was lost in thought. Ideas of a rasmalai cake or even a gulab jamun cheesecake were forming in her mind. Why hadn't she thought of these fusion cakes earlier? They could put her on the map. Shilpa opened her eyes and took a breath. This was what New Year was about: trying something new.

'Ow,' she heard Robin yelp up ahead. She saw that he was squatting, clutching his ankle.

'What's the matter?' she asked, hurrying over to him.

'Think I've twisted it,' Robin said, his face contorted in pain.

'Can you stand?' she asked, that sense of foreboding surfacing again. The skies were darkening and she swallowed down her anxiety. The feeling of being watched returned, but no one else was in the vicinity.

Robin tried, but his leg gave way. 'Come on,' she said. 'Rest on me. If that helps, you can limp the rest of the way. I can take some of your weight.' Albie's premonition came back to Shilpa as they struggled together. Gina's fiancé had said that someone was going to get hurt, and although it could have been a throwaway comment, it felt like there was some prescience in what he had said. Was it as simple as Robin spraining his ankle, or was there something more to come?

'Do you want me to take a look at that?' a voice said from behind them, making Shilpa jump.

A man with short grey hair and grey stubble stuck his hand out, and Shilpa reluctantly shook it.

'David,' he said. 'I'm a resident on the island.' A small dog with grey fur eyed her suspiciously from the man's side. 'I'm guessing you're not in the Graves party. You're in the cottage, and Millie and Duncan have filled you in.'

David didn't wait for a response. 'Here,' he said. 'Let me help.' He walked around the other side of Robin and took his weight. Robin had little choice but to lean on him. 'Let's go to my place. It's just over there.'

David must have sensed Shilpa's hesitation, as he stopped. 'I was a doctor,' he said. 'I can examine your friend's leg and give you something warm to drink.'

Shilpa glanced towards David's cottage and then towards the mansion. Rose Cottage was much further than David's house, and she had no phone signal to call the others.

'Don't worry,' David continued. 'I'm not going to drug you and hold you hostage. It's not like there are many houses here they could search if someone went missing, and you have friends staying with you at Rose Cottage, no?'

Shilpa nodded, a little concerned at how David knew so much about their party. But she couldn't argue with his logic, and despite her reservations and what Millie and Duncan had said, David didn't seem cantankerous. His living situation was far from normal, but he appeared to be a sensible and caring retiree, someone that even her mother would warm to, and that was saying something.

Together, she and David helped Robin into the cottage. Once inside, Shilpa was pleasantly surprised.

'A far cry from Dreamcatcher Mansion,' David said as they lowered Robin into an armchair. David put a small stool under Robin's leg whilst his dog curled up next to an unlit fire. 'Wait a minute, boy,' David said. 'I'll get that going in no time.'

'But not too dissimilar from Rose Cottage,' Shilpa said, stretching her shoulder and standing straight. She glanced around the living room and craned her neck to look into the kitchen. The layout was almost identical. There was a large range cooker in the open-plan kitchen, low, exposed wooden beams and a well-used fireplace. A bottle of Barolo sat on the kitchen table.

David told Shilpa to make herself comfortable, and she sat down on the worn leather sofa. 'You said you were a doctor?' she asked.

'A plastic surgeon, can you believe,' he said. 'I even had a practice on Harley Street for a time.'

'So you haven't lived here long?' Shilpa asked, knowing full well that he had. You couldn't commute to London easily from Dreamcatcher Island though, and she was curious to know more.

'I've lived here long enough. Always worked locally. Mainly Exeter. I had a lock-up there when the hours were long. Harley Street was before that. I kept this place but rented in London. I soon found out that London wasn't for me though. Shame, because that's where the money is.'

'And now you're retired?' Shilpa asked, eyeing his sleek television and Bang & Olufsen sound system.

'Just,' he said. 'The grey hair is a giveaway.'

Shilpa studied the man attending to her boyfriend's leg. He certainly had the physique of someone younger. He was right: his grey hair aged him. She put him in his late fifties. Young to retire, but she supposed if he had made his money, he probably had no need to work.

'Does that hurt?' he asked Robin, who winced in pain. His dog looked up before dropping his head on the rug again, patiently waiting for the fire to be lit. 'Just a sprain,' David said. 'I'll get an icepack and put a bandage on it. When you get back to the cottage, keep it elevated.'

'There goes the cooking for tonight,' Robin said.

'Tanvi'll be pleased,' Shilpa said. She turned to David. 'So what's it like?' she said. 'Living here.'

'Peaceful,' said David. 'It suits me fine. When I need some entertainment, I take the ferry across to Parrot Bay. I know Josh, the so-called ferryman. If I need to get away, I give him a call, and I have a boat, of course, so I can leave when I want to. Can I get you a coffee or something stronger?'

'Tea would be great,' Robin said. Shilpa asked for the same.

'Do you ever meet the house guests?' Robin asked as David put the kettle on.

'Now and again. Most stick to the house. Some are nosy, understandably. I'm sure Duncan and Millie do a good job of warning them away from me. I do a pretty good impression of a cranky old man.'

After their tea, David offered to walk them back to the cottage. Robin was hesitant, but Shilpa gratefully accepted. She liked David. He appeared genuine amidst the Graves. As they edged towards Dreamcatcher Mansion, Shilpa noticed that David kept his eyes to the ground.

## Chapter Ten

S hilpa and Tanvi left the compound of Rose Cottage and headed towards the swimming pool in what little light remained of the evening. The uneasiness Shilpa had felt on Dreamcatcher Island had dissipated after their run-in with David. He wasn't the least bit grouchy as Millie had made him out to be, and even though Shilpa got the distinct feeling that the house manager would have disapproved of her talking to David like that, she was glad she had. Since their conversation, she had felt a certain lightness about the place and felt a little bit more daring too.

Millie had warned them to stay away from the guests, and so far they had tried their best. A cold wind had picked up over the course of the afternoon, and Shilpa and Tanvi expected the pool to be empty.

There was a large rosemary bush at one end of the swimming pool, and Robin had sent them on a mission to collect some sprigs, declaring he had to have it for the lamb even though he wasn't really cooking but just directing Tanvi in the kitchen. Shilpa had offered to step in, but Robin wouldn't hear anything of it. Shilpa was glad of the fresh air. Thanks to Tanvi, she had started drinking a little too early, and she wanted to stay awake to bring in the new year.

'Hey, they're over there,' Tanvi said as they approached the pool. She pointed to the large earthenware urn under a portico to the far end of the pool.

Shilpa's eyes followed Tanvi's finger. Albie and Richard, Felicity and Gina were huddled together under one of the outdoor heaters, smoking. 'Should we just go back?' Shilpa whispered.

'What? And risk Robin blaming his poor cooking – or should I say directing – on the lack of rosemary? Come on, live a little. They can't see us from up there where they're sitting.' Tanvi motioned towards the plant they were about to attack.

'This rosemary bush is in a precarious position. We are risking life and limb for our supper.'

Tanvi sighed. 'You're usually more gung-ho than this,' she said.

Shilpa shrugged. 'I think it's the time of year. New Year is about new beginnings, but…' She trailed off. 'Do you think I rushed into things with Robin? This place is lovely and luxurious to say the least, but something about it is making me so anxious about everything, it seems.'

'It's the detective in you,' Tanvi said, holding Shilpa's arm. 'Come on.'

The two walked to the rosemary bush, and Shilpa retrieved from her coat pocket the scissors which she had picked up earlier from the kitchen. They set about their task in silence so as not to disturb the guests, but as Shilpa walked to the far side of the bush, she could distinctly hear Felicity's voice.

'Come on,' Tanvi whispered. Shilpa silenced her by placing her finger on her lips.

'He's not well,' a man was saying. 'You can tell.'

'D-don't worry,' said another. Shilpa had heard the stutter during her baking class and knew it was Richard. 'I'm sure he's put money aside to support your venture.'

'I'm not in the least bit worried about that, mate,' the other man said. It had to be Albie.

'A-and your mum and Rashmi are close, Albie,' Richard said. 'That's got to count for something.'

Richard's insensitive comments appeared to be ignored, and a silence fell upon the group until Felicity's voice came through again. 'Do you have another rich investor?' she asked in that shrill tone of hers.

Shilpa heard a shuffling of feet.

'Felicity, I never wanted to ask Alan for any investment—'

'I asked,' Gina interrupted. 'It's my project as much as his, and Albie is practically family. You know how Daddy is always going on about family.'

'I think what Daddy has said is that blood trumps everything,' Felicity said. A silence fell upon the group. 'Has Daddy said anything about his health?' Felicity asked. Her tone was a mix of concern and something else that Shilpa couldn't quite place.

'No,' Gina said. 'Not to me anyway.'

'What's that supposed to mean?' Felicity asked.

'Well, you're his blood, aren't you?'

'S-so if he were to die, do you think Felicity would get it all?' Richard asked.

'The Grave tradition is that the firstborn inherits the lot,' Gina said in a clipped voice. 'It's been like that for generations.' An awkward silence followed.

'I was only j-joking,' Richard said. Someone attempted to laugh it off, but Shilpa could sense an atmosphere.

'The one thing about Daddy,' Felicity said, 'is that he's fair. Whatever he chooses to do will be the right thing.'

'Unless there's a condition in the will that prevents Alan from leaving the money to whomever he wishes.'

'Puh-lease,' Albie said. 'With all his money, I'm sure he could hire a team of lawyers to find a loophole to break any kind of conditional clause.'

'If he wants to,' said a small voice. Shilpa took this to be Gina. 'And then there's Mum,' Gina said a little louder.

'And J-Julian,' said Richard, clearly without shame from his earlier comment.

'Yes, Julian,' Gina said, stifling a laugh.

'I think I'm going to head in,' said Felicity. 'Check on Daddy.'

Shilpa could hear the click of her heels as Felicity left through the archway back to the house.

'She's so tetchy of late,' Gina said.

'Richard hasn't stepped up to the mark,' Albie said. 'Don't keep the lady waiting, mate.'

'Tonight would be perfect,' said Gina, her voice shrill with excitement. 'The whole family's here. Well, not quite the whole family, but those who count and it is her birthday.'

The three burst into laughter. 'You're gonna do it, aren't you, mate?' Albie said.

Shilpa felt a tug on her arm. 'Come on,' Tanvi said. 'I'm freezing my bits off out here.' Shilpa cut off a few stalks of rosemary and slipped the scissors back into her pocket. She followed her friend back towards the cottage, her head down, rosemary in hand.

'Got what you wanted?' said a sharp voice from behind her.

Shilpa turned. She held out the rosemary to Julian, who didn't even feign interest. Instead he sniggered and stared at her for longer than was necessary. Shilpa averted her gaze, searching for Tanvi, who had been a few steps ahead of her. She couldn't locate her friend anywhere, and it was dark now.

She put her hand in her pocket and clutched the scissors. When she turned back, the guest had disappeared.

Shilpa let out the breath she didn't realise she was holding.

'There you are,' Tanvi said from up ahead. 'What's gotten into you today?'

Shilpa didn't say anything; she just hurried along.

## Chapter Eleven

It was supposed to be innocent, the murder mystery, but something was off from the moment they started playing. Felicity could feel it in her bones.

She had taken a walk earlier in the afternoon while it was still light and had passed the hut where the old man lived. She remembered it from when she was a child. Had she visited herself? With her mother and Julian? She didn't recall, but she remembered that the old man had been kind. At least she thought he had been. She hadn't spoken to him in years. He never came anywhere near the house, although she was sure she had seen someone pottering around the garden the other evening. It could have been him, but it could have also been one of the guests at Rose Cottage.

Felicity had stopped outside the hut, which wasn't really a hut but a small cottage. It was just so tiny compared to Dreamcatcher Mansion. Enough for one person with low expectations, she supposed. She didn't know what had drawn her to the house, but when she reached it, she had the compulsion to knock on the door. She didn't. Instead, she turned and started to walk back to the main house.

'Hello,' she heard a man call behind her. Felicity stopped and turned back. 'You don't remember me?' he had asked.

'I do,' she said, returning his smile. 'David,' she said, pleased that she recalled his name. She was terrible with names. A memory of a filling bowl of soup presented to her by a roaring fire came back to her.

Her dad always joked that the old man didn't know how to smile, that he didn't know how to live, but there was something warm about him and what she remembered about his home. Perhaps it was all in her imagination. Felicity never was a good judge of character, especially if any of her ex-boyfriends were anything to go by, but there was something about David that made her want to talk to him.

'Have you got a big evening planned?' he asked. 'You're not usually here for New Year.'

Felicity nodded. 'It's my birthday,' she gushed, like a child. 'And you? Is anyone…?' She trailed off, realising a little late how insensitive she had been.

'No, love. Not as yet,' he said.

Felicity wondered if, by his words, he meant that someone was on their way. He stared at her for a moment. Felicity pulled up the zip on her coat and crossed her arms.

'Happy birthday. Is it a big one?' David asked.

Felicity nodded. 'It's why we are all here.'

'It's going to get much colder tonight,' David said. 'Make sure you wrap up warm for those fireworks.'

'I'll need something,' she said. 'I'm supposed to be playing dead later for our hide-and-seek murder mystery. The rest of the family have to find me.' Felicity raised a hand to her mouth. How mean she was to talk about her plans when David was going to be all alone on New Year's Eve. 'Perhaps you could join us?' she said, regretting the invite as she uttered the words. Her father would be furious. Not that she was inviting someone back to the house – she was always inviting waifs and strays home, as Alan put it – but because it was David.

David; the man who had refused to sell up when Alan bought the island; the man who had rights and stood his ground, no matter how much money Alan Grave threw at him, or so Daddy had told her. Felicity was sure that David was the only man who had resisted her father's charms and money, and she had a certain respect for David because of this.

'I can't,' David said. He offered no explanation, and she didn't press him, relieved at his response.

'I'll be going then. It was nice to see you,' Felicity had said, and she meant it. She turned to leave.

'Felicity,' David had called out. 'Have a good evening,' he had said. 'And be careful.'

At his words, a chill ran down her spine as she walked towards the main house.

~

Felicity took her place on the hessian sack in the boathouse. Earlier, in the light of day, it had seemed a good idea to hide in here; but now, in the darkness, it felt dank and icy, not to mention the smell of petrol and dried fish.

'I don't like that you know more than us,' Gina had grumbled about the murder mystery earlier. Felicity loved her sister, but she could be so petulant at times. She said as much to Richard.

'Pot calling the kettle black, don't you think,' was all he had said. She watched her so-called boyfriend gazing at Gina in her chartreuse dress and white rabbit fur that complemented her skin colour perfectly. What Felicity would give to have sun-kissed skin like that. No tan in the world came close to what Gina had.

'So who's your dad?' Felicity had once asked her when she

was young enough to get away with it. They had been away from their parents, sitting on a rug on the front lawns at the house in Suffolk, eating strawberries and cream laced with sugar. Felicity had overheard her mother talking about Gina being adopted and had outright asked her sister about it.

'A prince,' Gina had replied as she dunked another strawberry in cream and then into the bowl of sugar. She put the fruit in her mouth and bit it. Strawberry juice dribbled down her chin and stained her jeans.

'Why didn't he marry your mum then?' Felicity had asked.

'He died,' Gina had said. 'Otherwise he would have.'

Felicity heard two people walk towards the entrance of the boathouse, rousing her from her memory. 'Drat,' she mumbled to herself; she was going to be found. But the people at the entrance to the boathouse didn't seem the least bit interested in finding her.

'Isn't that something?' Gina was saying. Felicity adjusted her position on the ground so that she could observe them. The moon was full tonight and illuminated the couple in the doorway. Albie was practically holding his fiancée up. Gina kicked off her shoes and sipped her martini, the contents of the glass sploshing about and dripping onto Albie's white shirt.

Gina's diamond ring caught a light and flashed at Felicity, making her wince. From what she had heard, Albie couldn't afford a diamond like that. His antiques business was practically bankrupt, which was why he was so desperate to marry Gina. And then, of course, there were the gambling debts he needed to pay off. His family were no longer going to keep the sharks away, or so her best friend had told her, and she should know – she was some distant cousin of Albie Leafield.

Felicity didn't know what Gina saw in him. Okay, so he was tall and just the right amount of muscular, and he was connected. He knew people. Not just the rich, but artistic types, bar owners, producers. He was a modern-day Lovejoy who everyone warmed to. Gina and Albie wanted to start their own antique jewellery store in central London – funded by her father, of course.

Felicity could hardly criticise. Her father had paid for all her ventures. The latest and the last, or so he said, was supporting her fashion line, which was slowly failing despite the hundreds of thousands that had been put into marketing and promotion. One mean but extremely popular designer at London Fashion Week had said that it didn't matter how much money she threw at her brand; if the designs were crap, they wouldn't sell. Felicity's nose twitched at the memory.

Her failing fashion line was something she didn't want to think about. Her father wouldn't cut her off like he had threatened, would he? She didn't think so. Alan Grave was too soft when it came to his firstborn. She smiled, feeling comforted by the sentiment.

Felicity gently opened the case she had previously stored in the boathouse and took what she needed. She opened the mini bottle of vodka and downed it in one. She didn't know why she was trying to be quiet. Gina and Albie weren't in the least bit interested in finding her.

Her hide-and-seek murder mystery had been the last in a string of bad ideas. She had wanted to bring the family together. She and Gina had practically been brought up together. They had spent nearly all the school holidays with one another except the trips Felicity, Julian and their mother spent at Dreamcatcher. Rashmi simply refused to come to the island. It was why Felicity was determined to get her here this time. She wanted Rashmi to admire how beautiful the place was, but more than that, she had wanted to know if Rashmi would back out, concocting some story to get out of visiting the place. What was it that Rashmi hated about it so much?

So far, Felicity was none the wiser. Rashmi seemed her usual indifferent self. Perhaps Rashmi had previously avoided coming to the island because there was a time when Julian had an obvious crush on Gina, and Rashmi hadn't wanted to encourage it by allowing the two of them to get lost on an island together. Thank goodness Julian's crush hadn't lasted. She had to thank Rashmi in a way for staying away for all those years. Because when they came to Dreamcatcher, it was just them, and it was what Felicity liked so much about their trips to the bay.

'But isn't it?' Gina slurred. 'And to think I had thought he was dead, all this time.'

'And she only just told you?' Albie said.

Gina nodded.

'Why here? Why now?' Albie asked. 'This changes everything.'

'It doesn't change anything.'

'The will,' Albie said.

'Shh,' Gina said. 'What's that in there?' she asked, looking in Felicity's direction.

Albie held Gina's wrist and pulled her back.

'What?' she said, pulling her hand away. 'Don't talk like that.' She straightened herself and headed inside the boathouse.

Gina was drunk, as was Felicity, but their talk had instantly sobered her up. She wanted to spring to her feet, embrace her sister and friend and ask Gina who she had been talking about. Felicity was certain that they were talking about Gina's biological father, and Felicity wanted all the details.

Felicity screwed her eyes shut as Gina walked past the wooden boat towards her. As she lay there waiting to be found, a thought occurred to her as to who Gina had been talking about. Felicity suddenly felt the chill in the air.

Gina screamed. Her scream turned into a giggle. 'Found you,' she shouted. 'Albie, I found Flick. I win.'

'You've been in here the whole time,' Albie said as Felicity struggled to her feet. 'You must have heard us.'

'Heard you?' Felicity asked. She crossed her arms across her chest to stop her hands from trembling.

Albie stared at her for a moment, then he turned back to his fiancée. 'You win,' he said with a laugh. 'You win.'

## Chapter Twelve

Julian stood by the water and ripped the naked image into several pieces. He took a step closer to the oncoming wave and then opened his hand, letting the tiny pieces fall into the sea. He despised her. She had made him the person that he was. She had made him do those things, those unthinkable things. He ground his fists into his pockets.

'Damn her,' he whispered to a wave as it rolled towards him, stopping to recede just before the water licked his shoes. He despised her and yet he still loved her. It wasn't right what she had done, what she was now threatening to do. Would she expose him in that way? He wouldn't put it past her.

The crowd had dissipated after Gina had located Felicity's 'body'. What a palaver that had been. Everyone obeying Felicity's orders as usual. As the eldest of Alan's children, she was the one who everything would come to when he passed, and they all knew that was going to be soon. No wonder everyone had agreed to come to Dreamcatcher Mansion over New Year. Perhaps Felicity had been testing them. He wouldn't have put it past her.

Julian made a face. It was clear to him that Gina did not

love Albie; their relationship was a joke. But then Gina had always been the type to need someone in her life. Albie had just been there at the right time, and he was in desperate need of her money, so there was no chance that he was going to leave anytime soon.

Julian closed his eyes and took in a lungful of sea air, thinking about Gina in her green silk dress. Cloaked by darkness, except for the light of the moon, he felt safe out here with his thoughts. He couldn't deny that at one time he had been infatuated with Gina. They had had a thing, if you could call it that. They had been young, too young to do anything sexual. He had wanted to, but she had refrained, and he was glad she had, because given what had happened later, it wouldn't have cast him in a good light. They held hands, they kissed. She even let him fondle her breasts in the large grounds of their father's estate during weekends and holidays.

Every summer, Julian had looked forward to spending it with Gina, until the year she completely blanked him and spent all her time with Felicity instead. The two became inseparable and spoke in whispers around him.

Later that summer, at their father's annual party, it became clear that both Felicity and Gina had boyfriends. Julian had spied both Gina and Felicity making out with two spotty teenagers behind the pool house. Julian would have laughed at the memory if it didn't still sting. Still, the boys had unfortunately crashed their car on the way home from that party, and that had put an end to those love affairs, and for that Julian allowed himself a small smile.

He recalled how Rashmi had broken the news to Felicity and Gina the next morning over their poached eggs.

It was then that he realised he liked seeing women distressed. He had comforted his sisters at the time. Gina had burrowed her head into his shoulder and gripped him tightly, but Julian had vowed never to go near her in that way again, and he hadn't. No, he had chosen someone else instead. On reflection, it had been a good decision. If he and Gina had fallen in love, he would have had to deal with her mother, and he didn't think he could handle that.

Rashmi had avoided the celebrations at the boathouse after Flick had been found. Gina's mum had come to Devon to keep Alan happy and that was it. There was no chance she was participating in anything the least bit outdoorsy. Julian couldn't understand what his father saw in her, but he supposed at least she spoke her mind. She wasn't afraid to call people out on their lies.

He recalled one summer at the Suffolk house when Felicity and he were younger, Rashmi had taken their father to task when he had promised to take them all out for the day to a local bird sanctuary but failed to do so.

It wasn't the first time Alan had promised to do something with them and then failed to turn up, instead sending a load of presents from Harrods or a chauffeur to take them somewhere. They had grown used to it, but Rashmi wasn't going to let their dad fail to show up every time.

It was years after that that Alan next skipped out on them. Rashmi's wrath hadn't been worth it in the interim. Julian had wondered at the time what it was that Rashmi had over their father to make him listen to her. He never listened to anyone. Perhaps, he reasoned, Alan just respected Rashmi. He certainly never respected Jane.

From where Julian was standing, Jane had never been treated well by Alan, but then he couldn't blame him. His mother was erratic, irrational at times. In front of the others, any others, she played a part. The perfect host when they were at home; the perfect mother at school events; and of course, the wounded divorcee. She was great at attention-seeking in this last role, throwing herself at rich men, but had never been able to succeed in her plan. She was still single even though she and Alan had been divorced for decades.

Jane had been engaged several times, but each time the engagement had been called off. Julian couldn't work out if it was his mother, who couldn't imagine being married to anyone other than the great Alan Grave, or if the men she had been with figured out how crazy she was before they said 'I do'.

He assumed it was the latter, especially in recent years. Jane was becoming demented with the brushing of her hair and turning the light switch on and off.

Julian didn't think to offer his mother any support, because, quite frankly, he didn't think she deserved it. Jane was no different to the annoying cat that Julian's next-door neighbour owned. It was always mewling about something insignificant, and one day someone was going to take a bat to its head because they wouldn't be able to take its whining. His mother would probably meet the same fate.

Julian's teenage years were fuelled by drinking too much vodka and smoking too much weed. Jane had hardly noticed. The excess had done something to his brain though. He never admitted as much, but he was almost certain of it. Sometimes his thoughts wouldn't fuse together correctly, and he found himself halfway through a sentence with nothing more to say. Often he found that he couldn't read a social situation.

It was like he had forgotten how to behave, especially with women. A sudden urge came over him, and he couldn't focus. It was like everything around him was blurred out apart from the woman he had set his sights on. At first, some of his female friends laughed it off, but then he found he was getting aggressive, or so he had been told.

Two women he had once been friends with had cut him out of their lives, and another had filed a police report. He couldn't believe it. It took some quick thinking and the pulling of several favours to get himself out of that one.

Julian needed help, more so than his mother. But Jane wasn't going to get any help, and neither was he.

His eyes searched the water for remnants of the photo. Nothing. Then he turned towards the house. They would be down any minute now, the whole lot of them, ready for the fireworks. He focused in on a woman standing at her bedroom window on the first floor of Dreamcatcher Mansion. Could she see him? And if she could, would she be shaking inside with excitement or fear? He didn't know, and that thrilled him a little. He stepped back into the shadows.

## Chapter Thirteen

The passion fruit and chocolate cake stood half eaten on the glass and driftwood table at the end of the room. Shilpa had spent hours crafting the marzipan flowers that were now carelessly strewn on the silver platter on which the cake stood. Shilpa made a face, but what did she expect? After all, it had been a commission and her client hadn't ordered the cake just to look at it. The cake had been devoured and there was no better compliment to a baker than that.

It was a surreal feeling being inside the mansion once again, this time with the owner and his family, his extended family. The enormous dining room was a mix of traditional and modern, with a solid, dark wood dining table and chairs.

The staff were nowhere to be seen. Shilpa was surprised that they had been allowed to leave. She had noticed them retreat after the fireworks, but maybe the Graves were kind, knowing full well that the same staff would be up at the crack of dawn ready to serve them their breakfast. At the other end of the room, just before the French doors that led onto the patio, was a makeshift bar.

Countless paintings adorned the walls. Shilpa wasn't an expert in art, but she had read an article in *ArtHouse* about a Rothko being in the main dining room, and the block of red paint splashed across one of the canvases was vaguely familiar. She studied the painting and then turned.

The guests were seated around the table. Rashmi was sitting to her right and had just given her the third degree on her Indian heritage.

'Goa?' Rashmi had asked. 'Your name isn't Goan.'

'Delhi, originally,' Shilpa had said, which seemed to satisfy her. Rashmi had smiled at this and had said no more, her attention taken by her daughter's display of affection with Albie at the table.

'Gina,' Rashmi scolded, glaring at her daughter. Gina seemed not to care. Albie removed his hands from Gina and put them flat on the table.

Alan Grave eyed Shilpa and her friends with suspicion. She was staff, and there were no other staff around. Andreas the chef had no doubt cooked his best meal ever. There were no tell-tale remnants. The staff had done a good job to clear everything away from dinner before the guests returned.

Duncan and Millie would be back at their cottage too, congratulating themselves on a successful evening. Shilpa glanced at her watch. It was one in the morning. They were probably fast asleep now.

Of course, Alan Grave had his reservations. Shilpa, Tanvi, Brijesh and Robin were interlopers in this private family gathering, but they had little choice as to how they ended up at the house.

Despite Robin's twisted ankle he and Tanvi successfully presented a scallop starter. But the rack of lamb was difficult to taste under the charred edges so they had stepped outside Rose Cottage to view the spectacular firework display. Shilpa could hear laughing and talking from the family below and thought they were safe to step out of the grounds of the cottage to sit on the pool loungers.

The storm that had threatened earlier had failed to materialise, and the night was relatively still and clear. 'Perfect for fireworks,' Tanvi had said as she swirled her champagne around her coupe. The group had huddled together in their puffer jackets as the display started just as midnight struck.

Ten minutes into the display, Shilpa noticed that Richard and Felicity were engaged in some sort of argument on the beach. Felicity appeared distraught and then she disappeared. Moments later she was walking up the steps towards the pool.

'Oh,' Felicity had said in between fireworks, as if surprised to see them, but her eyes lit up as soon as she recognised who they were. 'Serendipity,' she said, swaying as she walked towards the group with a bottle of Krug in her hand. 'Supplies are running low. I offered to get some more. Duncan and Andreas are busy with that...' She trailed off and pointed upwards as pink, gold and green flashes of light filled the sky.

Felicity walked away from them towards the house. There was something about Felicity Grave that intrigued Shilpa. She was old enough, yet she seemed so young in her manner and her words. Shilpa imagined her to have had a sheltered upbringing, her parents making sure her every whim was met. She came across as naive and spoiled, but Shilpa could hardly blame her.

Shilpa turned back but then heard a crash. Felicity had tripped over a pot.

'The murder went perfectly,' she shouted as they all turned towards her. 'They took ages to find me. They were fooled,' she said with some exuberance.

As her face lit up from a flash of white in the sky, Shilpa noticed that Felicity wasn't as enthusiastic as she sounded. It could have been because her make-up was smudged from playing the part of the murder victim, but there was a lost look in the woman's eyes that told another story.

'Great,' Robin shouted back. He held on to Shilpa's hand and gave it a squeeze. 'Who was the killer?'

'My father,' she said. In another flash of light, Shilpa saw a single tear run down Felicity's face. At least she thought that was what she saw. Seconds later the light was gone and so was Felicity as she headed into the house through the French doors.

Shilpa had turned her attention back towards the fireworks, which were as spectacular as promised, and leaned into Robin. The cold air was refreshing after the heat of Rose Cottage with its modern log burner that Brijesh insisted they lit to keep the cottage cosy. The burnt lamb hadn't helped, filling the cottage with the smell of cinder. They had opened all the windows and had decided to return to Tanvi's tiramisu after bringing in the new year with another glass of champagne as they watched the fireworks.

Twenty minutes had passed when Felicity had stumbled towards them again empty-handed. If she had been into the house for supplies, she had either forgotten them in her drunken stupor or had been distracted by something else. The staff perhaps. A few of the employees who had been on the beach helping with the fireworks had headed into the house not long after Felicity.

'Where's the booze?' Richard had asked from the steps to the beach. 'What's taking you so long?'

'I was just trying to persuade this lovely lot to come and join us back at the house for a nightcap, wasn't I?' Felicity said, smiling brightly. 'So you'll come to the house?' she asked.

'Flick—' Richard started, but she cut him off.

'There's plenty of space in the dining room, and I think you'll love it. You don't want to stay all cooped up in that little cottage all night.'

Tanvi was first behind Felicity as they headed into the house. She had been desperate to catch a glimpse inside the mansion since they arrived at Dreamcatcher Island. There was no way that she was going to pass up an opportunity now.

# Chapter Fourteen

'So once you get malaria you can relapse. It's always there, dormant in your system,' Albie was saying as he took a long sip of his drink.

'No, no. That simply isn't correct,' snapped Richard. Rashmi rolled her eyes at the two.

*They are no different to my family,* Shilpa mused as she relaxed into the dining chair and sipped her Amaretto.

She hadn't wanted another drink, but Felicity had insisted, and she didn't want to appear rude. It didn't take Shilpa long to recognise that Felicity was one of those people that took offence if someone refused her hospitality, a trait that Felicity shared with Shilpa's mother.

Shilpa noticed that while everyone had someone to talk to, Felicity wasn't talking to anyone. The birthday girl's drink of choice, after the fireworks, had been a Negroni, 'to warm me up,' she had declared. She hadn't hesitated with the measures of Campari, gin and vermouth and used a short, dark-green swizzle stick to give the ingredients a stir.

Richard was trying to talk to her, but she had that same

lost-girl look that she had earlier in the evening before they had been invited over.

'How was the murder mystery?' Shilpa asked when Albie temporarily sat opposite her.

'Great,' Albie said, his eyes glazed over, like he was on something.

'Did anyone get hurt?' Shilpa asked, repeating his premonition back to him. Albie stared at her with his icy blue eyes, and that ominous feeling that had disappeared earlier returned. Another night and they would be off the island, and that moment couldn't come soon enough for Shilpa.

'Sorry?' Albie asked, turning away. She followed his gaze towards Felicity. Albie turned to her again, but Gina sat down next to him.

'Am I interrupting?' she asked with a wicked laugh.

Shilpa shook her head. 'Your partner was just saying–' she started.

'How beautiful you are, my darling,' Albie said, 'and that I can't wait for us to get married.' He nuzzled his fiancée's neck.

Shilpa was about to say something when the sound of a chair being pushed back over the wooden floor made her turn.

'Excuse me,' Felicity said, standing up. Her face was pensive and purposeful. Felicity put her drink down and cleared her throat. Jane tried to catch her daughter's eye, but Felicity just turned. Felicity tapped her knife on her glass and waited for silence to descend. 'I've something to say,' she said.

Everyone quietened except for Tanvi, who was laughing at something Brijesh was saying. When Tanvi realised, she quickly closed her mouth and suffered a look from Alan Grave.

'I'm ever so tired,' Alan said to Felicity. 'I wouldn't normally stay up so late. I can't recall the last New Year's Eve I was awake for, but as it's your birthday and we are all here together, I thought I'd make an exception, but you've probably noticed that I've been nodding off.'

Felicity studied her father's face then made a show of acceptance. Even though Shilpa hadn't been in the room for long, she had seen Alan close his eyes and jerk his head back more than once.

'Daddy,' Felicity started as Alan stood up. Alan took his daughter's hand. He examined the shiny timepiece on her wrist, which Shilpa assumed had been his birthday present to her, then he released her. 'We'll speak in the morning,' he mumbled as he turned to leave, as if he knew what she was about to say but would rather she didn't. Rashmi followed and then Jane. Felicity appeared defeated but only for a moment before her bright smile reappeared.

The younger Graves made their way to the patio despite the time of year. Wrapped in cashmere scarves and full of champagne, they didn't seem to feel the cold. Shilpa had to admit she didn't feel it either, which was unlike her, but she had had enough to drink, and for New Year's Eve it wasn't as icy as it could have been. Brijesh and Robin, who had been talking to the other young men, followed. Brijesh had now mastered taking Robin's weight on his shoulder as he limped behind them.

'I think I'm done,' Shilpa said to Tanvi.

'That's not like you. What's wrong?' her friend asked.

Shilpa glanced at the house and shrugged. 'Something about this place just doesn't feel right.'

'Not that again. Don't be such a spoilsport,' Tanvi said. 'One more drink on the patio won't *kill* you. We can sleep all day if we like.' Tanvi stood up and made her way towards the patio, and Shilpa reluctantly followed with their coats. She was so tired though; she could barely keep her eyes open.

One drink on the patio turned into three. Shilpa and Tanvi found they had much in common with Gina, who frequented some of the same bars as they had when they lived in London.

Felicity told them all about her fashion line and how she

was using unique fabrics from Rashmi's company in Mumbai to stand out from the rest. Shilpa and Tanvi had eventually wandered off towards the loos. They had taken their time admiring a few other rooms like the cinema suite and games room on their way. She laughed in the hall as they peered into each room, holding on to each other in drunken delight at their finds. On their way back they made their way to the kitchen, and the last door they opened appeared to lead to a cellar.

'Let's go down there,' Tanvi said. 'I can imagine there are the most exquisite bottles of wine all stacked up, like in the movies.'

'What do you know about wine?' Shilpa asked. She was sceptical about snooping in her employer's house, but it was late, and the older family members had all retired to bed. 'Come on then,' she said to Tanvi, the alcohol in her blood giving her some Dutch courage.

'Ah,' Tanvi said. 'There's the Shilpa that broke into a crazy woman's apartment and jumped into the estuary that one time. I knew she was hiding somewhere.'

They began to descend the stairs. 'Isn't there a light?' Tanvi asked, putting on the torch from her phone. As they got to the bottom of the stairs, it was clear they were not alone. There was a shuffling noise from behind the shelving that held the wine bottles.

'Rats?' Tanvi asked, turning towards the stairs.

'Shhh,' Shilpa said. 'Listen, music.' Something old and French was playing. The shuffling was followed by giggling. Shilpa motioned for Tanvi to put her phone away, which she did. Shilpa held her breath as she peered around the cabinet. Then she turned back to Tanvi, her eyes wide. She made her way back up the stairs in silence, Tanvi following.

When they were safely on the other side of the cellar door, Shilpa started laughing.

'What?' Tanvi asked. 'What?'

'It was Felicity,' Shilpa said. 'Candles around them, Negroni in reach.'

'With the chef,' Tanvi said. 'I knew it. I saw them exchange a look earlier. I thought it was one of hatred, but maybe it was passion,' she said with a laugh. 'Check this out,' Tanvi said, holding a dusty bottle of red.

Shilpa put her hand to her mouth. 'You didn't,' she said.

'We can hardly return it now, can we?'

Shilpa shook her head. 'I don't know why I bring you to places like this.' She walked towards the kitchen, and Tanvi followed.

'Should we have a glass?' Tanvi asked. She started opening cupboards in the kitchen to locate a couple of wine glasses. Failing to find any, she pulled out two mugs and found a corkscrew. Tanvi opened one of the rear kitchen doors, and the two of them sat at a small, green wrought-iron table where Shilpa imagined the staff took their cigarette breaks.

Tanvi opened the bottle of wine and poured a generous measure into each mug. She took a sip. 'This is pretty rank. Goes to show money can't buy you taste.'

Shilpa sniffed at the mug and put it back down. 'There he goes,' she said, watching a figure retreat from the house.

Tanvi strained to look at him. 'That's not the chef, is it? He's shorter and stockier than that.'

'No,' Shilpa said, although she had noticed the look between Felicity and Andreas that told of more than an employee/employer relationship. 'That isn't Andreas.'

'Then who is it?'

'Duncan,' she said.

'Duncan as in Duncan and Millie?'

Shilpa nodded. Tanvi swallowed her wine.

By the time they had rinsed their mugs and returned to the patio to find the others, it was empty. 'Maybe the boys have gone back to the cottage,' Shilpa said.

'They wouldn't have gone without us,' Tanvi said. 'You know what Brijesh is like. He's so traditional.'

'You're right,' Shilpa said. 'They'll be back for us, wherever they've gone. Should we open this last bottle?'

'This is the Shilpa I know and love,' Tanvi said. 'Finally, you're relaxing a little.'

'I know I've been uptight. I'm the paid help here though, not a guest, and it makes me feel uncomfortable. Especially with that talk from Millie and Duncan that we are to stay away from the guests.'

'Duncan is one to talk,' Tanvi said with a laugh. 'Felicity invited us to the house,' she added, taking another selfie with the large dining room behind her.

'Exactly. And I've come to realise they are not too dissimilar from us despite their wealth. I don't know why I've been so tense the last couple of days.'

'You're not pregnant, are you?' Tanvi asked.

Shilpa laughed, but something tightened in the pit of her stomach.

## Chapter Fifteen

The room was dim with only her bedside light to guide her. Rashmi got into bed beside Alan and put her arms around him, wanting his warmth more than anything else.

He flinched. 'You're so cold. Where've you been?'

Rashmi was silent. 'Just on the balcony,' she said eventually.

'Hmm,' he said, half asleep. 'I didn't hear you come in. It's much too cold to be out at this time in the morning.'

Rashmi made a noise in agreement. She had slipped in and out of the bedroom while Alan was sleeping. It never took him long to fall asleep these days, not with the cocktail of drugs he was on. She watched him every morning and evening swallowing various tablets in yellows and greens. Tonight he had taken his pills with whisky. A little unorthodox, but what did it matter?

As she had crept back into the room, she had gently opened the balcony door, hoping to hear the youngsters talking. Julian and the two men staying at Rose Cottage had been chatting earlier, but she hadn't had time to listen in to what they were saying. The men were long gone, and for a while there was silence below. There was something about the quiet that had set her teeth on edge. She had waited, then she checked her watch and considered a quick shower before getting into bed, but she didn't think she could afford the time.

Rashmi closed her eyes. She thought about her daughter, her Gina. She had loved her more than anything from the moment she was born. With a child out of wedlock, she was certain her parents would disown her, but they hadn't. They had proved themselves that way. What she had done was revolutionary in India at that time. Yes, she was talked about, sneered at. Some of her mother's friends stopped inviting her mother to their kitty parties.

'How could you have been so stupid?' her mother had asked. 'And now refusing to have a clean-up.' Rashmi cringed thinking of her mother's term for an abortion. Had Gina come to her in the same way she would never have spoken to her like that. No, she would have spoken to her with compassion. Gina *had* come to her with another problem though. Something more sinister than a love-child. Rashmi had known very well what she had been doing; she just couldn't tell her mother that. It made her wonder if Gina had known what she had been doing too.

Rashmi pressed her fingers to her eyelids and took a breath. She hadn't wanted to come to this godforsaken house, but she had done it for her daughter and Alan. Earlier that day she had grown tired of everyone's effusive appreciation of the house, which she considered to be average in its facilities and decor.

When she had seen Gina sitting alone in the cinema room watching an old movie, she decided to join her, carefully turning the lock on the door behind her. Had she known then that she was about to shatter her daughter's world?

'What's wrong?' Alan asked.

'Nothing,' Rashmi whispered. She opened her eyes, picked

up the remote to the night-light on her bedside table and pressed a button. Darkness.

'I can hear you thinking. It's unsettling,' Alan said.

'Shhh,' she said. Rashmi turned away from Alan and closed her eyes once again.

## Chapter Sixteen

'Ah, you're back,' Millie said as Duncan came through the front door of their cottage. He rubbed his eyes which had dark circles around them. 'New Year is always a killer,' she said, draping her arms around him. Duncan shrugged her off and picked up the brandy bottle from the silver tray in the lounge to pour himself a large measure.

'What took you so long?' Millie said, returning to the sofa and picking up her magazine. She feigned disinterest in his answer, but inside she was all nerves. It was a good job she had taken acting classes in school. Her performances were at least better than Felicity's. She had witnessed her rehearsal death the other night from the security of the boathouse and had to refrain from laughing. Felicity Grave was quite something, and it irritated Millie that the pretty little darling hadn't really been killed. Nevertheless, there was always time.

Duncan drained his glass and turned his attention towards the lights of Dreamcatcher Mansion which were visible from their living room window.

Millie stood up, padded over to the window and closed the curtain. 'The one thing I dislike about this cottage is that it overlooks the main house. It's like we can never get away from it, from them,' she said.

'You love that house and the guests.'

Millie smiled. 'These have been particularly trying.' She sat back down, pulling her feet up. 'So what did take you so long?'

'The guests.' Duncan sat next to her, and taking her feet in his hands, he gently pressed them. 'One of the guys wanted a bottle from the cellar. Took them an age to find what they were after.'

Millie turned towards her husband, but his eyes were on her feet. She waited a moment before she spoke. 'Bet it was Richard. He's not part of the family and yet he acts like he owns the place.'

'It was,' Duncan said.

'Well, that's another New Year's Eve done. Who'll grace us with their presence next year? Just imagine, if we don't get many bookings, the Graves may well come down next year too. Things have to pick up this year, surely.'

Duncan ignored her. Millie pulled her feet away. She straightened. 'Do you think there'll be another New Year here? This job is perfect for me, for us. I don't think I could manage living back on the mainland, running another hotel. I definitely couldn't go back to London,' she said.

Duncan shook his head. 'No, you couldn't.'

'What's that supposed to mean?'

'You were much too delicate for London,' said Duncan. 'I was worried about what you were going to do.'

'I was okay until you started...'

'Playing around?' Duncan asked.

'Please, Duncan, not tonight. My nerves couldn't handle it. They couldn't.'

Duncan smiled at Millie. 'I'm sorry,' he said. 'I shouldn't have brought it up. Can you forgive me?'

Millie returned his smile. 'I can never be angry at you for

long.' She stood up and listened for a moment as the wind whistled through the upstairs windows. 'What a joke,' she said.

'What do you mean?'

'The Graves,' Millie said. 'The whole lot of them.' Millie reached for her husband, but he was lost again. 'Mind if I take a bath?'

Duncan nodded. 'I might work on my novel,' he said. Millie asked how he was getting on with it, if she could take a peek at it sometime soon, but he shut her down. He wasn't ready, he said.

Millie left him in the sitting room and walked up the creaky old stairs of the cottage to the lemon-yellow bathroom. She drew herself a bath and used a capful of Felicity's lavender bath oil. No one noticed if additional beauty products were added to the bill for the running of the house. Millie considered it one of the perks of living on the island. She took off her clothes and sank into the warm water.

Her mind drifted to Felicity and she thought back to the scene she had witnessed: a young, beautiful, rich thing gazing at Duncan wantonly while his wife unpacked her underwear like a maid. A tear slipped down Millie's cheek. She took a breath. She had been strong before; she could be strong again.

She heard a noise from downstairs. It could have been the study door, but it was a little too loud for that. On second thoughts, she had left a window ajar, and it had probably slammed shut with the wind. She put Felicity out of her mind and thought about her husband instead. They had met more than fifteen years ago. They were both in the hotel trade and started working together. He was a handyman of sorts, and she was a front-of-house in a small hotel. She knew he was the one the minute she saw him.

They were married less than a year later. Millie had done great things with Duncan; he had gone from handyman to concierge, and now he was as much house manager at

Dreamcatcher Mansion as she was. He ensured the estate was maintained and the books were in order as well as doing his best to welcome their guests and make them feel at home. *Hotel* magazine had named them hosts of the year a few years ago.

When Duncan had started writing his novel, several years ago now, he alluded to it being about his time in the hotel industry – the guests and what they got up to. He had been vague in his description, and the more she asked him about it, the less he told her. She had surprised herself by not peeking in the folder called *manuscript* on his desktop, but in her darkest moments, she wondered if her husband really was writing a book.

Of course he was busy with his novel. If she went downstairs right now, he would be sitting at his machine, tapping away like he had been all those nights she had woken to find him away from their bed. His writing always made him so distant, and today Duncan was already withdrawn, more so than usual. Spending his time finding wine in the cellars of Dreamcatcher for someone else couldn't be nice. She closed her eyes for a moment, but they quickly snapped open.

Duncan had said Richard was after a bottle of wine, but Richard didn't drink wine. Alan Grave had commented on it the night before. 'Who in this day and age doesn't drink wine, unless they're in nappies?' he had said, and the room erupted into fake laughter to humour the old man.

Richard could have been getting the bottle for someone else. Then again, maybe Duncan was just lying. It wouldn't be the first time.

The bath water was turning cold. Millie thought about adding more hot water to the tub but then thought again. Instead, she stepped out of the bath, dried herself and wrapped her pale pink dressing gown around her.

She tiptoed downstairs to the study. Duncan had always given her strict instructions to leave him alone when he was working. It was his time, he had said, and she respected that, only knocking on the door occasionally to offer him a coffee or a nightcap.

Millie stood outside the closed study door. She put her hand on the handle and pushed down.

'Duncan?' she said into an empty room. She went from room to room in the cottage but couldn't find him, then headed back to the study. She seated herself at his usual chair and turned on the computer. Minutes later, she put in their password and viewed his clean desktop. Duncan liked to keep things tidy. It was what made him an excellent manager. There was one folder titled *manuscript*. Millie took a breath and double-clicked on the folder. She expected it to open, but it was password protected. 'Why, Duncan?'

She sat there motionless, staring at the password box for minutes, not even attempting to put a series of letters and numbers in. When she woke from her stupor, she realised she was shivering with cold. Millie pulled the dressing gown cord tighter around her waist and then made her way back upstairs.

Methodically, she put leggings and a black vest on. She covered herself with a cashmere poncho and then made her way back downstairs. She slipped on her cape and felt in her pocket for her backup plan. It was still there, as always.

She let out a breath as she felt the security of it in her hands. Then she looked up to the mansion and made her way towards it.

## Chapter Seventeen

'There you are,' Robin said as he hobbled towards them from inside the house.

'We came back to find you and you were gone,' Tanvi said.

'You two were gone ages,' Robin said. 'We couldn't just hang around.'

'So where d'you go?' Shilpa asked, peering behind Robin. 'And where's Brijesh?' she asked, a little panicked.

'He was here when I left him. He was talking to Richard. Albie and Gina went to bed.'

'And where did you go?' Shilpa asked again.

'To the bathroom,' he said.

'Okay, guys,' Tanvi said. 'How's the ankle?'

'Not too bad, but it'll probably kill tomorrow. I think the alcohol is having an effect.'

'It's late. Should we just find Brijesh and go back to the cottage?' Tanvi said.

'That's the best thing you've said all evening,' Shilpa said as the sense of foreboding returned.

Tanvi made a face. 'Come on. I'm actually tired.'

'I should think so, the way you were knocking back that

wine,' Shilpa said. 'Which way did Brijesh and Richard go?' she asked, turning to Robin.

'They didn't,' Robin said. 'They were right here.'

'So they'll be back,' said Shilpa. 'They probably went for a walk or something.'

'Richard was talking about the antiques here. There are a few priceless pieces like that vase over there,' Robin said, pointing to a green-and-pink vessel on a tall console table. 'He's probably gone to show Brijesh a few. It's getting too cold and blustery to go for a walk. We could just go back to the cottage. Brijesh is a big boy. If he notices we've gone, he'll return to the house.'

Shilpa and Tanvi shared a look. 'You guys head back,' Tanvi said. 'I'll just wait here. You're right, Shilpa. Something does feel off about this place.'

Robin laughed. 'Don't listen to this one,' he said, putting his arm around Shilpa. 'Solving a couple of crimes has gone to her head. She's seeing suspicious behaviour everywhere.'

Shilpa playfully pushed Robin away. 'If you're worried, let's go and find him,' she said. 'They couldn't have gone far. And for what it's worth, I'm with you. We need to wait for Brijesh. He's the one person who would never leave any of us behind.'

'Ouch,' Robin said, his hand on his heart. 'Come on, let's work our way through each room starting out there.' Tanvi and Shilpa followed Robin as he limped out of the vast dining room and into the hall. They arrived at the closed door to the left and gently opened it. Robin flicked the switch on inside the room.

'The house has gone eerily quiet,' Tanvi said. Less than an hour ago, the house had been filled with music, merriment and laughter, and now it was deathly silent.

Shilpa peered over Robin's shoulder into the room. There was a large mahogany table and a laptop set up. The walls were covered with bookshelf panelling, and a circular wooden table stood in the centre.

'No one here,' Robin said, moving aside to let the others in. They took a cursory glance around the room before filtering out again. They were about to open the door to the next room along when they heard a loud thud from upstairs.

Tanvi, Shilpa and Robin shared a look before heading for the impressive imperial staircase. Tanvi and Shilpa quickly walked up the right-hand side, taking two steps at a time, whilst Robin stayed at the base. When they reached the top, they stopped. The bedroom doors were open. In the doorway of one of the rooms stood Rashmi in a vibrant aqua and cream silk dressing gown. In the doorway of another stood Jane, her hair under a silk cap, a towelling dressing gown wrapped tightly around her slight frame.

Shilpa heard a scream as someone rushed past her towards the third open door. Before she knew what was happening, she saw Jane, her hand to her mouth, running towards the same door. Shilpa followed, her heart pounding.

'It can't be,' she said, realising the person who had run past her, giving a blood-curdling scream, had been Tanvi. 'It just can't be,' she mumbled.

There was another scream, this time deeper and more mournful than the last.

Jane and Tanvi were crouched over something – no, someone. Tanvi caught her eye. Tears were streaming down her friend's face. Tanvi walked over to Shilpa and embraced her. 'Thank goodness,' she whispered to her friend. 'Thank goodness it isn't him.'

Jane crumpled over her dead daughter, saying her name over and over between deep sobs.

Shilpa looked at the body. Felicity didn't appear that different to when she had found her the previous night, lying on the beach, her face twisted, her make-up smeared. Any minute now she expected the enthusiastic young woman to blink and let out a laugh, saying, 'Fooled you.'

That wasn't going to happen. There was an air of death in the room.

Shilpa had read about it before, the sense of morbidity lingering when a person passed, but this was the first time she had encountered it. It filled the air with a staleness, one she was desperate to walk away from, and yet she stayed. She had known that something untoward was going to happen this weekend. She could feel it in her bones. Her friends had laughed at her and her amateur sleuthing, but she had been right all along.

Shilpa took a step closer to Felicity's body. There were, perhaps, lesions around her neck, but without squatting next to the body, Shilpa couldn't be sure, and it wasn't her place to do that. The others would think her ghoulish and march her off Dreamcatcher Island. There was no pool of blood around Felicity's body, no apparent sign of struggle, so it wasn't something obvious like a stabbing or a gunshot wound.

But when she strained her neck to get a better look, she noticed a trickle of blood on the girl's lips and around her nose a white residue, which Jane quickly wiped away.

Shilpa's eyes shifted to Felicity's dressing table. The table was void of any potions or lotions, but it contained a bottle of mineral water. These green bottles had been everywhere around the house. The Graves, it seemed, couldn't drink ordinary tap water. The cap was off the bottle. They had all been drinking heavily. Drinking water was a sensible thing to do, but Shilpa wondered now if Felicity could have been given a poison.

The chair to the dressing table, covered in a rich red fabric, was at an angle. Shilpa studied it and then focused her eyes back on the body. It was conceivable that Felicity had been sitting on it and then fell off, which was the thud they'd all heard.

She heard someone call her name. It was Tanvi. 'We should go. Leave the family to it.'

'What about the police?' Shilpa said, her eyes drifting to the green bottle on the table. 'Shouldn't we stay to help?'

'They'd take a while to get here,' another voice said. It was Duncan. Millie was standing behind him, wide-eyed, like she had never been to bed. And come to think of it, how had Duncan and Millie got here so fast? They had only just found Felicity.

'Thank you for coming so quickly,' said another voice. It was Alan Grave. Wearing a silk dressing gown over his pyjamas and navy velvet slippers, he looked a little like Hugh Hefner.

'Rashmi came and told me,' Alan said, as if sensing Shilpa's curiosity. 'Naturally I called them to sort this out.' Alan spoke like he was tending to a business matter, not the loss of his firstborn.

Minutes later, Gina burst through the door to Felicity's room in her green silk dress. Alan closed the door behind her. 'What's happened?' she asked, pushing past Duncan and Millie. 'My sister,' she said, her voice catching.

'Should there be so many people in here?' Shilpa whispered to Duncan. 'Surely it's contaminating the scene.' Millie stared at her. Shilpa hadn't been as discreet as she had thought.

'The scene?' Rashmi said. 'This is a family matter. Isn't that right, Alan?'

Alan's eyes shifted from his wife to Shilpa and then to Duncan and Millie. His eyes eventually rested on Jane. A silence fell on the room as the family waited for Alan's verdict.

'You have to call the police,' Jane hissed. 'This isn't just a family matter.'

'Mum,' a voice came from the hall. 'What's going on?'

'Mate,' came Albie's voice outside the bedroom door. 'Don't go in there.'

'Move,' the other voice said, and then the door creaked open and Julian walked in. He stood in a crumpled shirt and trousers, the same he had been wearing just hours ago when they had all been drinking on the patio.

Jane cradled her daughter's head in her hands, and Shilpa suddenly felt the need to speak to her own mother. Tanvi reached out for her hand, and squeezed it. Why did it always take a tragedy to make you realise what was important in life?

'I think you'd better leave,' Duncan said. 'You shouldn't be here.'

'You should never have been in here,' Millie said from behind him. She shot Shilpa a look, reminding her of her initial warning to stay away from the Graves.

The balcony door of Felicity's room was open. The curtain moved as a gust of wind came in. Shilpa nodded at Millie, but Millie was already busying herself with another task: cleaning up Felicity's room. Shilpa stood aghast as Millie pulled out a small packet of white powder from Felicity's cupboard and disappeared into the en suite with it. She was desperate to say something, but she could feel Tanvi pulling on her arm.

'Okay, let's go,' Shilpa said.

Tanvi was deathly quiet as they stepped out of the room. Robin had made his way up the stairs and was waiting for them outside Felicity's bedroom. 'We still haven't found him,' Tanvi said, her voice barely audible.

'Who?' Shilpa asked.

'Brijesh,' Tanvi said. 'Where the hell is he?'

# Chapter Eighteen

A light was on at Rose Cottage as the three made their way back.

'He wouldn't just leave us,' Tanvi said. 'I know he wouldn't. Something must have happened.'

'There's absolutely no reception,' Shilpa said, holding her phone up.

'You still trying to get hold of the police?' Robin asked, putting an arm around Shilpa's waist. She nodded. 'Use the wifi in the cottage.' He turned to Tanvi. 'You're jumping to conclusions,' he said. 'It's Brij. He'll be fine.'

'He's not used to this weather. It's so cold and dark and so slippery everywhere. What if he's fallen down there?' Tanvi said, pointing past the infinity pool towards the bay. 'He was drunk. He never drinks that much. I made him drink more than he wanted to.'

'You make everyone drink more than they want to,' Shilpa said, thinking of Tanvi's earlier comment. As they approached the cottage Robin leaned on Shilpa and she turned and kissed his head with a sudden rush of love for him.

Tanvi was the first to reach the cottage door. She pressed

the bell and then fumbled with a key she had taken out of her pocket.

'Here, let me,' Robin said, taking the key from her and inserting it into the lock.

'Brijesh,' Tanvi shouted once inside, but there was no response.

'The lights are on; he must be here,' Shilpa said. She wanted to believe her own words, but if Brijesh was around, he must have passed out not to have heard Tanvi's shouting. Shilpa glanced at her phone. There was no wifi signal. Previously she had always had a connection when she was as close to the router as this.

'Check upstairs,' Shilpa said to Tanvi, who was fretting. Tanvi didn't need to be told twice. She slipped off her shoes and took the stairs two at a time.

Robin and Shilpa shared a look before they made their way upstairs. Shilpa's pace was slowed by having to help Robin. They could hear the slamming of doors as Tanvi checked the bedrooms. Then there was silence. Robin and Shilpa quickened their pace, and then they heard a scream.

Brijesh was sitting on the sofa, wrapped in Tanvi's towelling dressing gown, a mug of hot chocolate in his hands.

'I was just taking a bath,' he said in that innocent way of his.

'After an evening of drinking, *and* your eyes were closed,' Tanvi said, hitting him on his shoulder. Brijesh had to steady his hand to stop his drink from spilling.

'I was trying to relax. What an evening that was. I can't believe that woman's dead. She was annoying and conceited, but she didn't deserve to die.' Brijesh shook his head.

'You were drunk,' Tanvi said to Brijesh. 'You shouldn't have gone off on your own.'

'I barely had three drinks,' he replied. He was telling the truth. Brijesh was completely sober and not suffering any after-effects from excessive alcohol consumption. Shilpa hadn't drunk half as much as Tanvi and Robin, but she still felt weary and wanted her bed.

'And I didn't go off on my own,' Brijesh said. 'I was with Richard, remember?' He turned to Robin. 'You ladies left us, and we were stuck with Richard, who wanted to show me some precious antiques. I'm not sure how Robin got out of it.'

Robin smiled. 'I was scrolling on my phone, not giving him any attention. You, on the other hand, seemed interested.'

'I was,' Brijesh said. 'At first. And I have to admit, when he offered to show me some antiques, I thought it was a good excuse to check out the rest of the house. But then, while we were admiring a wooden sculpture of the head of a monkey, Richard said he had to go. He was mid-sentence, telling me something about the piece's origins, and then he just stopped talking, as if he had remembered something important that he had to do or someone he had to meet. He checked his watch, mumbled something and left me there.'

'Where?' asked Tanvi.

'The cinema room,' Brijesh said. 'To be honest, if I knew no one would notice, I would have made myself comfortable and put on a Bond movie.'

'You didn't know how to work the player, did you?' Robin asked.

'Really?' Tanvi said. 'That's what you were doing.'

'No,' Brijesh said. 'I wasn't. Like Robin said, I couldn't get the movie player to work. Anyway, I decided it would have been rude in any event, so I went back to the dining room to find you, but none of you were there.'

'And you didn't think to wait for us?' Tanvi asked.

Brijesh shook his head. 'Maybe I had more to drink than I remember. I just assumed you had all headed back here. I mean, what harm could come to you? We're on a secluded island.'

'You might want to rethink that,' Shilpa said.

~

The sun was rising and the birds chirping by the time Shilpa made it to bed. They had filled Brijesh in on what had happened back at the house.

'I can't believe she's dead,' he had repeated. Neither could the rest of them. 'Murdered?' Brijesh had asked.

Shilpa had to admit that she didn't know, and it worried her that the family were considering not calling the police.

Brijesh had tried to get the wifi hub working again but couldn't, and so they had no choice but to wait for a reasonable hour to go back to the house. Shilpa reassured herself that the Graves would do the right thing. Even with all their money, they couldn't just make Felicity's death go away. There were witnesses, including Felicity's mother and brother. Any sudden death had to be investigated, especially for someone as young as Felicity. The coroner would conduct a post-mortem to find the cause of death if it wasn't apparent. Shilpa's knowledge of police procedure was limited, but even she knew that the authorities had to be informed.

'Don't overthink this,' Robin said as she got into bed. 'Get some sleep. Something tells me tomorrow is going to be just as eventful.'

'Today,' Shilpa said. 'Today is going to be eventful.' She put her hand on her chest, slowly letting it fall to her stomach. Her hand rested there for a while, then she closed her eyes and tried to sleep.

## Chapter Nineteen

Rashmi took her cup of coffee to the drawing room. Her eyes were drawn to the swimming pool. Her daughter was standing alone to the right of the pool, staring out over the bay. She had spent her whole life protecting Gina. She was her mother, after all, and that was her job. That role would never come to an end, not until one of them died, but things were going to change soon, and Rashmi wasn't sure if she was ready for that.

The weather was coming in now. Thick grey clouds hung in the air, and a drizzle had started – the type that was light enough to walk through but made your hair frizz. Gina didn't seem bothered by it. She hadn't even put up the hood to her rain jacket. Rashmi wanted to go to her, but now wasn't the time. Richard and Albie were outside too, sitting on the loungers, talking about something inane, she imagined.

Rashmi put her coffee cup on the cream leather table and sat on the white sofa. She wrinkled her nose. White was a terrible colour for guests, no matter how much they paid. She supposed it was showy, and that's what paying guests wanted. She could have designed the house much better. She would have put brass lamps in the room and maybe an Osborne & Little feature wall with some vibrant colours. As it was, the room was too white. What did she care anyway? She was never coming back to Dreamcatcher Mansion. Once was enough, and after what had happened last night, how could any of them return? Alan would certainly want to leave the godforsaken island as soon as he could, and she couldn't wait. But would the police let them?

Felicity had been foolish to invite the guests from Rose Cottage into the house last night. They should never have been there in the first place. Duncan and Millie knew better than that, but there was no telling Felicity what to do. Those guests had seen far more than they should have. Rashmi was suspicious of the Indian woman, Shilpa, and the way she wanted the police to be informed immediately. She was nothing more than a baker. She should have known better than to meddle in another family's business.

Shilpa had got her way though. After much deliberation, the police had been called, at Duncan's insistence. This had surprised her, because she didn't think much of the house manager, who lacked gumption. To add to his poor character traits, he was practical and law abiding too. He would have been branded a poor excuse of a man had he lived in Mumbai and roamed in her circles.

Millie, on the other hand, had shown that she could cater to the Graves' requirements. Rashmi watched as Millie swiftly tidied away things the Graves would not want the police to see, such as Felicity's stash of cocaine, which was swiftly flushed down the toilet. She had even managed to convince Duncan to call the family lawyers and delay calling the police.

'Why the delay?' Jane had asked.

'So that we can all get our stories straight,' Rashmi wanted to say, although she had hers well rehearsed already. She was in bed with Alan; that's all there was to it.

Jane couldn't reason. 'Call them, now,' she shouted. 'There's nothing to discuss.'

Alan had looked at Duncan. Jane wouldn't have even thought of the police if that Shilpa Solanki hadn't mentioned it. To Rashmi it was obvious that Felicity had overdosed.

'There's no sick,' Jane said. 'She'd have been sick if the drugs had caused this.' Julian put his hands on Jane's shoulders then and pulled her away from Felicity's body.

Rashmi had Googled overdose symptoms. Vomiting wasn't always a symptom of an overdose. It's what they portrayed on television to make it more graphic.

An hour later the police were called. How Duncan had explained the delay to the police she didn't know, but maybe he was more resourceful than she had given him credit for. No one had briefed her before she spoke to the police, but she knew to be vague with the times. Maybe that's what they had all expected, that no one would actually know what time it was.

The ferryman had been summoned to collect the police. They had only arrived a few hours ago, and Rashmi had to refrain from rolling her eyes when she saw the senior investigating officer and detective arrive.

'Never been on this island before,' the taller and more senior of the two had said, gawping at the moulded ceilings. 'It's quite something in here.'

Rashmi noticed that the corner of Alan's mouth had begun to turn upwards. He didn't want the police here, but given that he had no choice, at least he could work with this pair.

The police had spoken to each of them individually. First, Jane. She had calmed down a little by the time they had arrived, and she wanted to get her interview over and done with. Rashmi had been in the adjacent room and tried to listen in, but she couldn't hear a thing.

Felicity's room was out of bounds, as a forensic team had arrived ready to collect and photograph everything. Thank goodness for Millie's quick thinking. Although in hindsight the white substance in the bathroom would have provided evidence that Felicity was an addict. Without that, it could be construed that someone else in the house had given the drugs to her, that they had possibly been tampered with. Rashmi's heart started to race a little.

After speaking to Albie and Richard, they had questioned Alan. He didn't know anything. How could he? He had been fast asleep at the time, hadn't he? And he had always turned a blind eye to his daughter's indiscretions.

It was Rashmi's turn next. She had answered their questions as best she could. Of course, she hadn't told them that Felicity had found her in the cinema room earlier in the day, that she had accused and threatened her. It didn't suit Felicity to be filled with so much rage. Rashmi had tried to calm her, to explain the reasoning behind her actions, but there was no telling the girl. Rashmi had wrung her hands together, and in desperation she had gone to find Alan.

Felicity couldn't see sense, at least not when Rashmi tried to talk to her, but Alan had a way with her. He knew how to speak to her, unlike Jane. Julian and Felicity walked all over Jane; but Alan was an effective father. Of course he was; he held the purse strings.

Rashmi tried to be truthful, knowing full well that sticking as close to the truth as possible was the best way to get away with a lie. The questions were basic. They had asked about Felicity's mood. It had seemed usual to her, but then Rashmi had been preoccupied. She hadn't said this, of course.

'Wasn't Felicity excited, it being her birthday?' the detective had asked.

'I suppose,' was Rashmi's reply. 'She was certainly animated at dinner. She was telling everyone about her fashion line.'

'The one you supply the fabric for?'

'All the way from Mumbai,' Rashmi said.

'And there was a murder mystery game?'

'Felicity's idea. I was supposed to be a wealthy gold dealer or something. It was all a little childish. I eventually retired to the drawing room with a brandy. I think everyone knew Felicity was the victim, and there was a big thing about finding her body. She added that bit in, wanted someone to find her. I don't think that happens in a murder mystery usually, but I can't say that I've played before. I don't even know who the killer was in the end.'

Rashmi swallowed hard. She managed a smile and nodded. 'Felicity played the victim so well, and now it seems she is one. A little ironic.'

The detective had raised his eyebrows at that.

Rashmi didn't tell them that Felicity's mood had deteriorated after the murder mystery, that she had stormed back into the house shouting for her mother. She did tell them that there had been a heated exchange between Jane and her daughter but added that it was probably something trivial, like the way she and her daughter rowed.

'Your daughter, Gina?' the detective had asked. 'Were she and Felicity close?'

'Very,' Rashmi had said, her pulse quickening. Gina and Felicity had been inseparable at one time.

'Did you see Felicity again that night?' the officer asked.

Rashmi explained about the fireworks at the bay. All their other interviewees must have told them the same thing. They wanted to know who was there and what time people started to leave the beach. Rashmi recalled watching Felicity with Richard from her bedroom window. She was talking to him and he was trying to comfort her, but when she walked off he didn't follow.

'Was Richard her boyfriend?' the detective asked.

Rashmi had shrugged. 'There was a rumour that they were

about to get engaged,' she had said. 'I can't say I knew much about Felicity's relationships. We all ended up back in the dining room for games and some more drinks. But I left them to it after a while. I couldn't carry on drinking like that.'

'Was Felicity on good terms with everyone?'

'Do you think her death is suspicious?' Rashmi asked. She explained that Felicity had white residue around her nostrils, which her mother had wiped off. The shorter man, the investigating officer, scribbled furiously in his book. She would have thought police these days would use iPads or something similar.

'We have to consider all the possibilities at this stage,' the detective said. 'We'll know more after the autopsy.' Rashmi smiled as best she could given the circumstances. The detective and the officer thanked her for her time and said goodbye, but just as they were leaving, the detective stopped and turned to her. 'The guests at Rose Cottage?'

Rashmi had nodded.

'You didn't mention them.'

Rashmi laughed. She put her fingers to her temples. 'With everything that's happened, I must have forgotten. Sorry.'

'Not to worry,' the detective said. 'We'll go and speak to them now.'

Rashmi smiled as the two men left. She had been careful. She was certain none of the other members of the family had seen anything they shouldn't have, but the other guests, the ones at Rose Cottage, she wasn't too sure about them.

## Chapter Twenty

'Have you noticed anything unusual whilst you've been on the island?' Detective Sergeant Sharpe asked.

So far Shilpa had answered the detective's questions as best she could. She wouldn't normally have wavered, but she had been thrown by Millie's sudden appearance. There had been a brisk knock on their door just an hour before the police arrived.

Shilpa had opened it in a daze. The last twenty-four hours had taken it out of her. The preparation for the cookery class, the class itself, which had been a disaster, and then seeing Felicity's body like that. It had just been too much, even for an amateur sleuth like her.

Millie hadn't waited to be invited in. Instead, she pushed past Shilpa and seated herself on the oversized sofa like it was her home. 'Are you all in?' she asked.

Shilpa nodded.

'Well, can you call the others?'

Shilpa didn't need to move. The others, being Brijesh, Tanvi and Robin, appeared from various rooms as if they had been listening in. Shilpa didn't put it past them.

Millie didn't stop to make any small talk; instead she cut to the point. 'The police are here. I don't need to tell you that the Graves are important people and they have power.'

Brijesh was nodding. She, on the other hand, couldn't believe what she was hearing.

'So is Felicity's death suspicious?' Shilpa asked.

'The police have to investigate a sudden death like this, naturally. And they're interviewing everyone at the house.' Millie fixed her eyes on Shilpa like she was an annoying fly she was getting ready to swat. 'They're nearly done with the family,' she said, crossing her arms under her cashmere poncho. 'The police will ask you some questions too. You were at the house, despite my request,' Millie had said.

'We were invited,' Shilpa said.

Millie didn't acknowledge the comment but instead carried on with her monologue. The gist of it was that they were to be economical with the truth. If they felt something was better not said, then they were not to say anything. Millie didn't quite use these words, but her tone and that deadly serious look in her eye conveyed to them exactly that.

Shilpa had wondered if she had been sent by someone in the family to brief them or if Millie had taken it upon herself to do the deed. Neither option would have surprised her. She had seen how deftly Millie had cleaned Felicity's room, without so much as a word being uttered by anyone in the Grave family.

DS Sharpe prompted Shilpa for an answer.

Anything unusual? The whole event had been bizarre. Firstly, there was the man she had seen loitering around the estate. She had managed to convince herself he was a figment of her imagination but now she wasn't so sure. DS Sharpe made a note.

Then there was Felicity with her mysterious case that she had enlisted Robin's help with the day she arrived.

'It could have been drugs,' Shilpa had said to Tanvi earlier. 'Although Felicity didn't come across like an addict.'

'Of course, she wouldn't show any signs of being a drug addict,' Tanvi had said when they were discussing the green water bottle and the obvious white powder around Felicity's nose. 'Addicts are pretty good at covering it up. And those closest to them are always the last to know because of that, and the fact that they don't want to notice it. Isn't that right, Brij?' Tanvi had said, turning towards her boyfriend.

Brijesh, being a pharmacist, had been grilled by both her and Tanvi for a good half hour after the discovery of the body. They wanted to know just what could have killed Felicity. The residue around Felicity's nose could have been a clue, but it was too obvious, almost staged. The water bottle could have held a variety of poisons. Brijesh's poison of choice in this instance was potassium cyanide. 'Although she would have been able to taste it. It's bitter,' he had said. 'So water wouldn't be the best disguise. And the blood you mentioned in her mouth. Was it bright red?'

Shilpa nodded.

'Cyanide stops the body's cells from being able to use oxygen, so the victim's blood is always bright red. But it could have been some other toxin. It sounds like Felicity had some kind of arrhythmia and bit her tongue as it happened. It would explain the trickle of blood from her mouth.'

'How do you even get your hands on cyanide or any poison that can kill?' Tanvi had asked.

'The dark web,' Brijesh said. 'If you are tech savvy. Some industries use it too, like in jewellery making to electroplate items.'

Tanvi and Shilpa had shared a look. Albie and Gina were venturing into a jewellery business together, but they were jumping to conclusions. It could have been a drug overdose, even suicide, although there was no note – none that Shilpa was aware of, at least.

'A Negroni would have masked the taste,' Shilpa said. Felicity was drinking the cocktail after they had come in from the fireworks. Shilpa recalled her stirring the drink with a short, dark-green swizzle stick.

Shilpa thought about the Graves and their guests as the detective waited in anticipation. There had been a certain animosity between the group, and there was the overheard conversation between the younger members of the family and their friends talking about Alan's life expectancy and who was to inherit his fortune, but she had just been eavesdropping at the time, so she wasn't sure if it was right to mention it.

There was also the argument between Richard and Felicity whilst the fireworks were going off which had prompted Felicity to come up to the pool. From where she was standing, she noticed the upset on their faces every time a firework lit up the sky.

And then there was the whole scene with Felicity and Duncan in the cellar. She detailed this to the detective, who showed every professionalism and didn't even raise an eyebrow.

Shilpa also mentioned the water bottle, in case it had been removed after she and her friends had left Dreamcatcher Mansion.

'You're observant,' the detective said.

Shilpa paused. She was uncertain whether to mention the 'cleaning' of Felicity's room after her body had been found, where Millie had flushed away the white powder found in Felicity's drawer. Leaving out such vital information would discredit her if the others mentioned it, but to expose Millie like that just felt wrong. For all Shilpa knew, Millie could have been doing just what she had been told to do. But then again, Felicity had been sleeping with Millie's husband. The cocaine could have been cut with something else, something that killed Felicity, and Millie had used her opportunity and position in the house to flush away the evidence.

'Anything else?' DS Sharpe asked. She shook her head, and he passed her his card.

'Wait,' she said as he turned to leave. She told him what she knew.

'If you recall anything else…' the detective said as he was leaving, and Shilpa nodded. She had half expected him to tell her and her friends not to leave the island, but he didn't, and when she closed the door behind him, it felt almost surreal, like they were free to go and leave this place even though something terrible had happened there.

She turned towards her friends. They were as exhausted as she was. 'So,' she said. 'Do we leave now, or later?'

They looked at each other, not knowing what was the better option, then Tanvi spoke. 'Let's sleep,' she said. 'We don't even know if Felicity was killed or if it was an overdose. We could all do with some sleep.'

She nodded. Tanvi was right. They returned to their bedrooms. Shilpa could hear Robin snoring gently beside her. She closed her eyes, but sleep wouldn't come.

Shilpa's mind returned to Felicity's drink. How easy it would have been to dispose of a cocktail glass from Felicity's room. If foul play was suspected, and it sounded like it was, her drink could have been spiked. Felicity's cut-glass cocktail glass with the green swizzle stick had been with her when Shilpa saw her with Duncan in the cellar. The Negroni could have been tampered with then, or perhaps whoever wanted Felicity dead had taken a freshly mixed drink to her room for her.

Whoever wanted her dead could have easily entered Felicity's room via the imperial staircase and left by the open balcony. There was a porch directly under Felicity's balcony. It wouldn't have been difficult for someone to jump down from Felicity's bedroom to make their escape, throwing out Felicity's laced drink as they went.

How long did cyanide take to kill someone from the time it was ingested? Shilpa didn't know, but she was going to find out.

## Chapter Twenty-One

Jane turned on the shower and waited for the steam. She undressed and stepped inside the cubicle, closing the glass door behind her. The water was hot, scalding almost, but it was just what she needed.

She picked up her washcloth and started to scrub her legs as the tears began to fall. She couldn't believe that Rashmi was at this very moment having a massage, salt scrub and facial in the spa room. Her ex-husband's wife had called Devon's finest therapists to the house for the morning as if it were perfectly normal under the circumstances.

What was she thinking? And how had she managed to get a therapist to come to the house on New Year's Day? 'Money,' Jane grumbled. It was all down to wealth and how much you had.

Her daughter had just died, and Rashmi Grave was acting like nothing had happened. Rashmi's holiday was not going to be inconvenienced by death, it seemed. Jane let out a scream.

She hated the Graves. Why had it taken them so long to call the police? And what were they talking about in hushed tones around her? Her daughter wasn't a user. Jane had taken a keen interest in going through her daughter's phone lately, and surely there would have been something to suggest she was buying drugs from someone had she been addicted.

But what did she know? She was never good with technology. It was more than likely that she had only just scratched the surface of her daughter's private life by snooping in her phone whenever her daughter stayed over. And what had she actually gleaned from the deception? That Felicity thought her mother sweet but overbearing; that her daughter had been sleeping with Richard long before she had told her. It was information a mother should never know, and yet Jane's life was so dull, going through her daughter's phone had been one of the highlights of the last few months.

Jane knew her own faults, and she had many. Paranoia was one of them. The prying became an addiction, and she found herself arranging lunch dates with Felicity just so that she could go through her daughter's device when she nipped to the loo. Her passcode wasn't hard to guess. Her daughter was as bad as her with technology and had selected her birthdate as her passcode. She used it for everything.

The Graves were up to something though. Jane was certain of it, and she wasn't going to let them use their power to cover up how her daughter had died. White powder around her nostrils! Like that wasn't the easiest thing to plant. And so what if her daughter occasionally dabbled in drugs? Didn't all the rich kids do it these days? A dabble didn't make you an addict.

They thought she hadn't noticed Millie flush the drugs away, but she had, and she had told the police exactly what she had seen. Those drugs could have been laced with something, something meant to kill her daughter. She considered the various house guests and who could have wanted to harm her daughter. Everyone had a motive, even Gina.

They all believed that Felicity was jealous of Gina's engagement, but it was Gina who had been jealous of her daughter. Just two days ago, she had overheard Gina telling her mother that she would never compare to Felicity in Alan's eyes because she wasn't his flesh and blood.

Alan could be so obtuse by referring to blood being thicker than water all the time. He had made a show of adopting Gina and treating her the same as his own children; and yet he still kept quoting this famous saying. Alan Grave was two-faced, that was all.

Jane had overheard Rashmi consoling her daughter, telling Gina it wasn't true, but she had said something else too. 'Don't you worry about that girl. She's going to get what's coming to her very soon.'

Alan Grave wasn't the only two-faced person in the Grave household. Rashmi had been in business with Felicity for some time and Jane could feel the animosity she had for her stepdaughter.

Tears began to fall afresh as Jane realised she would never hold her daughter again. She would never stroke her soft curly hair and tell her that everything was going to be okay; she would never just be there for her on the phone whatever time she called because Felicity was feeling blue. It had been a regular occurrence when Felicity had started university, but over the years Felicity had called less and less, until last summer. Then the calls started again, and Jane had to admit she liked it, even if it was late. It was good to feel needed again after years of nothing.

Jane had been so foolish telling Alan her secret, last night of all nights. She had had years to do it, and yet she had picked her daughter's birthday. It was true that this holiday was the perfect setting for disclosing to him what had happened all that time ago. Jane had wanted to tell Alan the day they arrived, but she found she didn't have the courage. She never did have the courage, did she?

Last night, her hand had been forced. Felicity had

approached her before the fireworks and had told her what she believed to be the truth. Jane listened in stunned silence, but instead of telling Felicity it was a lie, instead of taking the coward's way out, which was usually her way, she refrained. She let Felicity believe what she knew to be true.

Jane pinched the skin on her upper arm until a small welt appeared, then she selected another area on her other arm and did the same. It didn't make her feel better. After she had spoken to Felicity, she should have missed the firework display and gone straight to bed. They wouldn't have missed her. Instead, she had gone to see *him*. She couldn't help herself.

Jane had had no choice. She had to confide in Alan before Felicity did, and she had to choose her moment carefully, but her options were limited. The house was busy, and the guests were not so preoccupied with themselves that they wouldn't notice if she did something out of character. She waited for her moment, and then she saw it.

She had found Alan in the library alone. She walked into the room, and he turned towards her, putting his leather-bound journal down. She checked the room, to ensure that no one was lurking in the shadows, and knew this was her time.

'What?' he had asked without any concern for her, despite her pale face. She didn't bother with any small talk.

In hushed tones, she told Alan what she had kept hidden from him for so long. The tears came. She waited for a reaction, but there was nothing. She reached out to him, but he turned away from her. She had felt sick to her stomach then, but something had shifted inside her, and she knew exactly what she had to do next.

Later, she went down to the beach for the fireworks, watching her ex-husband and daughter from afar while they gazed up at the skies, desperately trying to distract themselves from what they knew.

She left them to it and retreated to the house. By the time

she was back in the dining room, the guests from Rose Cottage were making themselves at home. She couldn't just sit there all night like nothing had happened. She had turned to Felicity, but her daughter had blanked her, and then Felicity expressed that she had something to say, an announcement which had chilled Jane to the bone. Jane had given Alan a look, and he returned it with one of hatred.

Jane hadn't been able to sleep last night, despite the wine she had consumed. Two hours later, the world as she knew it ended.

She turned the water off and stepped out of the shower. She wrapped the soft grey towel around her and stared in the mirror. She had aged ten years in the last twenty-four hours, but what did it matter? What did anything matter anymore?

She observed her bright pink skin, raw from the scrubbing and scalding hot water. She felt her body tense. She was clean, but she didn't feel it.

Disgust came over her. She let her towel drop to the floor and turned the water on again, this time setting the temperature half a degree higher, then she stepped inside the cubicle and closed the door.

Julian opened the door to the bedroom and gently closed it behind him. He sat down on the blue velvet chaise longue and listened to the murmurings of his mother as she chided herself in her usual way. He couldn't hear much above the noise of the water, but he could tell she was angry. Of course she would be. Her daughter, her beloved daughter, was dead.

Julian knew the door to the en suite wouldn't be locked. He could walk in there right now and tell his mother what he knew. He considered it, but then he thought again. It wasn't the right time. Julian stood up, walked over to the bathroom door and listened in, tilting his head to one side and closing his eyes.

He took a deep breath and inhaled the aroma of the lavender in his mother's shower gel, the fragrance of which had escaped under the bathroom door. Then he left the room as quietly as he had entered it.

## Chapter Twenty-Two

'Why are we out here? It's freezing,' Tanvi said.

Shilpa glanced over at her friend, who was pulling her thin cardigan around her. 'You should have worn something more suitable.'

'I thought we were nipping out for some fresh air, not snooping.'

'We're not snooping,' Shilpa said. She walked towards Dreamcatcher Mansion, Tanvi following. 'Felicity's balcony is up there,' she said in a low voice. 'Anyone could have climbed up to that balcony or down it.'

'You're doing it again,' Tanvi said.

'What?'

'Investigating a murder that has nothing to do with us.' Tanvi walked up to the police tape that had been pulled across the patio under Felicity's bedroom.

'We were in the house last night,' Shilpa said. 'We may have witnessed something that could be helpful. We might find something that the police have missed.'

'Like what?'

'Like that,' Shilpa said, pointing to the hebe.

'A plant?'

'Take a closer look,' Shilpa said.

'I don't know…' Tanvi started, but then trailed off. 'I see it,' she said with excitement. 'It's the swizzle stick you were on about.'

'The one that reminded me of our holiday.'

'So what about it?' Tanvi asked flatly. 'Am I really freezing my butt off for this?'

'It was in Felicity's Negroni. Don't you remember?'

'And?'

'It suggests that Felicity had another drink that night up in her room. The Negroni would have been easy to spike,' Shilpa said.

'You're jumping to conclusions here. It could have just been an overdose. And where's the glass? That swizzle stick could have fallen out from her drink at any time.'

'Felicity wasn't an addict,' Shilpa said. 'The killer must have chucked out the glass, but the swizzle stick must have fallen out when he or she disposed of its contents.'

'Let me guess, when he or she was fleeing the bedroom?'

'Exactly,' Shilpa said.

Tanvi shook her head. 'This island has finally got to you. You're seeing what you want to. I don't think foul play was involved. You've been suspicious since you got here. I'm freezing. Let's get back to the house and pack.'

'Can I help you?' came a voice from behind Shilpa. Shilpa turned and found herself face to face with Rashmi Grave.

'Just out for some fresh air,' Tanvi said, taking Shilpa by the hand.

Rashmi didn't say anything; instead her eyes locked on them as they retreated to Rose Cottage.

～

Shilpa folded a red jumper and put it in her holdall. It felt good to be packing, to be leaving Dreamcatcher Island and the Grave family. The ferry was due in an hour, and they didn't want to miss it.

She would have thought Alan Grave would have wanted them off the island as soon as possible, but he didn't seem bothered. After Rashmi had caught them snooping, she and Tanvi had hurried back to the house. Tanvi had bolted through the front door seeking warmth. There was a cold wind blowing and the sky was dark. Any excitement about staying on Dreamcatcher Island had disappeared, and whilst they had arrived full of hope for a promising start to the new year, they were leaving with a feeling of fear, or at least Shilpa was. Their luxury trip away had turned into a disaster.

Shilpa had paused at the front door to Rose Cottage, turning towards the house and gazing up at Felicity's room, wondering what had happened after her rendezvous in the cellar.

She had been about to look away when she saw Alan in a waxed jacket heading towards the cottage. She turned to him.

'Can I help?' she asked.

Alan Grave stared at Shilpa as if meeting her for the first time. 'Sorry?' he said.

'Were you coming to the cottage to visit us?'

He shook his head and stared at her.

'We're staying at Rose Cottage. I gave the baking class yesterday,' she said gently. When that didn't register any recognition, she tried again. 'I made the cake for your daughter's birthday...' She trailed off, realising how ill-timed it was to mention his daughter, and expressed how sorry she was for his loss.

Alan didn't say anything at first, but after a moment he blinked. 'Oh yes,' he said and gave Shilpa a small smile. Shilpa wasn't sure if the elderly tycoon had remembered who she was, but she didn't press the issue. Instead, she again asked if she could help.

'I wasn't coming to the cottage,' he said, turning towards the sea. 'I was heading down to the bay, just for a walk.'

'Good idea,' Shilpa said, now feeling a little awkward.

'It was a terrible idea to come back to this island. It's cursed. Do you know that? It's why I never returned after my party all those years ago. This place will haunt me till my dying day. I should never have listened to Felicity and came back here after all this time,' Alan said. Shilpa noticed his frail hand shaking as he steadied himself on his walking stick.

'A previous owner died here,' Shilpa said, recalling the local legend that Robin had told her about.

Alan stared at her blankly.

'Do you know why Felicity wanted to come back here to celebrate in the middle of winter?' Shilpa asked, moving the conversation along.

'I do now,' he said with rheumy eyes.

Shilpa waited a moment, wondering if the old man was going to say anything else, but he didn't.

Alan continued on his journey.

Shilpa winced as his walking stick balanced precariously on the edge of one of the steps that led down to the bay. She couldn't just watch. Shilpa turned towards the house. No one seemed to be concerned for Alan. After the conversations she had overheard about his health, she wondered if some of the household were hoping for an accident.

Shilpa followed him. 'Can I help you down to the bay?' she asked.

Alan didn't say yes, but he didn't say no either, so Shilpa accompanied him to the bottom of the steps. She asked if he had heard anything from the police about Felicity.

Alan didn't respond, although Shilpa was sure he had heard her. She left Alan staring out over the bay, but as she turned and started up the steps, she heard a shout. She turned back to Alan, fearing the worst, but he hadn't fallen. He was forsakenly standing by the water's edge.

'That wretched man,' he cried. 'That wretched man.'

Alan wanted his privacy, and despite wanting to stay and listen to what else the businessman had to say, Shilpa had thought it best to leave.

Now she put her wash bag on top of her folded clothes and zipped up her black leather holdall. She sat on her bed staring through the Crittall window out over the bay. Alan wasn't there. It was far too cold to have loitered after his bout of cathartic shouting, she imagined. Who the 'wretched man' was, Shilpa didn't know.

She took a breath. Tanvi was right. Shilpa wasn't her usual self. She had arrived on the island filled with anxiety, almost as if she had been anticipating something terrible. They hadn't yet heard anything from the police or the family to suggest that Felicity's death was suspicious, but Shilpa had been desperately searching for something to put her mind to.

Shilpa stood up. She put her hand on her belly and knew where her first port of call would be when they got back to Otter's Reach. Then she picked up her bag from the bed and made her way downstairs.

## Chapter Twenty-Three

R obin took Shilpa's holdall from her as she reached the bottom of the stairs. 'Should we walk out to the bay? Tanvi and Brijesh have already gone, and it's going to take me some time with my ankle. It's worse after last night.'

Shilpa scanned the cottage one final time to make sure they hadn't left anything and to check that Tanvi had kept to her end of the deal by cleaning the kitchen. Shilpa smiled. Tanvi was getting more and more responsible every day.

'There he is,' Shilpa said to Robin, pointing through the window.

'Who?' Robin said.

'That man,' Shilpa said.

'Where?' Robin asked, but as he glanced through the window, he saw a retreating figure. 'Oh yeah,' he said. 'Was that the same man you saw the other night?'

'I think so,' Shilpa said, staring at the disappearing figure. 'Hang on. I think it's David.' Shilpa watched for a moment, then she turned back to Robin. 'He's gone. I didn't see his face very well. But I'm sure it was him. Why would he come into the grounds of Rose Cottage? What was he doing?'

'Maybe he keeps an eye on things. He seemed harmless enough when we met him.'

Shilpa took her bag from Robin. 'This place gives me the creeps,' she said. 'Let's get out of here.'

'Terrible business,' the ferryman said as they got onto the boat. 'The whole of Parrot Bay is talking about it and the rest.'

'What are they saying?' Tanvi asked. They had all boarded the ferry, but they were waiting for one more passenger.

'The poor lass,' the ferryman said. 'In all them years of hifalutin parties here on the island, there's never been a fatality, and then the owner's daughter meets her maker at the house.'

The group were silent.

'If it weren't natural – and let's face it, a young girl like that wouldn't just keel over so soon – it must be sinister. If you ask me, I wouldn't put it past them two to do it to bring the place back into popularity.'

'Them two?' Brijesh asked.

'Tweedledee and Tweedledum. Duncan and Millie. They lord around the island like it's theirs. They're very protective of it and wouldn't want to see the life they have taken away. Rumour has it Dreamcatcher isn't attracting the clientele they're used to, and so they could be out of a job. There are a lot of people out there that like the macabre. People would pay good money to stay on an island where a real-life murder took place.'

The ferryman's words echoed Alan Grave's declaration that the island was haunted.

'Dreamcatcher Mansion is always fully booked,' Tanvi said.

The ferryman laughed.

'What?' Tanvi whispered to Brijesh. He gave a half shrug, but Shilpa had worked in marketing and public relations before she abandoned that life for one of a baker. She knew the tactics companies used to make a place appear busy just to garner further attention. Was there any truth in what the ferryman was saying?

'Ah, here he is,' the ferryman said, motioning towards the sand. 'Our last passenger.'

Andreas flung his blue holdall into the boat and climbed in. 'Josh,' he said to the ferryman in greeting and sat down next to him.

'They letting you leave so soon?' Josh asked as he started the engine.

Andreas studied his interrogator. 'The family are leaving later today,' he said in a low voice. 'Duncan can take care of any final requests. I need to get back; my mum's not well.'

Josh raised his palms up. 'Okay, man,' he said. He turned the craft around, and Shilpa looked out over the spray as the vessel cut through the water. 'You knew her though, didn't you?'

Andreas let out an audible sigh. 'What's your point?'

'It's sad when you lose someone. You were at that school together, weren't you? The cooking one.'

Andreas was silent.

'Felicity was a chef?' Shilpa asked.

'Sorry?' Andreas said.

Shilpa had to shout over the noise of the engine, but she repeated her question.

'She fancied a go at being a chef,' Andreas said with a small smile. 'Alan Grave made it possible to attend the school, but she didn't last long.'

'Isn't that how you got the job here?' Josh asked. 'She put in a good word?'

'I was on the cruise ships, but I got tired of all the travel. I was searching for something different. London wasn't for me, and then Felicity suggested this place. They were recruiting a chef.'

'So you stayed in touch?' Josh asked.

'What's with all the questions?' Andreas said. 'Your wife put you up to this? I know just how nosey she is.'

'Listen here,' Josh said. He leaned towards Andreas. Andreas stared at the ferryman, his eyes defiant. Shilpa noticed Josh's fist clenched by his side.

Andreas turned away. 'Sorry, mate,' he mumbled. 'It's been a bit of a shock, that's all. And now with my mum...'

Josh put his hand on Andreas's shoulder and gave it a squeeze. 'No mind. Like I said, it can be tough losing someone. And it sounds like you knew Felicity Grave well.'

Andreas was silent. His eyes shifted towards the water, and Shilpa followed his gaze. Robin gently pressed her knee, and she leaned into him.

## Chapter Twenty-Four

They would all leave separately from the island. Rashmi and Alan would be the first to go. It appeared that they didn't want to travel with anyone else. The ferryman would return to take Albie, Gina and Richard, and finally she and Julian would go.

Jane loved Dreamcatcher Island, and despite what had happened here, she wasn't ready to leave. Felicity had loved it through the decades. Jane recalled her daughter splashing about the bay as a child in her frilly blue-and-white-striped bathing suit that she loved; reading a book on a sun lounger by the pool as a teenager when she insisted on wearing black lipstick at all times of the day; and later, when she was older, enjoying hand-dived scallops and drinking white wine on the patio with Jane.

Jane stared out of her bedroom window over the bay. All this could have been hers. It should have been hers. She had been distraught when she hadn't got the house in the settlement, but her solicitor had been foolish and Alan had been smart.

'The title isn't clear,' her solicitor had said. 'Alan doesn't own the land in its entirety. It will be hard to prove that it is one of his assets. He hasn't declared it on his financial statement, and you've said yourself that Alan only ever celebrated his birthday there in the early nineties but never returned. In the eyes of the law—'

Jane had put her hand up to stop her solicitor going any further. Alan knew how much she loved Dreamcatcher Island. He was punishing her. Instead, he offered her a sizeable settlement. Her solicitor had told her to take it, but she wasn't going anywhere without the house. Her solicitor told her to sleep on it. Jane had drunk a bottle of wine for good measure before her head hit the pillow. She was determined to reject the offer the next morning, but then doubt crept in.

As dawn arrived, the consequences of her prior deception had hit her. Her therapist had told her that she catastrophised. 'The worst won't always happen,' he had said to her. But Jane was certain that Alan knew of her past and what she had kept hidden from him. Jane believed that because of it Alan was determined that she wouldn't get the house, and she couldn't compete with that. The next morning, she had phoned her solicitor and accepted what Alan had offered.

Jane went from one lover to the next after that, but she had never settled. She couldn't. She tried to forget about him, but it didn't work. They had shared too much together, and now this. Jane lifted up the little silver locket she carried with her. It held two pictures, one of Felicity and the other of Julian. She rubbed her thumb over Felicity's smiling face, and a tear slipped down her cheek. She wiped it away and turned back towards the bay.

She caught a movement from the corner of her eye which drew her to the walled garden of Rose Cottage. Earlier, she had observed the guests who had been staying there making their way down to the boat. A man was standing in the garden.

He wasn't one of the party that had been staying at Rose Cottage.

Dreamcatcher Mansion had eyes everywhere when it suited, but not when it really mattered. When her daughter had been wronged, nobody had witnessed anything. She had wanted to thank the Indian woman from Rose Cottage for suggesting that they call the police. Without her interference, without the interlopers into the Grave house, the police may never have been called. The Graves always thought they were above the law. Not this time. She wasn't going to let them get away with what they had done to Felicity. She would make them pay.

For too long Jane had allowed the Graves to side-line her, believing they knew her secrets, but they were ignorant of what she had done. She had found that out last night.

A figure on the patio made Jane's eyes shift towards the pool. Rashmi had appeared in a hot-pink trouser suit and freshly coiffed hair. Alan eventually joined her with his walking stick, which had become his permanent aid since Felicity's passing. They walked together down the steps to the beach. Two members of staff walked behind them with their luggage. Jane noticed how the couple walked straight past Rose Cottage without so much as an inkling as to who was sitting in the garden observing them through the narrow stone window.

Jane pocketed her locket and adjusted her hair. She headed to the door, put a hand on the lever and took a breath. She was stronger now; she could do this. She would speak to the man watching from Rose Cottage. It was time.

Jane opened the door and gasped. 'You're here?' she said, a little stunned.

'Going somewhere?' he asked.

Jane reached out and stroked his face. 'N-no, Julian,' she said with a stutter. 'I was coming to find you.'

'So we're the last to go,' he said. 'As usual. Even the skanks from Rose Cottage left before us.'

'It doesn't matter,' Jane said, putting on her brightest face.

'I hate this family,' Julian said like a petulant child. 'It's not fair, Mother.'

Jane shook her head. 'You're right; it's not.'

'But you're not going to do anything about it.'

'And what would you like me to do?'

'Never mind,' Julian said. He ran his big, clumsy hands through his hair and sat beside her, resting his head on her shoulder. 'I miss her,' he said.

Jane put a comforting hand on her son's head. 'Shhh,' she said as Julian started to sob. 'It'll be okay. It will.'

'Do you promise?' he asked.

She nodded.

Julian stood up. 'Liar,' he said, before walking out.

Julian wiped away his tears and grinned at Duncan as he struggled with his heavy suitcase. He didn't offer to help; instead, he made his way down to the boathouse. He found Felicity's case and took out three mini bottles of vodka, then one by one he opened them and drank them straight. He flung the empty vials on the floor and laughed. 'Thanks, sis,' he said. 'I needed that.'

His mother was making her way down the steep steps. She was weak. Any minute now a gust of wind could blow her over and she would fall to her death. Two deaths in one weekend wouldn't look good.

He smiled at his mother and waved.

When she finally stepped onto the beach, she missed her footing and almost fell, but Julian made sure he was there to catch her.

## Chapter Twenty-Five

S hilpa drew back the curtain, her eyes scanning the estuary. It was overcast, the tide was out and the seagulls were squawking. It felt good to be home.

Robin had returned to London to organise an exhibition of his photos which was taking place later in January, and Shilpa was keen to savour her alone time.

She made herself a coffee, and opening the bifold doors, she took her hot drink out to enjoy on her recently purchased patio chairs. She inhaled the salt-laced air as a black-and-white avocet with its upturned beak pecked at the sand, searching for lugworms.

Every so often her eyes were drawn to a white paper bag in the sitting room. Shilpa had woken early this morning and had dropped Robin at the station. Tanvi's jokey question about her being pregnant was still echoing in her ears, and there was no sign of her period. So on her way back, she had picked up a pregnancy test and a newspaper. She was going to give herself the day off and start real work tomorrow.

The question was whether she was going to take the test today or not. If she did take it and it was positive, it would set the course for the rest of the day. She would be filled with panic, maybe regret; all kinds of emotions would be running through her. She wouldn't get a day's peace like she had wanted. But by not taking the test she couldn't concentrate on a thing.

A little voice inside her said to take the test, because if it was negative she could just watch box sets all day and not think about it, but she didn't feel like listening to the voice of reason. Instead, she took the paper bag out to the pantry and put it behind a twenty-four kilogram bag of plain flour.

Shilpa had time. Robin was away for at least forty-eight hours. That allowed her to take the test and get clear in her mind what she wanted to do before she spoke to him. She threw away the contents of her coffee cup and, vowing not to think about pregnancy or babies until tomorrow, she picked up the paper she had purchased and began to read the local news.

Her interest was piqued when she saw that a new bakery had opened on the high street. Maybe she would ask Olivia if she wanted to join her and sample what the competition was offering.

Shilpa picked up her phone, messaged her friend suggesting afternoon tea and then turned the page. An image of Felicity Grave was staring back at her.

Shilpa's eyes scanned over the article, searching for answers to the questions she had. The article didn't say that Felicity's death was suspicious. It did say that Felicity was engaged to Richard Cole though, which was news to Shilpa. Is that what Felicity was going to announce the night she died? Or had someone in the Graves' publicity team made it up to make Felicity seem more... more what? More settled? Was there any point?

Shilpa continued to read. The article talked about Felicity's fashion line. Curiosity got the better of her, and despite promising herself to stay away from anything to do with the

Graves, Shilpa found herself searching online for the brand. The webpage had a black banner saying that The House of Felicity was in mourning for the loss of its founder, but that it was business as usual. Shilpa checked out the selection of tops and dresses. The fabrics were certainly different, and she recalled that Felicity and Rashmi were working together on the line, or rather Rashmi's company in Mumbai was supplying the fabric. The prices were extortionate. As she clicked through the garments, her phone started to ring.

Shilpa noticed the number on the display and considered declining the call, but it was a new year, and she had to make more of an effort. It wasn't as if her parents were getting any younger.

'Hi Mum,' she said in the brightest voice she could manage. She braced herself for her mother's 'find a husband' lecture that usually accompanied every birthday and new year.

'Yes, yes,' Shilpa said when her mother had finished.

'Your brother is no better,' Mrs Solanki said. 'I don't know which one of you is trying to put me in an early grave.'

'We're trying to keep you alive, Mum,' Shilpa said. 'Once we get married and have children, you'll think your work is done.'

'Smart,' her mother said. 'Always the smart one. So, how was your trip?'

Shilpa explained about Felicity Grave.

'I know about her,' her mother said.

'You've read it in the papers?'

'I know of the family. They own that dyeing company in Bombay, no?'

'Her stepmother Rashmi Grave owns it.'

'Cleaning all their black money and using a fashion line to do it,' her mother said.

Shilpa asked her mother to stop being so cryptic and to explain what she meant.

Mrs Solanki didn't know the details, but she told Shilpa about the rumours she had heard. It was said that the Graves were cleaning their money using Felicity's fashion line. Black money was a big thing in India, her mother explained, where businesses were earning funds on the black market and not paying tax on that part of their income. 'It's how the rich get richer over there,' Mrs Solanki said. 'The divide between the rich and poor gets bigger and bigger each year, and these big businessmen or women have no ethics. They don't understand how their doings are affecting their own country, their people. All they care about is how big the diamond is on their finger.'

'Isn't that all you care about?' Shilpa asked.

'That's not the point, dear,' her mother said. 'I don't have any black money.'

'You sound as if you're jealous of their money and not really concerned with their ethics.'

'Listen,' her mother said. 'You asked me for information, and now you are criticising me.'

Shilpa was silent for a moment. 'So what else do you know?'

'That the clothing they were selling was useless. No matter how much her family put into her fashion line, it was going nowhere. Money can't buy you everything.'

'Not these days with social media,' Shilpa said. 'It isn't just celebrities that are endorsing brands, it's influencers and–'

'I see, I see,' her mother said, clearly not interested when there was better gossip to be had. 'So you were at the house?'

Shilpa told her mother what she knew.

'A drug addict,' Mrs Solanki said. 'I knew it was something like that.'

'We don't know that yet, Mum.'

'You were there. You saw it with your own eyes. Wait till I tell Elvina.'

'Mum, no!' Shilpa found herself shouting down the phone.

'Please don't tell anyone that.' The last thing Shilpa wanted was for that information to get out.

'Okay,' her mother conceded. 'But this is the first bit of interesting news we've had in ages.'

'Mum, someone is dead,' she said, wondering if the cocaine had anything to do with Felicity's death and not cyanide or another poison. Shilpa had asked Brijesh how long cyanide would take to work in someone as slight as Felicity, but he couldn't give her a straight answer. In the end she had resorted to her friend Google. The results were sketchy. It could have taken her killer seconds to minutes, and one site even said up to an hour depending on the dose administered. Shilpa put the thought to one side. She was jumping to conclusions.

'Yes, yes,' her mother said. 'But at least she died with a ring on her finger.'

# Chapter Twenty-Six

'So, you were there,' Olivia said conspiratorially as they stood in line at Jacinta's, the new bakery.

'*Urgh*, the queue,' said Shilpa, ignoring her friend. 'Her cakes must be good.'

'She may be Indian,' Olivia said, 'but she isn't doing anything like you – you know, the east-meets-west fusion thing.'

'What's that then?' Shilpa asked, admiring a rasmalai cake in the chilled cabinet. 'I'll have a slice of that,' she said, pointing to the white-and-yellow cake, 'to take away.' She smiled at her server, who was wearing a name badge. 'Jacinta,' she said. 'I'm looking forward to trying this.'

'I hope you like it,' the owner said with a smile. 'I love your shoes, by the way.'

Shilpa was wearing black velvet pumps with embroidered cupcakes on the toes. Shilpa thanked her for the compliment, ordered a slice of halwa cake for Olivia and paid up. They took their cake to Leoni's. Leoni's wasn't a place where you could take your own, but Leoni was a friend, and Shilpa needed to sample the competition in a neutral environment.

'What's that?' Leoni asked as she brought over two pots of peppermint tea.

'Jacinta's,' said Olivia, taking a forkful of the carrot pudding cake. 'What is this?' she asked.

'It's grated carrot, simmered in milk and sweetened with sugar and cardamom. Is it that good? Your face!'

Olivia straightened her expression. 'It's okay,' she said, taking another forkful.

'Let me try,' Leoni said. 'Oh,' she said after a mouthful. 'That is good. And she's doing teas and coffees. I don't want her taking my custom.'

'You're packed,' Shilpa said. 'I don't think you're going to have a problem.'

'On that note,' Leoni said, 'I better get back to it.'

Shilpa turned to Olivia. 'You don't think Leoni is going to change her cake supplier, do you?'

Olivia shook her head. 'She'll have me to deal with if she does.'

Shilpa glanced at her friend's nearly empty plate. Jacinta's was a better focus than worrying about the pregnancy test she hadn't taken. She decided not to tell Olivia about it in the same way she had decided to keep it from Tanvi. Instead, she brought up Felicity Grave.

'Danny knows about it,' Olivia said.

Danny and Shilpa had been in university together, and by coincidence he was Olivia's brother-in-law. He had recently been promoted to detective sergeant at Glass Bay. Danny never gave anything away, so when Olivia said that Danny had spilled the beans on the Felicity Grave case, Shilpa was keen to know what exactly he had said.

'It's definitely suspicious. They released a statement this morning,' Olivia said.

'Does Danny know how she died?'

Olivia pursed her lips. 'Poison,' she whispered.

'He said that?' Shilpa asked incredulously. This wasn't like Danny at all.

'Well, not exactly,' Olivia confessed.

Shilpa's shoulders dropped. 'I knew it was too good to be true.'

'I did overhear him the other day when I went over to help Lo with the baby.'

'What did you overhear?' Shilpa asked.

'You're doing it again,' Olivia said.

'What?' Shilpa asked.

'You're investigating this, aren't you? In which case, I should keep my mouth shut.' Olivia motioned pulling a zipper across her lips.

'I was there,' Shilpa said.

'You're making it a habit,' said Olivia. 'And I suppose your business is quiet at this time of year... Although Jacinta's—'

'Exactly. I have to worry about competition now. I don't have time to poke my nose into someone else's business.' Shilpa refrained from telling her friend it was the distraction she needed today to avoid thinking about the paper bag in her pantry.

Plus, Shilpa had a certain confidence now that she had successfully put away at least two killers. Despite her friend's jokes, Shilpa was actually beginning to believe she had a certain knack for catching killers, and she had been there at the scene of the crime. What better position to be in was there?

'So what did you overhear?' Shilpa asked, scooping up the last of the halwa cake.

'I think Felicity Grave died by ingesting a toxin,' Olivia whispered.

'Ingesting it? She wasn't injected?' Shilpa asked.

Olivia shrugged. 'It's just what I heard,' she said, pushing a stray blonde curl behind her ear. 'Do I look like I know anything about poisons?'

Shilpa sat back in her chair. If Felicity had ingested something fatal then Shilpa was convinced that whoever had given it to her had spiked her drink with it.

Shilpa took out her phone and pulled up the statement the police had released that morning about Felicity's death. She straightened in her chair and then checked the time.

'Do you have to be somewhere?'

Shilpa nodded. 'I need to meet someone.'

Olivia shook her head and then smiled at her friend. 'Go on then, Sherlock.'

# Chapter Twenty-Seven

'Someone could have laced her Negroni with cyanide. What other drug could have done it?' Shilpa asked.

'Softly,' Brijesh said as he stood next to her in his white lab coat, restocking the Micropore. Brijesh paused and turned to Shilpa. 'There are so many drugs out there that are fatal if administered with intent to do some damage.'

Shilpa considered this for a moment. 'Your drug of choice is cyanide, isn't it?'

Brijesh nodded.

'So what would it have done, exactly?' Shilpa asked.

'Cyanide prevents your body from using oxygen. It can cause dizziness, headaches, heart failure. It could have caused a lethal cardiac arrhythmia. Death could be instant that way.'

'Instant? So the killer would have had to have left via the balcony or hot-footed it back to their room, because Tanvi and I ran up those stairs pretty soon after we heard the thud.'

'Which you assume was Felicity falling to the ground. But what if she had taken time to succumb to the poisoning? It could have taken ten minutes or even more.'

Shilpa crossed her arms over her chest. 'So the killer spikes her drink and exits her room, leaving her to die on her own. The killer could be anyone. Most of the family were up in their bedrooms at that time. Come to think of it, Felicity could have taken the drink back to her room, drunk it and died. The murderer could be anyone who was there that weekend.'

'Exactly, Miss Marple,' Brijesh said.

Shilpa frowned. 'What a way to go, and on her birthday as well.'

'Not technically,' Brijesh said. 'She died after we brought in the new year, so technically she died on New Year's Day. Her poor mother though. What a terrible way to start the new year, every year. So, are you going to solve this one as well?'

'I don't know what you mean,' Shilpa said.

'You may as well give it a go,' Brijesh said. 'You've got nothing better to do now that Jacinta's will be stealing your business.'

'Have you already tried her cakes?' Shilpa narrowed her eyes at him. 'Traitor,' she said.

Brijesh turned. 'Who said there is no such thing as coincidence,' he said. Shilpa followed his gaze through the glass window. 'If you want to play detective again, you should go and speak to her.'

Felicity's mother Jane was standing outside an old building, mesmerised by a sign above the door.

'What's she doing here?' Shilpa asked.

'You don't know?' Brijesh said. 'Call yourself a detective. Felicity's mother lived here when she was younger. Could be visiting family.'

'I don't think she's visiting family today,' Shilpa said.

Shilpa checked the time as she sipped a tea in the window of Jacinta's. She hadn't wanted to give her rival any business, but it happened to be opposite Sloan's Solicitors, where Felicity's mother had been for the last hour.

'Twice in one day,' a voice said behind her. Shilpa turned. It was Jacinta. 'I know who you are,' she said. She stuck out her hand, and Shilpa took it. 'I don't mind,' Jacinta continued, 'if you're checking out the competition.'

'I–' Shilpa started. 'You have a great place here. I was away in December and missed the local announcement. I had no idea that a new bakery was opening here.'

'You don't have a shop here though,' Jacinta said. Shilpa explained that her main business was occasion cakes but that she did supply to local cafés and that she ran a market stall in the main square.

'I've got a spot next Saturday at the stall too,' Jacinta said, turning to walk away. 'May the best baker win.'

Shilpa stood up. She stepped out of Jacinta's, and as she did so, she turned to take one last look at the proprietor, still pondering Jacinta's last comment. Jacinta was waving, which made Shilpa cringe inside. She quickly turned back and bumped into someone.

'Ow,' she said under her breath and then apologised profusely to a tall gentleman in a suit. 'I'm so sorry,' she was saying when she heard her name being called. When she looked up, she saw Jane staring straight at her.

## Chapter Twenty-Eight

They didn't have a reservation, but it didn't matter. The Graves always got preferential treatment at The Standard. The maître d' had shown Rashmi to a table at the back of the iconic restaurant in Piccadilly.

At the table next to her a young couple were sharing a bottle of Bollinger and scooping up oysters laced with lemon and Tabasco. It reminded her of her days with Alan when they had first got together. They had spent many afternoons in the same restaurant drinking their way to dinner. She had marvelled at the grandeur of the place when she first arrived. Mumbai had its fair share of opulent eateries, but this was something special. The domed ceiling and black-and-white marble floors transported Rashmi to a different time and place.

She glanced at the ornate timepiece fixed to the wall in front of her and ordered a glass of champagne. Alan would be on time, but she was early. Rashmi couldn't help but think of the night before they left for Dreamcatcher Island. She and Alan were supposed to spend the night together in their London mews. Alan had an appointment with his doctor on Harley Street the following day, and so the stopover made sense before their car took them down to Devon. That evening, she had waited for Alan, but he was working late, or so he said, and it gave Rashmi a convenient excuse to visit a friend knowing full well that she wouldn't return till early the next morning.

A smile rose to her lips thinking about that night. They had certainly had fun, but then Catharine had given her an ultimatum, and Rashmi was torn. Could she leave everything she knew and loved, for her?

Gina was old enough, or so she thought. But after Devon, she wasn't so sure. Kids never stopped needing their parents. Would Albie care for her daughter? Her first impression of Albie hadn't been good. Gina had introduced him to her parents here in this very restaurant.

He had brought her a small silver something from Tiffany as a gift and had been charming, but there was something underneath that charm that unsettled her. With his thorough questioning about her business in Mumbai and Alan's sports cars, it felt like Albie was after more than just her daughter. Alan didn't see it. He had been fooled by the boy's charms and the fact that his father and he had attended the same school in Windsor.

Rashmi had later found out that Albie's father had been nowhere near Windsor, but the school he had been to was just as prestigious, so why had the boy made it up? Rashmi had kept the information to herself, because by this time Gina was convinced that her mother was trying to sabotage her relationship and sully the name of her future husband. When Gina had something in her mind, there was no telling her otherwise.

Gina aside, there was Alan to think about. She couldn't just leave him now. They were so close to the end, and she was so close to financial freedom. She had her own money, but, of course, it was stuck in India, and without Felicity's fashion business, her money was dirty. It was black, and the Indian government was cracking down on people like her. Bribery was no longer the easy way out. They wanted to set an example, and how better to do it than to use a wealthy Mumbaikar who had moved abroad.

There was another way; there always was. Rashmi could give up the wealth that she had amassed there and start afresh. Who was she kidding? That wasn't an option.

Rashmi glanced over at the young couple, who'd had their platter of oyster shells removed and were now being served; steak for him and lemon sole for her. Rashmi perused the menu before looking up to see Alan heading towards her. He had just had another appointment on Harley Street. He hadn't told her, but a quick call to his PA with the impression that she knew just where her husband was, was all it took for Yvonne to confirm her suspicions.

As a young woman, Rashmi had learned early on from her mother just how important it was to befriend your partner's personal assistant. Her father was no saint, but her mother wasn't either. Her mother just knew how to play the game better. She would berate her father for his indiscretions but secretly have her own lovers about whom her poor father knew nothing. Her mother called it 'double diamonds', because every time her father had an affair, she got a new jewellery set for his guilt, and her lovers often bestowed diamonds on her.

Rashmi's mother believed she had kept this hidden from her daughter, but with little to do in a big house in Malabar Hill, Rashmi was soon onto her mother's ways. She supposed, now, that this education would see her through better than algebra and geometry.

Alan kissed his wife on her cheek and took a seat opposite. The waiter was immediately at his side. He only asked for a sparkling water, not his usual measure, which silently alarmed Rashmi. She wanted to ask him how his appointment went, but she had to remember she wasn't supposed to know. The last thing she wanted to do was to alert Yvonne to her deception and have that door of information close on her. A new prognosis could change everything. Her spirits rose a little just at the thought of it. If Alan were to leave them sooner than expected, she may not have to take matters into her own hands.

Rashmi lifted her glass to her lips and took a sip. She waited for the waiter to pour Alan's drink and then asked how his morning's meetings went. He waved away her comment, and she could see that he was distracted.

'What do you think it was?' Alan said.

'Sorry?' Rashmi asked.

'That Felicity was going to say. What was her announcement going to be before she died?'

Alan knew. He was testing her. She thought back to her conversation with Yvonne. Had she just heard what she had wanted to hear? Had Yvonne let her believe Alan was with a doctor because Alan had been somewhere else?

Rashmi swallowed. 'It could have been so many things, dear,' she said. 'Do *you* have any idea what it was?'

Alan beckoned for a waiter and then ordered a bottle of the Bourgogne and the calves' liver. 'Lobster for her,' he said, motioning to Rashmi, 'and another glass of that.' The waiter nodded and went away. Rashmi waited for Alan to say something more, but he didn't.

'Felicity did come to me the day she died,' Rashmi said tentatively.

'It sounds like Felicity had been busy on New Year's Eve. She paid us all a visit. I wonder who else she went to.'

'Do you think she was going to expose the business in Mumbai?' Rashmi asked.

Alan leaned forward. 'Is that what she came to you about?'

'Isn't that what she came to see you about?' Rashmi asked.

'I'm her father,' Alan said, spitting out the words. 'Was,' he hissed.

The couple were silent.

'So she came to you about the money laundering,' Alan whispered. 'Clever girl found out. But she was stupid not to have known from the start. Her business was never going to win.' Alan opened his mouth to say something else, but the waiter was back at their sides.

The wine was poured and it wasn't long after that their meals were served. Once the waiter had disappeared, Alan took a sip of his wine and told his wife where he had been all morning.

'Your solicitor?' Rashmi asked. 'Why?'

'I'm thinking about making some changes,' he said.

'To the business? Personal?' Rashmi had to ask. 'With everything that's happened,' she said, trying to sound less like she was prying and more like she was a concerned wife.

'It's all the same, isn't it? Personal, business.'

'So what are these changes?'

Alan appeared to not have heard her. He pushed the slimy offal around his plate. Then he cut into it and put a piece in his mouth. Rashmi watched as he chewed. 'Delicious,' he exclaimed, noting her disgust.

Rashmi prodded her crustacean with a fork and then picked up the lemon wrapped in muslin. She squeezed it over the lobster with no intention of eating any of it.

## Chapter Twenty-Nine

Richard pulled his AirPods from his ears and shoved them into his pocket. He ordered a macchiato and sat on the bench. A group of silver-haired men jogged past him. This is what Richard loved about Regent's Park. Anyone and everyone was welcome. He checked his smartwatch and took a swig of water from his bottle.

'Nothing better than an early morning run, eh?'

Richard squinted into the sun as he looked up. Albie was looming over him, wearing a hoody and a baseball hat. 'This isn't your usual attire.'

Albie stared at Richard for a moment. 'I'm on my way to meet someone, mate.'

'Don't let me hold you up,' Richard said.

'Sounds like you're meeting someone too. So how's it going?' Albie asked. He perched on the wooden seat opposite Richard. Reaching over, he squeezed his friend's shoulder. 'She was a big part of your life. All our lives. I know Gina…'

'Yeah,' Richard said. He checked his surroundings and then turned back towards Albie. Two teenagers stood near their table, scrolling on their phones for a moment before they moved on.

'Gina and Flick were close,' Albie said. 'She's taken it really hard.'

'I-I heard she was at the club last night,' Richard said.

'She needed to get out,' Albie said. 'It isn't healthy to just mope around at home every day. Have the police called since—'

'N-nah,' Richard said. 'Not again, but I'm sure they will.'

'Why d'you say that?' Albie asked.

'B-because it isn't clear how she died, is it?'

'An overdose,' Albie said. 'And that fits. Not sure why that maid flushed the evidence down the toilet, but there you go. That's the Graves for you.'

'It's a murder enquiry now.'

Albie shifted in his seat. 'You know that for sure?' he asked.

Richard stared at Albie. 'I'm making an assumption. But I can't be far off. You should know better. You're marrying into the family, aren't you? Sooner rather than later, I've heard.'

Albie stood up. He made a show of checking the time. 'I better get on, mate. Listen, if you ever need to talk…'

'Should have married her sooner,' Richard said. 'I asked Flick the night she died.'

Albie sat back down. 'Shit, mate. I didn't realise. So that was what she was going to say that night – that you were engaged?'

'Did you know she was sleeping with someone else?' Richard asked.

Albie leaned forward. He put his hand on Richard's shoulder again.

'So you did know,' Richard said. 'Listen, it's best you go. Back to the Graves. That family's something else. Each and every one of them has their own agenda, and they don't care who they hurt as long as they get their way.'

'Mate,' Albie started, but Richard ignored him. 'Okay,' Albie said, standing up. 'I'm going. You've got company.'

Richard saw Julian heading towards them. Albie started to walk away. 'Be careful of them,' Richard shouted after him.

Albie turned and nodded before heading on his way. 'It's me they need to be careful of,' he muttered as he headed past the rose gardens towards Ulster Terrace.

'You wanted to meet,' Richard said, stepping away from the bench and leaving his half-drunk macchiato behind. 'Let's walk. If I sit any longer, my legs will cramp up.'

Julian grunted a hello at him in his usual unnerving manner. It was better walking alongside the man instead of sitting straight opposite him. At least this way he didn't have to suffer the penetrating stare that he always inflicted on his audience.

'Wanted to know what you knew,' Julian said, getting straight to the point. Richard shouldn't have expected anything else.

'I'd think that you know more than me. You're family. I was merely a friend.'

'Flick was poisoned. It implies the coke wasn't cut with anything. It suggests that whatever drug she was given, it was administered separately to the coke.'

'Flick never used,' Richard said.

'Never?' Julian said.

'On the rare occasion. But not recently.'

'You had a bad habit once, didn't you?' Julian said.

'Haven't touched the stuff in years.'

'But you know how to get some.'

'Julian, do you live under a rock? They say that you are never more than eight metres away from a rat. Well, in London it's the same for drug dealers. I imagine Devon is similar. If someone wanted to get their hands on some, it isn't hard. Don't pretend like you don't know that and like you don't have a past. We all know about the Priory.'

'That was a long time ago. And my addiction wasn't coke.'

'What was it?' Richard asked. A silence followed. 'So it's just you who can ask the questions then, is it? Typical Graves. The powder around her nose was a ruse. Someone wanted to get away with it.'

'Don't all murderers want to get away with it?' Julian asked. He stopped and gave Richard one of his insufferable stares. After a moment, Richard started walking in the direction of the zoo.

'I'm interested in motive,' Julian said. 'Felicity upset people. She said no when you asked her to marry you, didn't she?'

'Sorry?' Richard said.

'Must have been like a punch to the gut.'

Richard was silent for a moment. 'What are you trying to say?' he asked eventually.

'I want to know how angry you'd be if you knew Felicity was screwing someone else on New Year's Eve after rejecting your advances. Would it make you so angry that you'd...'

'That I'd what, Julian?' Richard said. 'That I'd kill her? Absolutely not.' Richard picked up the pace. 'What's wrong with you?' he mumbled, walking ahead of Julian.

Julian caught up with him. 'Just curious,' he said. 'She made me angry.'

Richard stopped. 'Who, Felicity? Why?'

'Sibling rivalry,' Julian said with a smile.

'Who was she screwing?' Richard asked.

Julian folded his arms across his chest. 'You want to know if it was the chef or the house manager?'

Richard kept his clenched fists by his side.

'I'm finding it hard to read you,' Julian said. 'You did know that Felicity was sleeping around, didn't you? That's what your fight was about on the beach during the fireworks.'

'You're ridiculous,' Richard said, walking off.

'Did you tell the police that you knew about my sister's indiscretions?' Julian called after Richard.

Richard turned and walked back to him. His nose was centimetres away from Julian's as he stepped towards him. 'What're you trying to do?' he asked.

Julian took a step back. 'Trying to find out who the most likely candidate is for killing my sister. You can't blame me.'

'Is this just one of your sick fascinations?' Richard asked.

A look passed across Julian's face, then he turned and walked away.

Richard took a breath. 'Bloody Graves,' he said to himself as he headed towards Marylebone.

## Chapter Thirty

'I'm glad I caught up with you,' Jane said as they settled in a corner table at Leoni's.

Leoni delivered Shilpa's pot of peppermint tea along with Jane's black coffee with a curious look.

'I wanted to thank you,' Jane said. 'For reminding the Graves of their obligation when my daughter...' Jane's voice caught and she trailed off. 'They're so entitled. Think they're above the law. They never learn.'

'Something like this has happened before?' Shilpa asked.

'Gosh, no,' Jane said. 'Well, maybe. I haven't been in their lives for some time now. I've no idea what they get up to, but you do hear things.' Jane stared into the distance and started picking at the thin skin around her thumbnail, which was red raw. She quickly closed her fingers over her thumb when she caught Shilpa staring. 'Bad habit,' she said. 'She was a lovely girl, Felicity. She really was.' Tears welled in Jane's eyes, and Shilpa passed her a tissue. 'Felicity meant the world to me. Now I only have Julian, and he's, well...' She trailed off.

Shilpa waited for Jane to compose herself.

'He's different, shall we say. His behaviour can be trying sometimes.'

'I briefly spoke to him at the house,' Shilpa said. She refrained from telling Jane that her son gave her the creeps.

'He can be difficult with me,' she said, turning towards Shilpa. There was a warmth in the woman's eyes; that and something else. Concern for her son, or fear? Whatever it was, it made Shilpa feel uncomfortable.

'Julian's behaviour with his sister could be quite peculiar.'

'Peculiar?' Shilpa asked.

Jane stared at Shilpa for a moment, as if she was weighing up whether or not to tell her the truth. She must have decided against it, because she turned away. 'Julian has some issues,' she said. 'No thanks to me, no doubt. It's always the fault of the mother, isn't it? I was there for my son when he was younger, but not present, if you know what I mean.'

'I'm sure that's a common feeling amongst mothers,' Shilpa said.

'Mothers can often turn a blind eye to the faults of their children, but Flick wasn't a drug user. She just wasn't. I was relieved when Detective Sergeant Sharpe called to tell me that they were treating her death as suspicious. They haven't told me much else though. There's a liaison officer that came over yesterday, but she doesn't say much. I feel like she's watching me more than anything else. It's like I'm under suspicion.'

'It'll get better,' Shilpa said, feeling Jane's vulnerability. Unlike Rashmi and Alan, Jane hadn't aged well. Was it because her life was infinitely more difficult than theirs? The creases in Jane's forehead told of a lifetime of worrying. She noticed Jane's frail hands as she lifted her cup to her lips. Shilpa wanted to bake her a nice comforting cake with coffee and walnuts and lots of buttercream.

'You have family here?' Shilpa asked, moving the conversation along.

Jane nodded. 'My family home's here, but I don't live here. It's a small place, and it's rented for most of the year, but it's empty now. Anyone who was here for the Christmas break has gone back home.'

'So you have memories here?'

'Sentiment will get you nowhere,' Jane said. 'It's what my mother used to say, and she was right. Look where nostalgia has got me.'

'What do you mean?' Shilpa asked.

'Felicity wanted her party at Dreamcatcher Island. The place where it all started, and it all ended there too.'

'You met Alan on Dreamcatcher Island?' Shilpa asked.

'Dreamcatcher Island holds a lot of memories. Felicity was born nine months after Alan's infamous party there.' Jane smiled for the first time. She took a sip of her coffee. 'It was the party of the century, Alan's thirtieth.' Jane looked away. 'I'm taking up far too much of your time. I'm sure you don't want to hear all about my life.'

Shilpa smiled. 'Believe it or not, I have nothing to do today. I've given myself the day off, and I have some serious competition on the high street that I don't want to think about.'

'Ah, the bakery you came out of when I saw you,' Jane said.

Shilpa nodded. 'It's good. Really good.'

Jane reached over and squeezed Shilpa's hand.

'So tell me about Dreamcatcher Island in all its glory. It must have been something.'

'I was just a young local girl who dreamed about fancy parties. I went along to Dreamcatcher Mansion with one of my friends who had actually received an invite. The young Alan Grave was turning thirty. He had recently been in the papers for doing so well with his father's money. This rich man from Suffolk had bought an island, or rather his father had bought it, just to host his thirtieth birthday party. My friend knew a friend of a friend of his, and so we went. I had my first glass of champagne that night,' Jane said with a laugh.

'You met Alan that night?' Shilpa asked.

'He was every bit as charming as the papers made him out to be. They also said that he was a bit of a Don Juan, so I was wary, but the champagne meant that I let my guard down. My friend came over to me and said Alan was staring at me. He was. Alan came over, asked me to dance and…' Jane had a distant look in her eye.

'And the rest, as they say, is history,' Shilpa said.

Jane leaned back in her chair, lost in the memories. Tears started to well up again in her eyes, and Shilpa gave her another tissue.

'I loved him,' Jane said. 'I did, but I don't think I ever realised, not until…'

Shilpa waited for Jane to finish her sentence, but she never did. Instead, she forced a smile to her lips. 'Well, it's in the past, and now it's too late.'

'Did you ever return to Dreamcatcher Island?'

'All the time. Alan hated it, believe it or not.'

Shilpa did believe it. Alan had told her the island was cursed.

'He had flown in for the event and flew out quickly the next day. He called me several times, took me to some fancy dinners. My parents were thrilled and made sure I had the best dresses to wear. I was in my twenties, late twenties, and I hadn't had many boyfriends. I was still living at home, and they were keen to marry me off. Alan and I just clicked, but I don't think he would have married me if I wasn't pregnant.

'My parents found out about Felicity, and they made sure I told Alan. I wasn't sure, you see. I didn't want to put him off. It had the opposite effect though. It turned out that Alan needed an excuse to settle down. That or his father wanted him to. I think it was the latter, because I don't think he ever loved me.

'I went back to Dreamcatcher Island to relive that night over and over again,' Jane said. 'When I realised just how foolish I was, it was too late. Dreamcatcher Island had stolen Felicity's heart. She associated the place with love and laughter. But in the end, it was Dreamcatcher Island where the laughter died.'

Shilpa waited a beat then saw her chance. 'Do you know what Felicity was going to announce the night she died?' she asked.

'Sorry?' Jane said.

'Felicity said she had something to say that night, but Alan said he was going to bed, and that seemed to thwart her plans.'

Jane frowned. 'I've no idea what she was going to say,' she said, her eyes drifting to the window.

Shilpa took a sip of her now cold peppermint tea. Jane knew exactly what her daughter was going to say the night she died, but it didn't seem like she was going to say anything more on the subject.

Shilpa thought back to when she had been sitting in Jacinta's, watching the solicitor's office. 'So what brings you to the high street?' Shilpa asked.

'Sorry?' she said.

'Do you come into town often?' Shilpa tried again.

'Oh no, just a couple of errands to run, and I needed to pick up some paracetamol. I'm getting terrible headaches since Felicity passed.' She turned away from Shilpa and started searching for something in her handbag.

Shilpa took in Jane's appearance as the woman fumbled about. Despite Jane's humble beginnings, she was wearing a gold Cartier watch and a Chopard necklace. The timepiece could have been years old – it was one of Cartier's timeless designs – but the Chopard design was new. Shilpa had seen it in a magazine recently. Shilpa was just about to ask about the piece as an easy segue into money matters when Jane stood up.

'I have to go,' Jane announced. 'I've taken up too much of your time. You're young and busy.' Jane gave Shilpa a wan smile. She touched her hand again. 'You are just so easy to talk to, and being there on that terrible night, well, I suppose that makes it easier too. Neither of us are Graves, and we certainly have that in common.'

'Take this,' Shilpa said, pulling a business card out of her old leather bag. 'My card. If you ever need to talk, or even if you just want some tea and cake, just give me a call.'

Jane took the card and slipped it in her handbag. Then she smoothed down her skirt, put on her scarf and jacket and stepped out of the café into the cold.

## Chapter Thirty-One

Rashmi opened the door, peered at her guest and then took a step back, letting him into her Marylebone mews.

She walked over to her coffee machine, popped in a blue capsule and pressed a button. 'So,' she said, placing the coffee in front of the man.

'I need money.'

'How much this time?'

Albie laughed. 'I don't just need money for dinner or a new Rolex. I'm tired of waiting.'

Rashmi shook her head. She thought she had done a better job than this with Gina. Her daughter didn't notice Albie's faults, and the more she tried to point them out, the more Gina pushed her away. There came a point when she had to stop or she would lose her daughter forever. She had to accept Gina was going to spend her life with this waste of space sitting in front of her.

'What's the hurry?' Rashmi said. 'Gina'll be left what is rightfully hers. We both know that it's only a matter of time.'

'You say that,' Albie said, 'but how can we believe you? There's no proof.'

Rashmi folded her arms across her chest. He had used the royal we. He was treading on thin ice. How dare he drag her daughter down to his level?

'Alan's stalling, and we need to pay our suppliers to date. Have you seen the demands we've received?'

'I've paid for most of those out of my own pocket,' Rashmi said. 'You could liquidate, file for bankruptcy.'

'Your daughter would be a laughing stock if she did that. Is that what you want?'

'I think Gina would cope.'

'Gina wants success. She wants what is rightfully hers. Alan bailed out The House of Felicity countless times.'

'Gina wants it to come easy. Nothing good comes easy,' Rashmi said, knowing from experience just how true that was. She herself had inherited a business that gave her the high life, but she was imprisoned by it. The black money, the bribery, the corruption, the day to day that came with running a successful business in India.

'You don't know your own daughter.'

'I know Gina better than you'll ever know her,' Rashmi snapped.

Albie raised his eyebrows. 'Hit a nerve?' he asked. He didn't wait for a response. 'Gina's spoken to you recently about the cash, but still nothing. She asked you just before New Year and again at Dreamcatcher. I don't think you appreciate just how dire the situation is. You promised your daughter but failed to deliver, and so Gina had no choice—'

Rashmi put out her hand to stop Albie saying anything more. She didn't want to hear what she knew in her heart. 'It's only a matter of time,' she said again through gritted teeth.

Albie stood up and walked around the kitchen island to Rashmi. 'We've been over this,' he said, staring at her. 'You need to facilitate matters.'

Rashmi felt the heat rise in her cheeks. 'You've no idea

what I've done for you both,' she spat. 'You just have to wait and, in the meantime, trust me.'

'We've waited too long. *We've* had to take matters into our own hands. What have *you* done?'

'It's difficult,' Rashmi said. 'Alan has only just lost Felicity, and she was the apple of his eye.'

'Yes, had she still been around, she would be in line to inherit the lot.'

'Don't be daft,' Rashmi said, her hands trembling as she replaced her cup on its saucer. 'Julian is his blood too, and there is Gina. Alan may be many things, but he is fair.'

'Julian's not right in the head. He'll get something. Enough to keep him quiet,' Albie said. 'He was meeting Richard as I left the park.'

Rashmi straightened. 'Why?'

'Felicity was practically engaged to Richard. Julian's family. Maybe they were sharing their grievances. Although did you know Felicity rejected Richard's proposal?'

'No,' Rashmi said. 'I thought the little dear was desperate to marry.'

'Looks like you don't know much about anyone.' Albie stood up. 'I, on the other hand, know far too much. You need to make something happen soon or… well, you know the consequences.' He put his baseball hat back on and walked to the front door. 'Give my best to my mother,' he said before opening the heavy black wooden door and leaving.

Rashmi made another coffee and took it to the sofa. She rubbed her lips as she considered what her future son-in-law was threatening.

Gina would never hurt anyone. Felicity was the big sister Gina never had. Although when Rashmi thought back to the two of them together, they were just girls, playing princesses and Barbies. So much had happened since. They had been to university together and had fallen out on more than one occasion. Rashmi remembered a particular wet and rainy Saturday morning when Gina had arrived back from university, mascara smudged and full of tears. She had mumbled in her drunken state that she hated Felicity and that she would kill her, and then she had stormed off to bed.

The next afternoon, when her daughter woke, she had told her the whole story. It was a fight over a boy. Felicity had won. 'As usual,' Gina had said bitterly. The next day, the fight was forgotten until the next time.

Gina always thought she was second best. Felicity was the flesh and blood of Alan Grave, something people around her were keen to point out. Rashmi hadn't helped matters. Years ago, when the children played together, she had let them treat her daughter like a second-class citizen. They had absolutely no right to, no right at all, but she let it continue.

She didn't even stop to question it. Let Felicity take first pick of the dresses, let Felicity have the last scoop of raspberry ice cream. It started with small things, but as the two had grown, the options presented to Gina were always inferior to Felicity's. Albie was right. Alan had bailed Felicity out from enough bad business ventures; why couldn't he be more generous with Gina?

Gina had carried her inferiority complex around with her for years, but recently, Gina was making her own mark on the world. She had stepped out of Felicity's shadow, and this jewellery business of hers was going to be the making of her. If only she had a better business and life partner. Albie was full of greed, and he was power hungry. Alan saw it as a sign of ambition and determination, but Rashmi saw the ugliness of it.

Albie loved her daughter, she couldn't deny that, and there was even a slim possibility that Albie was good for Gina. Since being with Albie, Gina was the confident young woman she was always meant to be. Rashmi wondered if what Albie said had any truth in it, that she didn't know who her daughter was. She put the thought aside. Albie loved her daughter, that much was true, but he loved money just as much.

Albie wanted to save her daughter, but that was her job. Rashmi had failed her daughter when she was young. She wasn't going to fail her now.

Rashmi looked up as she heard a key in the door. 'Leave them there,' Gina instructed. A man stepped inside with several large shopping bags and placed them in the hallway. Gina tipped the man with a twenty-pound note. The driver nodded his appreciation and stepped back outside. Closing the door behind her, Gina beamed at her mother.

'I thought some shopping would make me feel better,' she said. She retrieved a black credit card from her handbag and handed it to her mother. 'You don't mind, do you?'

Rashmi took the card and swallowed hard. How could she mind after what she had put her daughter through? Albie was right; she hadn't done enough to help them.

'Mum,' Gina said, walking around to the open-plan kitchen and pulling out a bottle of wine from the fridge. She poured herself a large glass of Sancerre. 'We're going to bring the wedding forward, and we are keeping the date of the engagement party.'

'After what's happened–' Rashmi started, but her daughter cut her off with a stare.

Rashmi took out another wine glass from the cupboard. Gina filled her glass. She would just have to go along with what her daughter wanted. Why hadn't she come clean to Gina all those years ago? This was all her fault, and she was going to have to live with it.

## Chapter Thirty-Two

Shilpa followed Brijesh into the tiny apartment that overlooked the estuary. Tanvi and Brijesh had moved in about a month ago, and there were boxes everywhere. Shilpa stepped over something wrapped in bubble wrap and put down a bottle of merlot.

'Smells good,' she said as Brijesh stirred something in a big saucepan simmering on the hob.

'How's Robin?' Brijesh asked.

'Still in London, and I'm enjoying the peace and quiet here, to be honest. His leg is still bothering him, so I told him to take his time before he returns. What's cooking?' Shilpa asked.

'It's a Keralan pepper curry,' he said. 'Tanvi'll be out in a moment. She's just getting ready.' Brijesh poured her a glass of red, and Shilpa made her way to the balcony. It was dark outside, and the tide was in. The golden lights from the houses on the other side of the estuary shimmered on the water.

Shilpa loved Otter's Reach when it was like this, peaceful and still. The tourists were long gone, and just the locals remained, braving out the long winter on the coast. In spring, the vibrant purple aubrieta and blue cornflowers would be in bloom, and along with the blossoming flowers, the tourists would return, bringing their custom with them. The whole of Otter's Reach seemed to come alive then, enjoying the town through the fresh eyes of the newcomers. Those days were good for business and for life, but they could be tiring too.

Tanvi appeared behind her with a glass of white and chinked glasses with her. 'You're here, finally.'

Shilpa gave her friend a warm smile and told her just how lovely her new place was as she was given the grand tour.

After that, they settled down to dinner. The curry was delicious, and Shilpa managed to avoid drinking. The last thing she wanted was for Tanvi to speculate about her pregnancy. She hadn't taken the test yet, and Tanvi would be on high alert if she noticed that her friend wasn't drinking. It was highly plausible that her friend would make her take a test there and then, and Shilpa wasn't ready for that.

Instead, when Brijesh and Tanvi were preoccupied, she poured half her glass into the soil of the succulent that was sitting proud on the table. She silently apologised to the plant.

'You never cooked like this when you lived with me,' Shilpa said.

'His mum's been giving him cooking lessons over Zoom,' Tanvi said.

'I suppose you stay well away when those are happening,' Shilpa teased.

'That's my time for box sets,' Tanvi said.

'My mum said she knows of Rashmi Grave,' Brijesh said.

'Mine too,' Shilpa said, raising her glass. 'She told me all about the black money.'

'Brijesh is convinced that's what Felicity was about to announce when she was killed,' Tanvi said.

'That her family were laundering money through her struggling fashion line?' Shilpa said.

'That would give at least two people motive to kill her,' Brijesh said. 'Her father and his new wife.'

'Rashmi is hardly a new wife. And do you think anyone in that dining room would have cared? None of them have ethics, or at least they didn't come across like they had any morals. They were all there to sponge off Alan Grave,' Shilpa said.

'That's what I said. Great minds, eh!' said Tanvi.

Shilpa gave her friend a sideways glance. 'Oh no,' she said. 'I'm even starting to think like you now.'

Tanvi smiled. 'Think about it. Everyone on that island was making money from Alan Grave in some way or another. I'm surprised he wasn't the one to pop his clogs that weekend. They would have all benefited from that.'

'Alan Grave probably has a watertight will that prevents people knocking him off to get to the cash,' Brijesh said. 'That's why he's still around and Felicity isn't.'

'I think you might be onto something there,' Shilpa said.

'What do you mean?' Tanvi asked.

Shilpa reminded her friend of their rosemary-picking outing, when they had overheard some of the group talking on New Year's Eve. 'Remember. One of them said something about Alan not being well.'

'And another explained that the Graves always leave their wealth to the firstborn. Some kind of tradition,' Tanvi said.

'You're not playing detective too, are you?' Brijesh groaned.

'No, silly,' Tanvi said. 'I'm just the sidekick, helping Shilpa out. It makes perfect sense though. If they thought that Alan was on his way out then to get rid of Felicity meant there would be more money for...'

'Julian,' Shilpa said. 'He's the biological son of Alan Grave.'

'And Gina? They can't be that old-fashioned that they wouldn't leave her anything just because she isn't biologically Alan's, can they?'

Shilpa shrugged. What she had learned was that anything was possible with old money. It was how it lasted generations.

'Alan legally adopted her,' Brijesh said. 'And he seems like a decent enough guy. I'm sure he would be fair with his kids.'

'When did you speak to him to get an idea of what he was like?' Tanvi asked.

'I didn't, but I did speak to Richard at length when you left me with him to go gallivanting that night, and he told me what a great guy Alan was, before he disappeared too.'

'Richard was after his money more than anyone,' Tanvi said.

'Why do you say that?' Brijesh asked.

'Because that evening he was the one asking about how the inheritance worked,' Shilpa said.

'Felicity and Richard weren't even married,' Brijesh said. 'What right would he have to the money?'

'He wouldn't,' Shilpa said, 'but maybe that's what the announcement was about.'

'Their engagement?' Tanvi said.

'Maybe Felicity and Richard had eloped. Maybe they were already married,' Brijesh said. He poured himself another glass of wine and gave himself a congratulatory smile.

Tanvi laughed. 'Felicity was jealous of Gina's engagement and upcoming wedding. Felicity was eyeing up that diamond. She wasn't married. A married woman wouldn't look on with such envy. Felicity would have been smug about being married before Gina. She wouldn't be able to contain herself. She'd have told everyone her news on Dreamcatcher Island as soon as they arrived.'

Shilpa nodded. What Tanvi said made sense. She had witnessed Felicity arguing with Richard on the beach during the fireworks display, and then she had spied Felicity and Duncan in the wine cellar together.

'What if it wasn't about money?' Shilpa said.

'What do you mean?' Brijesh asked.

'Felicity and Duncan were having an affair,' Shilpa said. 'When I spoke to her mother today, she told me that Felicity associated Dreamcatcher Island with love and laughter. I initially thought that she had happy memories growing up there, but maybe the love and laughter arrived when Duncan started working on the island. Felicity has been religiously visiting the place.'

'So you think Richard killed her in a jealous rage after finding out about her relationship with Duncan?' Brijesh asked. He stood up and started clearing away the plates. 'And for afters,' he announced, 'we have kulfi.'

'I'm glad you live just down the road from me. I'll be here most nights.' Shilpa loved the sweet, thick, Indian ice cream made with condensed milk and, in this instance, mango. 'Delicious,' Shilpa said as she swallowed her first mouthful. 'Next you'll be opening an ice-cream store in town, and then I will be out of business.'

'So Jacinta is giving you a run for your money?' Tanvi said.

Shilpa waved away her comment. 'I don't want to talk about it.'

'Yes, who killed Felicity Grave is much more interesting.'

## Chapter Thirty-Three

'It wasn't just Richard who could have killed Felicity in a jealous rage,' Tanvi said. 'Remember what Josh, the ferryman, said to the chef on the way home? Andreas and Felicity had been close. Although why didn't they just kill Duncan? That would be the better solution, surely.'

'Because if Duncan was dead, Felicity may have still gone after Andreas assuming Richard was the killer,' Brijesh said.

'So you're going for the *I'd rather she was dead* theory. It could have been a jealous wife that did the deed,' Shilpa said, thinking of Millie.

'Millie did flush key evidence away for no real reason,' Tanvi said. She shifted in her seat, her eyes drawn towards the dark water. 'Let's not talk about death,' she said. 'It always seems so much more eerie after dark. I don't want you to put me off my new home.'

Shilpa apologised, but she couldn't help but think about this last suspect. Millie had been so calm and collected when she turned up at Felicity's room. She had barely looked at the dead body and knew exactly what to do. Most people, Shilpa included, were freaked out by the sight of a corpse.

Shilpa walked home and drew herself a warm bath. She sank into the water and closed her eyes. She was exhausted. She had expected a restful day, but it had been eventful. She had sampled the cakes at her rival's bakery, had a long discussion with the mother of the victim and had a lovely dinner with her best friends. Shilpa tried to relax, but something was troubling her, and it wasn't the pregnancy test that she was still trying to ignore.

Wrapping her towel around her, Shilpa padded over to her bedroom. Opening a search engine on her phone, she typed in The House of Felicity.

An hour later, having scoured the internet for information about the young woman, she was no further forward. So she took ten minutes to draw a spider diagram, populating it with the names of the people who had been on Dreamcatcher Island at the time of Felicity's death.

She considered that someone else had been on the island too, someone perhaps that no one had been aware of. She had noticed someone lurking in the garden of Rose Cottage, but on reflection, she believed this stranger to be David, the old man who lived with his dog on the island. Could someone else have come across to the island with the sole purpose of killing Felicity and have been undetected? Shilpa shook her head. There were enough people on the island with motive to want the young heiress dead.

Shilpa thought about her conversation with Tanvi and Brijesh and the idea that Millie could have killed Felicity out of jealousy. Shilpa had herself witnessed that Millie's husband Duncan was having an affair with the victim. It was possible that Millie knew too.

Shilpa went to type Millie's name into the search engine but quickly realised that she didn't know her surname. She found the website for Dreamcatcher Island and clicked on the About Us page. There was a picture of Alan Grave and his parents, on the eve of his thirtieth birthday, she assumed. Another of Duncan and Millie she had previously seen when she had been invited to the island before New Year's Eve. Their full names were written underneath the frame, promising to cater for guests' every whim. Duncan had certainly fulfilled that role where Felicity was concerned.

Shilpa typed *Millie Stevenson* into Google, and a hundred results returned. She didn't know where to start, so she tried *hotel manager* along with Millie's name in the search box. Shilpa clicked on the first few links, but none of the pages were about the Millie she was looking for. After clicking through an entire page of results, Shilpa was about to give up. There was never anything useful on page two, but something made her click through. She tried the first link. It was about a Mildred Port. Mildred could have been Millie – after all, the article had come up on the same search – but it could have been a red herring. Shilpa decided to read on. A short article from a newspaper over fifteen years ago. Shilpa scanned it and then stared at her screen. This was something. It really was.

Shilpa studied her diagram then she picked up her phone again and this time opened her email. She started typing a message.

The next morning, Shilpa checked her emails. There was nothing from Dreamcatcher Island. She had expected a response to her request to speak to Duncan and Millie at the house. A flat no was the most likely answer; but nothing? Maybe it was a good sign; maybe they were thinking about it.

Shilpa pulled her hair up into a ponytail and set to work. After taking the day off yesterday, she had a fair amount to do today. Of course, there was still the question of the pregnancy test hidden away behind the bag of flour in the pantry but that could wait.

She needed to bake, or at least that is what she told herself. The bakeries she supplied were all due deliveries, and Shilpa wanted to try baking a rasmalai cake. Even though Jacinta had already done it, she had had the idea on Dreamcatcher Island, before she had even heard of her rival, so it was only fair that she gave it a go.

Jacinta would think she was stealing her ideas, and she couldn't blame her. Shilpa stared towards the estuary for a moment, then an idea came to her. She would try a rasmalai cheesecake. She would make two. That way she could try one with Tanvi and Brijesh, and if it was any good, she could give the other to Leoni to serve in her shop, at no cost, of course, just to monitor how it went down with her customers. Shilpa needed to do something different to keep her clients before Jacinta stole them all.

As Shilpa measured out the cream and cardamom powder, her phone started to ring. She wiped her hands on her apron and answered. It was Robin. A smile rose to her lips as she heard her boyfriend's voice. After a few minutes, Robin asked her if she had watched the news. As soon as she disconnected the call, she opened the local news app she had on her phone. The headline said it all.

It had been confirmed. Felicity Grave had been murdered.

Millie read the email again and frowned at her screen. It wasn't good to frown, not after those extortionately-priced injections she had had to smooth out the lines on her forehead. Instead, she tapped her perfectly manicured nails on the wooden desk while she thought about a suitable response to send the woman.

If there was one thing Millie hated, it was leaving emails unanswered. No matter how annoying the author was, Millie believed that it was her duty to respond promptly to everyone, even the presumptuous baker. How dare she think it her right to visit Dreamcatcher Island again? They were a busy resort. They didn't have time to cater to Shilpa Solanki, just because she had an interest in Felicity Grave's death. Half the country now had an interest in Felicity Grave's death, so what right did someone like Shilpa Solanki have?

Shilpa's email had requested a meeting, but Millie could read between the lines. Shilpa wanted more than just that. She wanted to interview her, informally of course. She was nothing but a baker, so there was no need to worry.

Millie could tell her that they were too busy. The website said that they were full, but in reality they were not. Andreas was away, and their usual fill-in chef had come down with something. It was a problem Millie would have been able to fix – of course she could; she could fix anything – but she didn't have to because they didn't have any bookings for January.

After Felicity's death, Alan had told them to keep it clear in case he wanted to return. Two visits in such a short space of time, well, they were lucky.

Last autumn, when the bookings had started to dry up, Alan Grave had sent an instruction to block out several weeks in the calendar to make the resort appear more popular than it actually was. It had worked for a time, but they still had large gaps in their bookings calendar, which they had never experienced before. It was worrying.

Millie had even tried to offer some regular guests a discount. It hadn't been authorised, but a few of the clients had bitten.

'You're usually here every quarter,' Millie had said to one

of the regulars at the resort. 'This year you've only graced us with your presence once.' She batted her eyelashes and waited for a response.

Bernard Roper put his magazine down and turned on his sun lounger. 'I'm here this year because my wife insisted.' He looked over to the platinum blonde asleep on the lounger next to him. 'Something about nostalgia. She's sentimental like that. If I had my way I don't think I'd have returned at all this year.'

Millie kept her head held high as she enquired why Bernard didn't want to return. Millie couldn't imagine anywhere else guests would rather spend their free time other than Dreamcatcher Island.

'It's lost its magic,' Bernard said, picking up his glossy.

Millie had bristled at the comment and had to refrain from spitting in his glass of Krug later that evening.

She loved her job on the island and would do anything to keep it, and now that Felicity had died here in true Agatha Christie style, well, the phone was off the hook. Millie had to check with Alan's PA that he did want to keep the place empty for the rest of the month. The response came that he did.

Millie accepted his decision reluctantly and started taking bookings for the rest of the year.

She smiled to herself. Felicity's death had been a double bonus.

Millie could respond to Shilpa's email telling her that she couldn't meet with her on the island. She could meet her in Parrot Bay or some similar place, but Shilpa had asked if she could look around the house again. Millie could say no, she was well aware of that. It would be quite normal to refuse. Shilpa Solanki wasn't a real detective, just someone with a curiosity, and she had taken enough calls from local crazies in the last couple of days to believe in her right to say no.

But Shilpa Solanki was different. She had been here at the time of Felicity's death. Not just on the island but in

Dreamcatcher Mansion. Millie convinced herself that Shilpa knew more than she was letting on. Had Shilpa witnessed something at the house that made her suspicious? Something perhaps she had failed to tell the police, but something she would reveal if she didn't have the chance to clear her suspicions at the house. The thought troubled Millie.

'And why did you dispose of the drug?' DS Sharpe had asked Millie not so long ago. Millie had to think quickly. Eventually, she said that she did it out of instinct to protect the girl. The detective seemed to buy it. The whole ordeal reminded Millie of Leicester, and she didn't want to go down that road again. She had to be more careful. She recalled Duncan's parting words to her this morning.

'They're saying she was murdered,' Duncan had said as he set off for the mainland.

Millie had swallowed the acrid taste in her mouth as she waved goodbye to him. She hoped he would be back soon. She should have asked his advice before he set off. She could message him now, call him even. She took her phone out of her pocket and called up his number, then she put her phone back down again. It was no use. Duncan needed time, he needed space. She hadn't seen him like this before. Since Felicity's death, he seemed distant and withdrawn, wary and suspicious. He hadn't touched her.

Millie stared at the email. Would it raise the baker's suspicions further if she denied her access to the house? Would she delve further into her suspect's past?

Millie hit the reply button and started to type.

# Chapter Thirty-Four

Shilpa had one more delivery to make to a small but popular café at Mermaid Point. It was halfway up the cliff to a spectacular viewing platform over the harbour, and it was a popular spot in the summer. It was late, and Shilpa was tired, but she felt buoyant as well. Leoni had loved her rasmalai cheesecake.

'Why on earth didn't you try this sooner?' she had asked Shilpa as she tasted it, sitting at the bar of her coffee shop. 'It's absolutely delicious and just the right amount of sweet for the winter.'

'Not too sweet?' Shilpa had asked. The condensed milk made the dessert sweeter than her usual fusion cakes.

'No, pet,' Leoni said. 'That's just what the punters will like. It's different and will give her up the road a run for her money. It's similar to what Jacinta is offering.' Leoni gave Shilpa a sideways glance.

'I realise that. I had this in mind before I found out about Jacinta's,' she protested.

'You know where my loyalties lie,' Leoni had said, and with that she had cut the cheesecake and placed it under a glass dome ready for serving. She playfully shooed Shilpa away, and Shilpa had left with a smile on her face.

Her deliveries in Dartmouth and Mermaid Point had gone well. As Shilpa entered the café at Mermaid Point, she saw a familiar face behind the counter. 'Andreas,' she said. 'I didn't expect to see you here.'

'You're the baker from the house,' he said.

'Dreamcatcher. You cooked some fine food for us the day we dined with Duncan and Millie at the mansion,' Shilpa said as she passed over three boxes containing mini mango and chocolate loaves and a banana bread.

'So the famous banana bread is served in my mother's café too,' Andreas said.

'I didn't realise you were Maria's son? I came by in October, and she was talking about her talented boy working at a big house,' Shilpa had said, although as soon as she said it, she chided herself for not making the connection sooner. Andreas was very much like his mother with her dark eyes and angular nose. 'How is she?' she asked. 'You said she was unwell when we left Dreamcatcher.'

'She's okay,' Andreas said, turning away.

'So you aren't working at Dreamcatcher anymore?' Shilpa asked.

Andreas shook his head. 'They're closed,' he said. 'To be honest, the island hasn't had many bookings this winter, and with everything that happened, Mr Grave said to just keep it closed.'

'Her death must have hit you hard,' Shilpa said.

Andreas put down the tea towel he had been fiddling with.

'I didn't mean...' Shilpa started, although she didn't know how to finish her sentence. She didn't mean to pry? Of course she was prying.

'I was close to her,' Andreas said in a quiet voice. 'She got me the job at Dreamcatcher. I was broke, and I was going to just work here with my ma, but she always said I was better than that. That was the thing about Felicity. I saw a side to her that not many saw. She wanted to do good with her money, and she liked helping people out. Her business...' Andreas started, but then he stopped.

'The one she had with suppliers in India,' Shilpa encouraged.

Andreas looked at Shilpa again, silently weighing up whether or not she could be trusted. 'Felicity thought she was helping out young artisans who were designing and dyeing the fabric.' Andreas lowered his voice. He scanned the empty bakery. 'When Felicity found out what her stepmother and father were really using her for, she hit the roof.'

'She told you?' Shilpa asked.

Andreas smiled. 'She came to me the day before she died. She was in tears.'

'Why?' Shilpa asked, leaning in. She could tell that Andreas liked an engaged audience. Andreas told Shilpa what Felicity had told him. That she had found out that her label was being used to clean their dirty money.

'But that wasn't the worst part,' Andreas said. 'Felicity found out that the fabric wasn't being designed by artisans or young women in impoverished communities like her stepmother's brand claimed. It was all done in a local factory where working conditions were hard. Poor lighting, few toilet breaks.'

Shilpa nodded.

'Felicity was angry,' Andreas said. 'I had never seen her like that. I tried to comfort her, but she didn't want to know.'

'Did she say anything else?'

'Only that she wasn't going to let them get away with it, family or not.'

'What was she planning?' Shilpa asked, thinking about the

announcement that Felicity was going to make just hours before her death.

'I'm only the chef. She didn't tell me.'

'But she already told you more than she told Richard, I can imagine,' Shilpa said.

Andreas smiled. 'I didn't tell the police any of this. Mrs Grave came to see me and made it clear that I didn't have any kind of relationship with Felicity. She said that if the police knew I was friendly with her stepdaughter, they would ask all sorts of questions about me and my family, about my past.'

'Your past?' Shilpa asked.

'It was nothing,' Andreas said. 'I was young. Never mind.'

Shilpa nodded, knowing exactly what Rashmi Grave was trying to do.

'Did Felicity say anything about marrying Richard?' she asked. A dark look crossed Andreas's face that told her everything she needed to know. He silently rubbed an invisible stain on the countertop with his dishcloth.

'Will you go back to Dreamcatcher?' Shilpa asked, trying to lighten the conversation before she left him alone with his thoughts.

Andreas looked up, not directly at Shilpa but some way past her through the glass window out towards the ocean. 'Maybe,' he said. 'Maybe.'

Shilpa pressed the phone to her ear. 'Rashmi can be intimidating,' she said.

'You think Rashmi Grave intimidated Andreas to keep quiet about her dodgy business?' Tanvi said. 'She's an intimidating woman. And if Andreas loved Felicity then maybe she did confide in him. You know what attention seekers are like. Always willing to talk to a ready audience. Andreas gave Felicity the attention she craved. She probably didn't think much of him. To her, he was just the chef. She knew he wouldn't blab to anyone, so her secrets were safe. He was in her pocket, and that's what she liked about him.'

Tanvi's ideas were always out there, but Shilpa had to agree there was some truth in what her friend was saying. Andreas was easy to manipulate, and Rashmi had deftly done it.

'Is it a coincidence that you keep bumping into people from the island?' Tanvi said to Shilpa.

'I'm not stalking them if that's what you think,' Shilpa said. As the words left her mouth, an idea started forming in her mind. Tanvi was talking to her about something involving tote bags and high heels, but Shilpa wasn't listening.

'So you think I can get away with it?' Tanvi was saying.

'Get away with what?'

Tanvi started repeating her quandary again, but Shilpa still couldn't concentrate on what her friend was saying. Her mind was elsewhere. She put the call on speaker and looking at her mobile phone she pulled up one of the web pages she had found earlier.

She read and re-read the article which named a hotel. Shilpa opened a fresh webpage and put the name of the establishment into the search box. She didn't expect much. The piece had been written years ago, and it was more than likely that the hotel didn't exist anymore, but to her surprise it did.

She glanced over at her table to the desk calendar that she had recently acquired with her Sweet Treats logo on it. Robin had extended his trip so she had time. And she could do with a change of scene.

Shilpa's focus shifted towards the pantry. The paper bag from the pharmacy still haunted her from behind the sack of flour. She could do with switching off from her thoughts for another day or so, and then after her trip, she would definitely take the test. She couldn't put it off forever.

'Listen, Tanvi,' Shilpa said. 'I've got to go.'

'Are you serious?' her friend asked. 'You've not even answered my question. Where are you going?'

Shilpa was certain her friend would try and stop her if she said anything. She would just tell Tanvi where she was when she got there. Shilpa pulled out her holdall and started packing her clothes, underwear and toiletries. Then she went online and made a reservation. She could barely contain her excitement, but she had to get to bed. She had a long drive ahead of her tomorrow.

# Chapter Thirty-Five

S hilpa pulled up to the hotel on London Road and got out of her little red Fiat. Taking her holdall from the boot, she made her way through the glass doors, past the hanging baskets with their fake green foliage and into the lobby of the boutique hotel.

'Welcome to the Goldsmith Inn,' said a young woman, her blonde fringe partially covering her eyes. Shilpa noticed that the lobby was somewhat different to how it had been pictured in the article all those years ago. The luscious array of succulents had been replaced with large potted snake plants and money trees and the red and brown carpet had been swapped for a navy blue.

The receptionist handed Shilpa her key, and she made her way up the flight of stairs to her room. Once inside, she lay on the freshly pressed white sheets of the double bed. The room wasn't luxurious, far from it, but it was a change, and they say a change is as good as a rest.

Shilpa felt lighter being away from Otter's Reach. So much had happened recently. Her best friend had moved into town and her boyfriend had moved in; not to mention Jacinta's bakery. Then of course there was the chance that she was pregnant; and the death of a young woman. Shilpa hadn't had time to process any of it.

Her life was busy, and yet Shilpa found herself drawn into investigating Felicity's death. Was she just avoiding the problems in her own life by investigating those in Felicity's? Shilpa shook away her thoughts. Seeking justice was just something she did.

Shilpa sat up and gazed out of the window onto the car park. The Goldsmith Inn was a far cry from Rose Cottage on Dreamcatcher Island, but there was a connection between the two, and that was why she was there.

The dining room at the hotel was stunning with its glass ceilings and marble floor. It was called The Orangery, named after its former use, she imagined, without caring to read the literature at the front of the menu. Shilpa arrived at her booked table in time for a late lunch. She glanced around at the staff to gauge whether anyone could help her in her quest. As her lunch was served, Shilpa asked the waiter who had brought out her food if he had known a member of staff called Millie Stevenson or a Mildred Port.

'I've only been here a few years,' he said and turned away from her. Shilpa tried another couple of staff, but they were all so young, and no one had been at the hotel for longer than two years.

Shilpa's phone buzzed. It was Robin. She hadn't told him or Tanvi where she was. It had been foolish of her. What did she think? That she could come to this hotel and within hours find out about something that had happened here more than fifteen years ago? She hadn't been thinking straight. Shilpa stood up, leaving her French onion soup untouched. She swayed slightly and held on to the table for support.

'Are you okay?' A waiter wearing a white jacket and black bow-tie was at her side and helping her steady herself.

'I'm fine. Low blood pressure,' she said as she sat back down again.

'Are you sure, miss?'

Shilpa nodded. She hadn't previously noticed this waiter, who appeared older than the others. Shilpa tore off a piece of her bread roll and popped it into her mouth. She swallowed it down with some water as the waiter observed her with some concern.

'Just need to eat something,' she said.

It was the waiter's turn to nod. Shilpa tilted her head to one side. 'How long have you worked here?' she asked. 'If you don't mind me asking,' she added, remembering her manners.

'Three years,' he said.

'Oh,' Shilpa said, her face falling.

The waiter spoke to her kindly. 'I can tell that wasn't the answer you were after. There is someone I know who has been here for yonks though,' he said. 'I'll point you in her direction after you finish here.'

Shilpa smiled and found she had an appetite. She tucked in, and when she was done, the waiter kept his word. Shilpa found an elderly woman sitting in the back room behind the dining room.

'Are you Beryl?' Shilpa enquired.

The woman, with thick white hair and an elegant neckerchief, looked Shilpa up and down. 'How can I help you?' she asked.

'What was this place like when it first opened?' Shilpa enquired cheerfully. 'Alfie in the dining room said that if there was anything worth knowing, you were the one to speak to.'

Beryl beamed, her demeanour instantly changing.

'Do you have a few minutes?' Shilpa asked in her sweetest voice.

Beryl glanced at her watch. 'I'm due a break,' she said. 'We don't normally allow guests back in the staff area, but if you're writing a piece on the hotel...'

Shilpa hadn't mentioned anything of the sort but didn't bother to correct her.

'I've given some of my best years to this place,' Beryl said. She sat down opposite Shilpa with a mug of tea and a chocolate digestive. She offered Shilpa one from the packet, but Shilpa politely declined.

Beryl started with her first day at the hotel and told her just what it was like to work in a grand hotel like the Goldsmith Inn. *There is nothing grand about this place,* thought Shilpa, but then again it's all relative. She had just stayed at an exclusive resort in south Devon which would have usually cost over £10,000 for a week, and that was just for Rose Cottage.

The Goldsmith Inn wasn't a patch on Dreamcatcher Island, but looking at it afresh, she could see it had a certain charm, and she didn't think any dead bodies were going to turn up any time soon. Although they'd had a near miss in the past, and that was what Shilpa wanted to ask Beryl about. She just had to bring the woman around to talking about it without raising her suspicions.

'And so now am I correct in thinking you manage the housekeeping staff?' Shilpa asked.

Beryl's smile went from ear to ear. 'I started as a housekeeper myself and now look at me,' she said. 'Do you need to be writing this down?'

Shilpa smiled and took out her notebook and pen from her bag that she always kept handy. 'I was reading an article the other day,' she continued tentatively, 'about this hotel, you know, for research, and I read something about a member of staff, a Millie something, who attacked another employee. Was it one of the housekeepers? Do you remember anything about that?'

'I don't want to stir all that up and bring the hotel into disrepute. It's hard enough in this day and age–' she started, but Shilpa cut her off by raising her hand.

'I don't want to go into any of that in the piece I'm writing, but just for my own knowledge I wanted to hear her story. It sounded ever so interesting,' she said, making a show of putting her notepad and pen down.

Beryl leaned forward, assessing Shilpa again, then she smiled. 'Ooh,' she said conspiratorially. 'It was an interesting event. I've worked here nearly two decades, and it's the most scandalous thing that has ever happened here.'

'So Millie was the house manager here then?' Shilpa said.

'She was here when the hotel opened. It was a big step up for her, from what I've heard. Mildred wasn't likeable, always had an air about her, you know, like she was better than you.'

Millie hadn't changed then.

'Her partner, the handyman Duncan, was a nice bloke. The other staff here liked him around. He was fun and carefree when Mildred wasn't standing over him,' Beryl said.

'Handyman?' Shilpa asked, trying to contain her surprise.

Beryl's eyes turned to the ceiling for a moment before she spoke again. 'Yes, that's right, he was definitely a handyman.'

'So what happened?' Shilpa asked.

# Chapter Thirty-Six

Shilpa listened as Beryl described the affair in detail. The housekeeper, a young blonde with a small waist and high cheekbones, who 'had a way with men', had lured Duncan away from Millie.

'She wanted to be called Mildred back then. A harsh name for a girl. I once tried shortening it to Millie for her, but she didn't take kindly to it,' Beryl said. 'And Stevenson was Duncan's surname. Hers was something else. Port, I think, or something like that. Mildred Port, yes, that was it. Quite a name.'

'And Duncan was having an affair with one of the housekeepers?' Shilpa asked, reminding Beryl of the story she was telling. Beryl nodded and told Shilpa that the relationships between staff in those days were not uncommon.

'Everyone knew about them,' Beryl said. 'Except Mildred.'

'They say the wife is always the last to know,' Shilpa chipped in.

'She wasn't a wife back then. I don't know why she didn't just leave him. I've come across men like that before. They can't keep it in their pants. You know what they say: a leopard never changes his spots; he only rearranges them.'

Shilpa couldn't help but nod. She hadn't heard that line before, but Beryl was right. She had seen it with her own eyes. Millie was possessive and Duncan had a wandering eye. Did she think he would change when they moved away from Leicester?

'I understand that Millie found out eventually,' Shilpa said.

'Oh yes,' the woman said, running her fingers through her thick white hair. Her cheeks were flushed, and she reached for her tea. 'It was a terrible business when Mildred came to know about the affair, and we never got to the bottom of how she found out. She may have heard some of the staff talking, that is certainly plausible, or she could have caught Duncan in the act. It wouldn't surprise me. Anyhows, she came to know about it, and the next thing we know, she has the poor housekeeper by the neck against one of the walls in the laundry room.'

'Did she cause any damage?'

'I saw the bruising the poor girl suffered at Mildred's hands. It wasn't a pretty sight,' Beryl said. 'And from what I heard, if one of the other housekeepers hadn't interrupted her, Mildred wouldn't have stopped her attack. She had to literally prise her off.'

'Why didn't she take it up with Duncan?' Shilpa asked.

'Maybe she did. No one knows if he suffered at her hands or not. She left soon after that.'

'The housekeeper?'

Beryl shook her head. 'No, Mildred. That little housekeeper may have come across like a pushover, but she wasn't. She was ready to press charges. She even went to the papers. Someone must have paid her off in the end. Probably the owners of this place or even Duncan and Mildred. It wouldn't surprise me. Mildred and Duncan left together under a dark cloud, probably less than a week after the incident.'

'Hmm,' Shilpa said, lost for words. What Beryl had just disclosed put Millie as prime suspect for killing Felicity. The woman had form. She had nearly strangled one of Duncan's previous lovers and may well have done if someone hadn't interrupted her. That was a long while ago. But Duncan was still up to his old tricks, Shilpa had seen him with Felicity with her own eyes. So if Duncan hadn't changed, what was to say Millie had?

Shilpa thanked Beryl for her time and made her way back to her room. As she closed the door behind her, Beryl pulled out her old Filofax. What was Mildred Port up to now, she wondered. She liked keeping up to date with her ex-colleagues, as she had little else to do in her free time. She surprised herself that she hadn't checked up on where the ex-hotel manager was.

Beryl found the name she was after and made a call.

The next morning, Shilpa was up bright and early. She left for Devon as soon as she had breakfasted, which she had little appetite for. Her lack of hunger was down to one of two things. One was her possible pregnancy, which she was still doing her best not to think about and failing spectacularly, and the other was the early morning call she had received from Rashmi Grave.

'I need a cake,' is what the woman had led with. 'Or a series of cakes, like mini loaves or cupcakes.' Her tone was dictatorial, like she expected Shilpa to oblige, and of course Shilpa did.

She did the obligatory checking of her diary and asking just what the occasion was, but she knew as well as Rashmi that Shilpa was making those cakes.

'So what can you make for my daughter's engagement?' Rashmi had said.

Shilpa suggested a selection of cupcakes with some of her fusion flavours like mango and saffron and rose and pistachio. Rashmi Grave had stopped her mid-sentence. Shilpa felt like she was on *Britain's Got Talent* after the first buzzer went. There was an awkward silence, after which Rashmi pronounced that she had got the job.

'The party had already been organised,' Rashmi said, by way of an explanation. 'I thought Gina had cancelled it all in light of what happened, but Gina's certain that Felicity wouldn't have wanted her stepsister to put her life on hold.' Rashmi informed Shilpa that there would be a hundred guests and gave her the time and location before disconnecting.

As Shilpa headed toward the M5, she considered what Beryl had told her. Millie was a prime suspect. She had motive and opportunity to kill Felicity Grave. Minutes after Alan had called Millie and Duncan to the house, she had arrived, dressed for the occasion in black leggings and a cashmere poncho.

Millie could have easily slipped a suitable quantity of poison into Felicity's Negroni as she discussed a private matter with her in her bedroom. It was possible that Millie had threatened Felicity in that passive aggressive way of hers, ignoring any consequences, knowing full well that her victim would soon be dead.

Millie knew Dreamcatcher Mansion like the back of her hand; she could have easily hidden in one of its many nooks and crannies after the deed was done, just waiting for a call to come through from Alan Grave, like she knew it would. She was the one who knew exactly what to do, disposing of the bag of cocaine like that. And by disposing of it in front of everyone, Millie was showing people that she had nothing to hide, but maybe the opposite was true. It could be that Millie had everything to hide.

Shilpa exited the motorway and breathed a sigh of relief. She much preferred trains because she didn't have to think of directions, but Leicester from Devon was one too many changes on the train for her.

Gina and Albie's engagement party was on Shilpa's mind as she headed towards Otter's Reach. She hadn't thought about how they could have been involved in Felicity Grave's death, but she certainly couldn't rule them out. Gina stood to gain financially from Felicity's death, she was sure of it, despite what articles had said about the Grave family will.

It was well documented that Grave family tradition meant that the firstborn direct descendant inherited the family wealth. By all accounts this was Felicity, but with Felicity out of the way, Julian was next in line to the pot of gold if they were going for the biological child.

Shilpa had done some research, and Gina was older than Julian, just. Would the fact that she was adopted affect her chances of hitting the jackpot? She wasn't Alan's biological child, but could a good lawyer argue that in this day and age that didn't apply? More importantly, would Gina know that?

Either way, Gina had a better chance of an inheritance pay-out with Felicity out of the way. So she had motive and opportunity given that Albie must have been her alibi for the time of Felicity's death. And Albie had warned Shilpa that someone was going to get hurt on the island. Had he been planning Felicity's murder the whole time? Albie and Gina could have been in on it together.

That just left Julian, Felicity's younger brother. He had sufficiently creeped Shilpa out during her time on Dreamcatcher Island, and it was clear that the siblings were not close. Julian could have wanted his sister dead because... Shilpa wracked her brain but couldn't think of anything. And being a creep didn't necessarily make you a murderer. She put a question mark over Julian's name as she pulled into her drive.

Shilpa sighed. At least it wasn't the end of her investigation. With any luck, she would be able to stay for the duration of Gina and Albie's party, where she would keep a close eye on her suspects.

Shilpa parked up and retrieved her bag from her boot. Opening her front door, she put her bag down and walked down the stairs to the kitchen. Making herself a tea, she groaned at the thought of making a hundred cupcakes in different flavours.

'Indians need to help each other out,' Rashmi had said, but it was clear this wasn't the case. Rashmi knew that Shilpa would deliver; and that her cakes tasted great – not that Shilpa wanted to blow her own trumpet, but they did. It was also likely that Rashmi couldn't find a decent baker in London at such short notice. Shilpa checked her phone for the full address of the party.

'London,' Shilpa said out loud. She had completely forgotten about that bit. Not only did she have all that baking to do, but she had to trek to London with her cakes. She wasn't sure if she could do it on her own, and Rashmi was paying her generously.

Maybe it was time to rope in some extra help.

Shilpa picked up her phone and dialled a number.

## Chapter Thirty-Seven

'I'm not sure how you convinced me to take two days off work to help you,' Tanvi said as she placed a mini rose and pistachio cake on a blue-and-white porcelain stand. 'Three days ago you managed perfectly fine on your own tearing up to Leicester and back.'

'You have leave to take and you're getting paid,' Shilpa said.

'A pittance,' Tanvi said. 'Look at this place.' She gazed up at the chandeliers and moulded ceilings painted in a shade of pastel blue. Large silver bowls filled with ice and magnums of champagne were sitting along the bar, where two waiters in black bow-ties were waiting to serve the guests. 'Must be worth millions in this postcode.'

'It's a private members' club,' Shilpa said. 'What did you expect?'

'This family has too much wealth for its own good.'

'Wealth you'd like access to,' Shilpa said.

'Any single Grave men about?'

'Julian,' Shilpa said.

Tanvi visibly shuddered. 'I'll stick to the impoverished Brij then,' she said with a laugh.

'And I pay you a decent wage, especially when I have to put up with your back-chatting.'

'I'm teasing,' Tanvi said. 'Although why you agreed to cater for a last-minute event in London is beyond me.'

Shilpa handed Tanvi a box of mango and dark chocolate mini loaves. 'Rashmi played the Indian card,' she said.

'These Indian mothers are so conniving.'

Shilpa stopped rearranging Tanvi's work and turned to her friend. 'She had me at *namaste*.'

Tanvi laughed. 'Bet that isn't the only reason you agreed to do this.'

Shilpa smiled. She had to admit it was too good an opportunity to pass up. She was hoping for an invite to stay beyond just setting up the cakes, but Rashmi had made no attempt to detain her. So much for Indians helping each other out.

Shilpa was fiddling with the tiered cake stand when Tanvi put a hand on her shoulder. 'Come on,' her friend said. 'We can't stay here forever. You promised me lunch, remember?'

'I don't remember, actually, as it was never my intention to leave.'

'Tough,' Tanvi said. She grabbed her coat from the back of a nearby chair and waited for Shilpa to follow suit.

The sound of the heavy wooden double doors from the main entrance of the club could be heard, and Shilpa waited in anticipation of who would be walking into the so-called living room.

Gina and Albie entered, and the string quartet started. Gina blanked Shilpa and pulled her fiancé towards where her mother was standing. Albie gave them a half smile in recognition and followed his bride-to-be.

Shilpa was looking back at the couple as she headed

towards the exit of the luxurious club when she bumped into someone. 'Sorry,' she said, turning to face the person she had offended.

Alan Grave took a moment to steady himself. Rashmi ran over to his side and gave Shilpa an icy stare.

'We were just going,' Shilpa said.

'The exit's over there,' Rashmi said, pointing towards the hall. Shilpa did her best to smile. Clients like Rashmi always boasted to their friends about their catering staff. This one party could be lucrative for Shilpa, although she didn't want to bake cakes for any more events in London. She had moved away from the city for a reason.

'Stay,' said Alan, as Shilpa was turning away. 'I hear you've done a fantastic job here, so you may as well enjoy it a little. It must have been a long drive from Devon for you and your friend, and you'll have been up early. The last thing you want to do is head straight back. Have something to eat and drink and then go.'

Shilpa could feel Tanvi's eyes boring into her, but she couldn't pass up the invitation. The party was a perfect opportunity to observe her suspects, as she was sure most of them would be here.

'I'm sure the ladies have to get back,' Rashmi was saying. 'This is a small family affair.'

'A small family affair isn't one hundred guests, dear, no matter how you dress it up. And it's too soon after–'

'I tried,' Rashmi said. 'You know what Gina can be like. She honestly thought it was what Felicity would have wanted.'

Alan looked like he wasn't convinced.

Shilpa turned away, fearful of catching Rashmi's eye during this private conversation, which wasn't so private.

The awkward silence between the couple was eventually broken by more guests arriving. Rashmi went off to greet them, and Alan pointed Shilpa and Tanvi in the direction of the bar. 'Go ahead,' he said.

Tanvi didn't need telling twice. A minute later, she was at the bar with two glasses of champagne. 'So what time are you meeting Robin?' she asked.

Shilpa took one of the glasses from her friend, pretended to take a sip and put it back down on the bar. She was careful not to catch Tanvi's eye.

'You have told him you're in London, haven't you?'

## Chapter Thirty-Eight

Shilpa hadn't told Robin of her trip to London, and she could understand why Tanvi was surprised. Robin was less than two Tube stops away from where they were, and she was desperate to see him, only she felt that she couldn't, not yet, not until she had taken the test.

Shilpa had been hoping not to get into it with Tanvi and she was amazed it hadn't come up sooner. Possibly because Tanvi had slept for most of the long drive down. Shilpa had been so preoccupied with making today's cakes that she had completely forgotten about the test, and the absence of her period. She needed to take the test before consuming vast quantities of champagne, which her friend clearly wanted her to do.

Shilpa had told Robin all about Gina and Albie's engagement party, but Robin hadn't asked where the party was, and so she hadn't told him.

It was foolish not to meet him just because of an inkling, but the more she dwelled on it, the more she magnified the situation. And she was sure that if she met Robin now, he would know something was up. Why hadn't she taken the test yet? Because the result, if positive, would seal her fate? It was likely, but she couldn't hold off forever.

'You always said I was a commitment-phobe, but I think you were projecting your issues onto me,' Tanvi said.

'What do you mean?' Shilpa asked.

'You and Robin are perfect together and yet since Dreamcatcher Island you've been weird.'

'Just drink your champagne,' Shilpa said.

'What about you?' Tanvi stared at her friend for a moment.

'I'm driving, remember? Oh look,' Shilpa said as a throng of young men and women entered the room. 'There's Julian.'

'Is that gel in his hair?' Tanvi made a face.

Julian slowly made his way around the room. He stopped for a soft drink at the bar and then stood awkwardly by one of the large windows overlooking the club's gardens.

'You should go and speak to him,' an unfamiliar voice said from beside her. Shilpa turned. She expected Tanvi to stay close, but her friend was nowhere to be seen. Albie was standing with a champagne flute in his hand, grinning at her.

'He's single, you know,' he said.

'I'm not,' said Shilpa.

'Oh yes, the floppy-haired journalist. You caused quite a stir at our New Year bash, although talk of your appearance was overshadowed by poor Felicity's death.'

'It was awful,' Shilpa said.

'And it's a good thing you were on hand to remind someone to call the police. We may never have thought of it otherwise.'

'I'm sorry—' Shilpa started to say but Albie cut her off.

'You do realise why you're here, don't you?'

Shilpa didn't say anything, but she could feel little beads of sweat starting to form on her upper lip.

Albie didn't wait for a response. 'Our dear Rashmi wants to know what you know now that Flick's death is a murder investigation. Rashmi likes to keep her enemies close, if you know what I mean, and we've all heard about your hobby. So who do you think did it?'

'Rashmi hasn't said anything to me,' Shilpa said. She didn't think that the super-rich had time to Google who their caterer was. On the other hand, maybe they had too much time.

'Rashmi plans everything, so if she wants to find out something, she'll have planned how to extract the information out of you and your friend without you even knowing. And if you're a bit short on suspects then Julian is your man,' Albie said with confidence. A man in a yellow suit walked past, and Albie raised his glass to him. 'Julian was obsessed with Flick. Gina told me all about it.'

'What do you mean?' she asked.

'A young man obsessed with his very beautiful sister can only mean one thing. Julian didn't like the person he was around Felicity. Gina said she once caught him staring at Flick while she was taking a bath. He was observing her through a crack in the door.'

'Did Gina stop him?'

'Gina was pretty sure Felicity knew her brother was standing there. Makes you wonder which one of them was more sick in the head.'

'Did anything ever happen between them?' Shilpa asked.

'It's interesting that Felicity refused Richard's proposal, don't you think? She was desperate to get engaged, or so we all thought, and then suddenly on New Year's Eve she tells him she just wants him as a friend. Although I don't think she used the phrase "love you like a brother", because who knew what that meant to her.' Albie laughed. 'But who knows if anything happened between the two.'

'Gina?' Shilpa offered.

Albie didn't bite. 'It must have felt so awful, to be attracted to your own sister like that,' he said, giving a mock shudder. 'It was why the two became so distant in the run-up to her death.

Julian stayed away from her because he couldn't control himself around her, and the one weekend they spend at the same house together in God knows how many years, well…'

'What are you trying to say?' Shilpa asked. 'That weekend on Dreamcatcher Island you told me that someone was going to get hurt. Like you knew something was going to happen.'

Albie hesitated for a split second and then laughed. He swallowed half the contents of his glass. 'Not too sharp, are you? I'm not sure why they made such a fuss about you in the local Devon rag. Rashmi'll be pleased.'

Before Shilpa could defend herself, Albie had put his glass down on the bar and, taking a cocktail from a tray, he left. Shilpa scanned the room for Tanvi. She was desperate to tell her what she had just heard.

If Albie was to be believed and Julian was in love with his sister then there was his motive for murder – well, that and a substantial inheritance. If being around Felicity made Julian ashamed and disgusted with himself then there was a high chance that he could have killed his sister just to stop feeling that way. Moving abroad would have been a simpler solution, although Shilpa was beginning to realise that rich families operated in a similar way to large Indian families. You could never escape one another. They would always track you down, desperate to be entangled in every part of your life.

'Where are you, Tanvi?' Shilpa mumbled as she pushed through the crowd towards Julian, who was still staring aimlessly out of the window. Shilpa followed his gaze. There was a group of young women wearing strappy sandals and long fur coats under a patio heater. They were laughing and smoking and had no idea they were being watched.

'It's you,' Julian said. Shilpa turned towards him. 'Why are you here? Why are you so interested in my family?'

Shilpa took a step back. 'I made the cakes,' she said, motioning to the table in the distance.

'They shouldn't be having a party,' Julian said. 'It's telling that they are. Gina insists it's what Felicity would have wanted, but I can guarantee that she would have hated this. Knowing my sister, she would have wanted a mourning period.' Julian smiled, and Shilpa reciprocated.

He was still creepy, but genuine, she supposed. She imagined Julian not knowing what to do with his love for his sister, and a part of her felt sorry for him. He clearly had issues, issues she didn't understand. Maybe Julian didn't understand them either, and that must have been tough.

Shilpa noticed that Albie was grinning at her from across the room. She turned away. It was possible that Albie had made up Julian's obsession with Felicity.

'You and Felicity must have been close?' she asked Julian, testing the water.

Julian fingered the rim of his glass.

'I can see why Gina and Albie celebrating like this so soon after her death is upsetting.'

'It's why Father didn't stay. He's made his feelings clear to Gina, but there's no telling her anything now. At least Felicity used to keep her in line, but now she won't listen to anyone or anything. The sad thing is that Father has lost one daughter, and he doesn't want to lose another. He knows just how short life can be, so he's letting Gina get away with anything right now.'

'Were Gina and Felicity close?' Shilpa asked.

'When they were younger. Gina was Felicity's plaything. Did whatever Felicity wanted her to do. As they got older, they drifted apart, or at least Gina tried to make her getaway, but Felicity had a way of making sure Gina never strayed too far. She needed Gina because she liked to lord it over people. Gina was a willing and sometimes not so willing subject.'

'Until Gina got engaged,' Shilpa offered.

'Something like that. We both lived in Felicity's shadow. Gina was trying to break away from my sister's spell.'

'And you?' Shilpa asked.

'Nothing was going to break that,' he said, his tone turning more sombre.

'Only death,' Shilpa offered. 'I can tell you loved your sister very much.' She waited for a response, but he was silent. 'She was very beautiful,' she added.

'What do you mean?' Julian asked.

'Nothing,' Shilpa said. 'I was just saying—'

'I think you'd better go. This is a family gathering, and you're not family.'

'Sorry,' Shilpa said.

Julian motioned something to someone in the distance. In less than a minute, a security guard was standing next to Shilpa and encouraging her to the exit.

## Chapter Thirty-Nine

Tanvi opened the cubicle door and saw Gina standing in front of the mirror. She rubbed her nose and grinned. 'Hey,' she said, turning to face Tanvi. 'I'm so glad you made it. When was it that we last met. Uni? Couldn't have been. Maybe Rob's Halloween party?'

'I think you've got the wrong person,' Tanvi said.

Gina studied her. Her expression changed. She opened her arms and embraced Tanvi with a half sob. 'You were with that group on Dreamcatcher Island?' she asked, taking a step back.

'That's right.'

Gina touched her hand to her forehead. 'I miss Flick. I didn't want all of this – this party – but I speak to my sister all the time now and she is so supportive of this, of today.'

Tanvi, who hadn't taken Gina for the spirit medium type, was surprised by this revelation and didn't quite know what to say. So she put her hand on the girl's shoulder.

'Your friend solves crimes, doesn't she?' Gina asked.

'Well, not quite,' Tanvi said.

Gina appeared not to have heard her and instead peered in

the mirror with mascara wand in hand. 'So who does she think did it?'

'We've not really discussed it.'

'I was with Albie at the time,' she said. 'We were busy, you know how it is, and then I heard a scream. It went right through me. I knew something was wrong. I ran to find out what had happened. You were there.' She observed Tanvi from the corner of her eye. 'You know the rest.'

'We left the house quite soon after we found Felicity.'

Gina nodded. 'You did,' she said pensively. 'Well, let's hope they find the monster that did this and put him away. We should get back. Coming?' she asked, slipping her make-up back into her handbag and turning towards the door that led back to the living room.

Tanvi nodded.

'My friend,' Shilpa said as the security guard ushered Shilpa out of the front door. 'I can't leave without my friend.' She gave the man a description of Tanvi, and he assured her that he would find her and tell her that her friend was waiting outside for her, but somehow Shilpa didn't believe him.

Shilpa stood outside in the bitter cold of January, desperately messaging and calling Tanvi. An hour later, the black-and-gold double doors of the club opened and her friend emerged.

'Where have you been?' Shilpa shouted.

'I was at the party *you* wanted to go to.'

Shilpa groaned and started walking towards the multi-storey car park where they had parked her red Fiat several hours ago. She paid for the parking, and once inside the car, she switched on the engine and turned up the heating.

'So?' Tanvi asked. 'What happened?'

'I need to thaw out first,' she said. Five minutes later, they were on the road again.

'Are you sufficiently warm?' Tanvi asked.

Shilpa nodded as she headed towards a McDonald's drive-thru. 'I thought you weren't interested in who killed Felicity Grave.'

'I wasn't,' Tanvi said. 'Until I had a drunken conversation with someone in the loos.'

Shilpa ordered a Quarter Pounder, a Filet-O-Fish, two medium fries and two strawberry milkshakes before turning to her friend. 'Who?' she asked.

'Gina and Albie were fully clothed in their partywear when we found the body and they came to Felicity's room,' Shilpa said.

'How do you remember? We were all so drunk,' Tanvi asked.

Shilpa hadn't been as drunk as the others. She had sobered up after Tanvi had freaked her out by mentioning that she could be pregnant. 'Gina was wearing the same pale green silk dress. I didn't see Albie. He wasn't let in the room, remember?'

Tanvi shook her head.

'If you were at it, so to speak, with your partner and you heard a scream and went to investigate, wouldn't you put on a dressing gown or pyjamas?' Shilpa said.

'Maybe she wasn't undressed,' Tanvi offered. 'It happens.'

'It's convenient that Albie and Gina were together when it happened.'

'Convenient or true. That's what happens when you're in a couple. What's their motive anyway? Do you think Felicity was going to expose Gina as a fraud and they had to stop her before it was too late? Newsflash, Shilpa. Everyone already knew that Gina wasn't Alan Grave's biological daughter. Can we head back home now? My head's beginning to spin.'

Shilpa gathered up their cartons and cups and walked to the closest bin. On the way back, her phone started to vibrate. She hoped it wasn't Robin. The last thing she wanted to do was to lie to him if he asked her where she was. Shilpa glanced at the display. She didn't recognise the number. She answered it.

'Hello,' she said for a third time as she opened the car door and sat back in the driving seat. There was a distinct crackle on the line. 'I can't hear you,' she said. Shilpa was about to disconnect when she heard a faint voice, one that she had heard before but couldn't place.

'Hello,' the voice came again.

'Who is this?' Shilpa asked.

'Jane, Felicity's mum. We spoke the other day. You gave me your card, remember,' she said. 'I hear from family that you're actually a detective of sorts.'

Shilpa tried to correct her, but Jane didn't give her a chance to speak.

'I think there's something you should know about Felicity. I realise now what she was going to announce before her death. I should have told someone sooner, but I haven't, and, well, here we are.'

'If you know something concerning Felicity's death, I think you need to tell the police,' Shilpa said. The line was breaking up again.

'I'm not sure about that. It's a sensitive matter,' Jane said. 'I suppose what I'm looking for is advice as to whether this information is relevant or not, because if it gets into the wrong hands, it could be fatal, and I'm in a hurry.'

'A hurry?' Shilpa said. 'I can't hear you.'

'I need to tell someone what I know because it's eating me up inside.'

'What was Felicity going to say?'

'I can't tell you over the phone,' Jane said. 'We can arrange to meet in Devon. Where are you?'

'I'm in London. Just heading out, actually.'

'I'm in London too,' Jane said. 'I don't have much time, but if I give you an address, can you make your way here?'

Shilpa turned to Tanvi, who was rubbing her temples. She had paracetamol in the glove box. She reached over her friend and retrieved it for her as she listened to Jane's directions.

'I'm on my way,' she said.

# Chapter Forty

'I miss London,' Tanvi said as they pulled up to a side street in Fitzrovia somewhere behind Goodge Street Station. Tanvi and Shilpa stepped out of the car. 'Smell that London air,' she said with a grin on her face as she followed Shilpa towards a block of apartments.

'All I can smell is fumes,' said Shilpa.

'And can you hear the hubbub of life on every street corner?' Tanvi grabbed her friend's hand and pointed to a bar across the road which was teeming with life behind the windows.

'What happened to your headache?'

Tanvi made a face. 'I just want to maximise my time in the city before we go back.'

'I thought you liked Otter's Reach,' Shilpa said.

'I do. I like them both, and I miss the city.'

'So come back for a long weekend with Brijesh. We're working,' Shilpa said.

'Are we?' Tanvi said.

'Come on,' Shilpa said. 'If we're successful here, maybe I'll buy you a glass of Malbec.'

'Is that a deal?' Tanvi asked.

Shilpa nodded. She stepped towards the apartment building and located the number she was after, then she rang the bell.

A tall man in a beanie hat and with a ginger beard was heading out of the apartment building as Shilpa and Tanvi waited by the intercom. Tanvi caught the door before it slammed shut.

'Come on,' she said.

Shilpa followed her friend into the lobby. Her low heels click-clacked on the grey porcelain-tiled floors. A large industrial mirror filled the space on the wall.

'Flat four?' Tanvi asked. Without waiting for a response, she headed up the stairs, which were covered in a grey cord carpet. 'This is it,' she said, standing outside a beech-wood door.

Shilpa caught her breath and rang the bell, but there was no reply. Tanvi tried, but still no answer.

'What did she say exactly?' Tanvi asked.

'That she knew what Felicity was going to announce the night she died. She wanted to tell me what it was,' Shilpa said.

'Typical,' Tanvi said. 'She's not here. Let's head back.'

'She wouldn't have made me drive all this way to just leave me here. Maybe she popped out to get some milk or something.' Shilpa listened at the next door along the corridor. She could hear two children playing a game.

'She'd have been back by now,' Tanvi said. 'There's a shop just across the road. Didn't you notice it?'

Shilpa shook her head as she made her way back to Jane's front door. 'What if something's happened to her?'

'Like what?' Tanvi asked. 'Like a trip or fall or something? She isn't that old. Or at least she didn't appear that way when we saw her on Dreamcatcher Island.'

'She's frail though,' Shilpa said, thinking back to when she had a drink with Jane in Leoni's. She recalled the delicate skin on her hands peppered with sunspots. 'I don't think life has been kind to her.'

'You don't know what kind of a life she's had. She could be one of those people that worry needlessly all the time, like both our mums. Come to think of it, all mums are probably like that. And she did just lose a daughter; no wonder she appeared worse for wear. So now what?' Tanvi asked.

Shilpa was staring at the door. Jane certainly hadn't sounded distressed when she had called, but she did sound like she was in a hurry. 'I don't have much time,' she had said. Did she mean she had to go somewhere, or was she worried that someone knew what she knew? Shilpa pushed the door gently.

The door gave and creaked open.

'Why am I always breaking and entering places with you?' Tanvi asked.

Shilpa explained that they were technically above the law, as the door happened to be open, and they had been invited over. 'Plus, we're checking on a friend.' She walked into the hall and then into the small sitting room, which was open plan with the kitchen.

'Well, this is certainly her place,' Tanvi said, picking up a framed photograph of Jane and Felicity.

Shilpa didn't respond; she was studying the other photographs that littered the mantelpiece. Most of them were of Felicity, but a few featured a solemn Julian in the background. There was one picture of the two siblings and Jane where Felicity was wearing a silver silk dress with spaghetti straps. Julian was standing in between his mother and sister and was turned towards Felicity. He had his arm around his sister's waist, his hand resting a little lower than it should have been.

Shilpa picked up the frame and examined it. To look at the

picture, you wouldn't think there was anything in it, just a brother and sister posing together for a photo on what appeared to be a happy occasion. It was one of the few pictures where Julian was smiling, but there was something else in his eyes. It made her flinch, and she quickly placed the photo back down.

'There's nothing here,' Tanvi said from the balcony as she peered at the bar across the road.

'There's a warm cup of tea on the table,' Shilpa said, touching the striped blue-and-white mug. 'Did you open this fridge?'

Tanvi shook her head.

'It was left open,' Shilpa said. 'Why would you leave a cup of tea and an open fridge?'

'I leave the fridge open all the time. It happens. I don't mean to do it. I just get distracted,' Tanvi said.

Shilpa returned a moment later with a black holdall. 'What about this?' she said. Shilpa unzipped the bag and pulled out a passport and clothes. It was Jane's passport. 'She was trying to get away. Something happened.'

Tanvi was by her side now. 'Like what?' she asked. For the first time, she had an element of concern in her voice.

Shilpa rifled through the contents of the bag. Jane had packed for a few nights away. It didn't make sense that she would do that and then put her bag by the door and leave without it. Surely wherever she was going, she needed her passport. And the open fridge and cup of tea. Something was wrong.

Shilpa turned back to the photo of Felicity, Julian and Jane on the mantelpiece; she thought of what Albie had said about the dead girl's brother; and the way Julian had removed her from the party the minute he felt threatened, but mostly she thought of the look in Jane's eyes when she had unintentionally mentioned Julian's odd behaviour to her the day they had a drink together at Leoni's.

Jane was in trouble, and Shilpa had to help her.

## Chapter Forty-One

Julian saw the text message and flung his phone at the wall. Why now? Why there? He stooped down and picked up his phone, which was miraculously intact, and read the message again. There were so many other places they could go. He swore at his dead sister and started to type a message, but it was no good. A car was on its way. He would have to go. They would all have to go.

An hour later, his bag was packed and he was ready to leave. The others would be drunk and high from the party, groggy and uncooperative. Is that why Alan Grave had picked this time – as some form of punishment? Julian had to smile at that. But he had his own issues to sort out before he left. He stared at the lifeless body on the sofa. Maybe if he gave her some time she would come to.

He waited, but she didn't move. He had no choice but to leave her where she was.

The phone rang, and Julian answered.

'Julian,' Rashmi said in that voice she put on when she wanted something, which was almost always. He was glad things never went any further with Gina. It would have ended badly. Badly for her, anyway. Julian stared out of the window towards the BT Tower. He couldn't bear to look the other way. 'You are coming,' she said. 'Alan's keen that you're there. He has something important to say, and he wants everyone to be there.'

Julian asked Rashmi what the rush was, but she was silent. So Alan was finally dying. He wondered if Rashmi had managed to speed up his father's demise. She certainly had it in her.

He had been observing her for some time now and noticed that she often stirred something into his drink. She had caught him once and laughed that fake laugh of hers. 'Helps him sleep,' she had whispered, and she had touched him on the small of his back, which had made the hairs on the back of his neck stand on end. He had let it slide. He should have warned his father.

Although what did he care? His father never cared for him. So what if Rashmi had been slowly poisoning him. Maybe they would all be better off when the great Alan Grave was dead.

'Dad was never interested in Dreamcatcher Mansion, and now he's there twice in less than a month. Why?'

'Something serious happened there, Julian,' Rashmi said. He could hear her sigh on the other end of the line. He imagined that she had had this conversation a few times tonight. 'It's important that he tells you all at the house.'

Felicity never got a chance to say what she had wanted to say. Maybe Alan would have better luck.

Julian disconnected the call and hovered by the window waiting for the black car to pull up outside. The weather was miserable. The car arrived. Julian grabbed his bag from the hall and made his way down the stairs.

~

It was late by the time Shilpa and Tanvi got back to Otter's Reach, and an icy wind was blowing as Shilpa stepped out of her car and made her way towards the front door. They had listened to the weather forecast on the journey home, and it sounded grim. They were talking about sleet and snow and even a storm; the first of the year. They were calling it Storm Alan, which was fitting for what was on her mind.

No matter how much Tanvi had tried to explain away the tea, the open fridge and the ready-to-go holdall, Shilpa couldn't quiet her mind about Jane's disappearance. She was certain that Jane wouldn't have left her apartment that way with the front door open, for anyone to enter.

Shilpa still had DS Sharpe's card in her wallet. She called him, but it went straight to voicemail. She disconnected and tried again. This time she left him a message explaining her concerns about Jane.

Sharpe called back fifteen minutes later. He didn't sound as concerned as she felt, but he told her he would put word out about Jane's disappearance.

'Have you called her family?' he had asked. Shilpa had to say she hadn't. Shilpa didn't have Julian's number, and she wasn't sure that he was the best person to call either. She didn't voice her concerns, but she had a strong suspicion that Julian had something to do with his mother's disappearance. It was more than likely that Julian was involved with his sister's death too. The motive was there, especially if Felicity was going to expose his feelings for her that night, although why she would do such a thing was beyond Shilpa.

Felicity did like to get her way though. Julian said she liked to lord it over people. If Felicity hadn't been having a good day, she could have taken it out on her brother just to make herself feel better. Had Felicity threatened Julian for her own amusement, leaving him with no choice but to end her life? Or had he, like Shilpa, witnessed his sister fornicating with the house manager? Was his jealousy too much to contain, so much so that he believed his sister should die?

It was possible that Jane knew what her son was capable of and she knew what her daughter had wanted to say the night she was killed. But why did Jane want to confide in Shilpa before the police? Was it because her revelation could ruin the Graves and she feared for her son who was still a part of that family?

It was feasible that after Jane had spoken to Shilpa and had given her directions to her home that she had called Julian and told him what she was about to do. He had been in central London at Gina and Albie's party. He would have easily been able to get to his mother before Shilpa and Tanvi did. Had he convinced his mother to leave her home, or had he snatched her away?

Shilpa disconnected her call to the detective, unsure whether speaking to him had reassured her or not. She filled the kettle and checked her phone. She had three missed calls from Robin and a voicemail. She expected it to be Robin, and she retrieved the message and listened to it as the kettle boiled. But the voice on the message wasn't Robin's. She listened to the message and then listened to it again.

She couldn't believe what Millie was saying, so she quickly opened up her email on her phone. There it was, the email she had been waiting for. It had arrived much earlier in the day, but she had been so busy with the party and then worrying about Jane that she hadn't checked her messages. Shilpa read the contents.

She quickly emailed her clients to say that she would be out of town for a couple of nights but that she would return to complete their orders that were due. Shilpa smiled. She couldn't have timed it any better. The wind was whipping up the water in the estuary below. Storm Alan was approaching.

Shilpa pulled up the weather app on her phone. Tomorrow was supposed to be overcast, but the storm wasn't due to come in till after lunch. If she woke early enough, she could make it to her destination in time.

# Chapter Forty-Two

At six the next morning, through the rain, Shilpa made her way to Parrot Bay. She wanted to catch the ferry to the island without having to call the house to send for one, because she had reason to believe that since Millie had invited her, she had changed her mind.

As she boarded the boat along with three staff heading to the house, her phone vibrated. She pulled it out of her pocket and glanced at the display, hoping it wasn't Kelly. Kelly ran the market, and Shilpa was due to have a stall today and give Jacinta a run for her money, but with Gina's party and everything that followed, the last thing Shilpa wanted to do was run a stall. Besides, she hadn't been organised enough to have some cakes ready. She had messaged Kelly yesterday and cancelled. She hoped Jacinta hadn't gone to too much trouble to try and show her up. May the best baker win, indeed.

The message wasn't from Kelly. It was Millie again. She had been ringing incessantly last night, so much so that Shilpa had turned her phone on silent. Shilpa would have been concerned at the number of calls, but she knew why Millie was desperate to get hold of her from the first voicemail she had left. Something had come up, Millie had said, and so she was retracting Shilpa's invite. Shilpa couldn't afford to wait around, especially with Jane missing. She had to go back to the island, and this was her only chance.

Her phone buzzed again. It was a message. It started with the words 'important, please read'. Shilpa wasn't going to open it. She would pretend that she hadn't seen it. It was too late anyway. She was on the ferry.

'You'll be lucky if you make it back,' Josh shouted to the passenger seated closest to him. She was wearing a waterproof mac in a charcoal grey like the other two passengers. She turned her face away from the cold wind and driving rain. 'It's coming in, and they say it's going to last for some time.'

'The boss lady wants us,' the woman sitting next to Shilpa said, but the wind carried her words away from the ferryman, and he didn't hear. 'When the boss lady wants us, we go,' she said.

'Is that Millie?' Shilpa asked.

The woman eyed Shilpa with suspicion.

'I'm not a guest,' Shilpa explained. 'I worked at the house over New Year.'

'Show us your hands then,' the woman said. She introduced herself as Clara as she folded her arms across her ample chest.

Shilpa held her hands out for inspection.

'Them don't seem like working hands to me,' the lady said.

'I make cakes,' Shilpa clarified.

'So you were up at the house when she died?'

Shilpa nodded. She gave Clara scant details of what had happened that night. Clara didn't seem the sort to keep things to herself.

Clara mulled over what Shilpa had told her. 'So what them

are saying is most likely true,' she said, when they were halfway across the bay.

'What are they saying?'

Clara stared at Shilpa as if weighing up whether she was worthy of divulging such information. 'That he did it.'

'Who?'

'The old man who lives on the island.'

Shilpa leaned in. 'Who?' she asked. Then she remembered. 'David?' she said, remembering the grey-haired man with his scruffy dog, who had helped Robin when he had twisted his ankle.

'He's not right in the head. We all knew it was only a matter of time before, you know, he took a life.'

'Do you think that?'

'He never wanted anyone in his house. I offered to do the cleaning and cooking for him once, and he said no. A man on his own for so long like that goes a little crazy in the head, if you ask me.'

'He's never had a partner?' Shilpa asked.

Clara shrugged. 'None that I've noticed, and I've been working here years. What I have seen is him watching that one that died though. Not just looking, staring, and that gave me the heebie-jeebies.'

'You saw him staring at Felicity Grave?'

'Not just the once either. He used to sit in the grounds of Rose Cottage staring through that window at her in her swimming costume, if you could call it that, with this lost look in his eye. He thought no one knew, but we all saw it. I saw him at it twice from the mansion. You've got a good view from the pink bedroom en suite. Why would an old man like that be staring at a young girl if he wasn't interested in something?'

Shilpa gave Clara a half nod. She had almost forgotten that she had observed David in the gardens of Rose Cottage the first night they had stayed there and again right before they left the island. She had been sufficiently freaked out that first time not knowing who he was, but when she saw him there the second time, she thought him harmless enough, having spoken to him before. Now she wondered if her instincts were wrong.

'What was worse,' Clara said, 'was her mother. She knew what he was doing and never said anything. I mean, why would the Graves let that man stay on the island when he was blatantly perving on their daughter? They must be sick in the head.'

'Was Alan on the island at the time?' Shilpa asked.

'Him? No, never. But her ma was. I once saw her staring at David, who was gawping at her daughter. I expected her to go and give him a good telling off, but she didn't. She just dabbed her face with her handkerchief and went back to brushing her hair. She didn't treat her children right,' Clara said. 'Both of them damaged goods. I don't like to criticise mothers, we have it hard, but Jane Grave was more interested in herself and winning Alan back than her children. Felicity was a madam and Julian, well, if you've met him, you'll know what I mean.'

Shilpa gave the woman another half nod.

'If I can't come get you, you'll have to wait till this clears,' the ferryman was saying. 'I'm sure they can put you up. It wouldn't be the first time that this place was cut off due to poor weather conditions.'

Shilpa had read the weather report before she left this morning and had packed a bag just in case. She checked her phone as the ferry neared the shore. She had one bar of reception that she was going to lose the minute she stepped ashore. She had forgotten about the poor signal on the island. She had meant to tell Tanvi and Brijesh where she had gone. Not last night, because she knew her friends would try and talk her out of it, but she should have messaged them this morning.

Her phone rang, and Shilpa glanced at the display. It was Robin. Her heart leapt, and she answered it.

'Hey,' he said. The line was terrible. 'Thought you'd be up for the stall today.'

'Oh that,' said Shilpa. 'I'm not doing that today.'

'Some more time off?' Robin joked.

'Something like that.' The right thing would be to tell Robin where she was, but she knew that if she did, he would come after her. She hadn't spoken much to Robin about her investigation, but her boyfriend was no fool.

He knew what she was doing to keep herself entertained in his absence. Last night, after she had slipped into bed, he'd called, and during their conversation he had asked her for an update on the case. When she told him that Jane was missing, he was concerned. It was only then that Shilpa realised that Robin had some serious reservations about the Graves and what they were capable of.

'You're not doing anything foolish, are you?' he asked. 'Felicity's death isn't like the other cases. Someone on that island killed her in cold blood, and they may well kill again. You said yourself that Jane had information on her daughter, and now she's disappeared.'

'I'm doing some research on leasing a premises in town,' Shilpa said, trying to change the topic as she shielded herself and her phone from the rain. Strictly speaking it wasn't too far from the truth, as she had decided that this was an avenue she wanted to go down. If Jacinta was making it work in the dead of winter, why couldn't she? 'Where better to showcase my cakes than in my own bakery,' she said. 'It was a childhood ambition, and somewhere along the line, I lost sight of that.'

'Oh right,' Robin said. 'It's a great idea.'

'Listen,' Shilpa said. 'I need to go. The line is really bad. I'll call you later.' She barely heard his response as she disconnected. Shilpa stood up as the other passengers disembarked. Shilpa picked up her bag from under the tarpaulin that had been tied over the luggage to keep it dry and stepped off the boat into the wet sand.

She stared at the imposing yellow house through the pouring rain. How different the mansion appeared today from when she had last arrived full of hope and awe. Now the house was nothing more than a symbol of greed and death. She cowered from the rain as she made her way towards the house.

# Chapter Forty-Three

Millie held her fists by her sides. Shilpa was standing on the boat, waiting to disembark, and her blood began to thicken. *How dare she?* It had been a shock to receive a call from an old colleague yesterday, one she had never wanted to hear from again.

'It wasn't hard to track you down,' Beryl had said to her in that voice which was still as irritating as ever. Millie had to use all her willpower not to slam the phone down on the old bat. And it was lucky that she didn't, because Beryl had been insightful, telling her about Shilpa's visit to the Goldsmith Inn and the article she said she had been writing.

After the telephone call, Millie knew she had to do something. She watched as the passengers stepped onto the wet sand. She should have been waiting on the shore, despite the rain, so she could tell Josh to take Shilpa Solanki straight back to Parrot Bay.

Andreas had arrived yesterday though, and he had needed her in the kitchen. She had tried to put him off, but he was insistent, and with no further food deliveries coming to the island and a handful of hungry and important guests, she had no excuse not to go and ask what he needed.

Andreas had been well behaved since his arrival back on the island, agreeing to all her instructions and hardly answering back, which was unlike him. It was surprising that he was being so pleasant when before it was she that had needed to be nice to him. They needed him to make their guests happy. Despite her contacts, she had struggled to find another chef of Andreas's calibre at such short notice.

Millie knew that by the time she made her way to the beach, the ferry would already be making its return journey. There was no way Josh would be returning later that day given the forecast. The weather was rapidly deteriorating and Millie was going to be stuck with the cake woman who seemed to know too much. Shilpa stepped off the boat. Just one misstep and she could easily slip, hit her head on a rock.

Sadly, Millie hadn't the time to make such things happen. She would just have to put up with the woman for now. Millie had no one to blame but herself. She had invited the amateur sleuth back to the island because she was desperate to find out just how much the woman knew about the night Felicity died. Only Millie hadn't expected the other guests to arrive. The house was supposed to be empty.

Millie needed to speak to Duncan, but he had been avoiding her. They couldn't go on pretending that nothing had happened on New Year's Day. Since Felicity's death they had not been intimate at all. It felt like Leicester all over again, and she had sworn she wouldn't let things get that bad. Only they had, and this time it was worse, much worse. Forget the intimacy; Duncan wouldn't even look her in the eye.

Millie didn't have time to dwell on it. There were other more pressing matters at hand. She was, after all, the head of house, and she needed to ensure that all her guests were comfortable, that all their needs were met, and with the Graves that was always a tall order.

Millie straightened her glasses and smoothed down her pink satin pleated skirt. She put on her best smile and went to make sure the breakfast room was set up to her liking.

~

Shilpa paced in her room. She thought she would have been assigned a room in Rose Cottage, but to her surprise she was given a small room in the main house.

'There's been a leak at the cottage. A burst water pipe with the frost, and so you're in here,' Millie had said begrudgingly. 'And you didn't get any of my messages?'

'My phone's been playing up,' Shilpa said. 'Intermittently.'

The house manager practically pushed Shilpa and her holdall into the pale green and white room and shut the door behind her.

The room was small, possibly a study at one point in its life, but at least there was an en suite with a bath and a well-stocked minibar. Shilpa squatted down and opened the intricately carved door to a small cupboard next to the fridge and noticed the same cut glasses and green swizzle sticks that Felicity had used in the dining room on New Year's Eve. Shilpa closed the door and stood up. She stared out of the window. The room was small, but it would have a lovely view of the bay, currently obscured by the incoming rain. Shilpa sat on the bed and took off her wet shoes that she had squelched up the stairs in.

Shilpa had come to Dreamcatcher Mansion on a fact-finding mission, but it turned out that Andreas had been misinformed. The house was very much occupied, and Shilpa felt like a spare part. Although she did feel reassured by the presence of other guests on the island, and she now understood why Millie had suddenly wanted to cancel her invitation.

Shilpa sighed with relief. With other people around, she was safe. She could tell her boyfriend and friends where she was without making them panic.

Shilpa opened her messaging service on her phone and started typing, but when she hit send, the message failed. Of course it wouldn't send. She didn't have any phone reception or mobile data, and the wifi code she had used the last time she was on the island didn't work. She hopped off the bed and frantically searched for the wifi passcode, but she couldn't find it.

Shilpa found a dry pair of shoes from her luggage. She stepped outside her bedroom and padded over to the stairs, listening for voices. She could hear the clatter of cutlery and crockery from the dining room below, and she could smell freshly baked bread and bacon. As before, was she expected to stay out of the way of the residents? Millie hadn't said anything.

Shilpa was about to go back to her room when she saw a chef passing the bottom of the stairs with a large ceramic tureen. It wasn't just any chef but Andreas. She was about to shout down to him, but something held her back. The wifi code could wait for now. Instead, she needed to consider what she wanted to find out during her stay and how she was going to go about it. Shilpa made her way back to her room, closing the door behind her.

## Chapter Forty-Four

S hilpa had woken far too early this morning. She lay on the bed and considered what Clara had said on their journey to the island. She hadn't considered David a suspect in her investigation, but after what she had heard, it was only right that she did. Shilpa pulled out her phone and stared at it. If she had wifi she could have accessed the Land Registry webpage for Dreamcatcher Island. There was a slim possibility there was something on the title that explained David's presence.

Shilpa must have drifted off, because the next thing she knew, she could hear doors opening and closing. The guests were up. She could hear voices too. She glanced over to the clock in her room. It was nine o'clock.

Shilpa sat up and thought about what Millie had said. If the guests were uninvited or expected then it could only be one family. As realisation dawned, Shilpa heard a familiar voice echoing down the hall. Rashmi Grave was at Dreamcatcher Mansion. Someone on this island had murdered Felicity, their own flesh and blood, and if they could do that to their own, imagine what they could do to her

Shilpa wasn't going to be a prisoner at Dreamcatcher

Mansion. She tidied herself up and got ready to go downstairs to the kitchen to fix herself something to eat. As she took a step towards the imperial staircase, she heard another door open.

'You,' the voice said. 'What are you doing here?'

It was Rashmi. Shilpa explained that she had been invited by Millie. She made it clear that her invite had come before the Graves had decided to visit the island again.

'You can't leave this family alone, can you? Don't you have a family of your own?' Rashmi asked, adjusting her white fur gilet. She took a step towards Shilpa. 'My husband wanted us to be here for today, and unfortunately, due to this weather, we are stuck here for longer than we would like to be.' Rashmi glanced at her gold watch. 'Alan's going to speak to us in the drawing room, and I don't expect you to interrupt us. Do you understand?'

Shilpa nodded, but she wasn't going to slink back into her room like a child. She stood straight and made her way downstairs to the kitchen. She opened all the cupboards and drawers until she had located a bowl, a spoon, some cereal and some milk. She poured the cold milk over a bowl of cornflakes and pulled up a bar stool to eat. Rashmi Grave had got under her skin because she was poking her nose where it didn't belong. She just couldn't help herself.

It had been a foolish idea coming back to the island. She thought that being back in the house would help her find out what she was missing about Felicity's death. She was hoping to speak to Millie again and find out a little more about her suspects and narrow them down, because apart from the guests at Rose Cottage, everyone who had been on the island had reason to want Felicity Grave dead.

'Back so soon?' said a familiar voice.

Shilpa saw Andreas. She smiled. 'So are you,' she said.

'They called and I came running. The family helped me out when I needed a job. It's only right I help them out the only way I know how, with food. So I've reason to be here,' Andreas said. 'And you?'

'I came to talk to Millie.'

Andreas didn't respond. Shilpa asked Andreas for the wifi code. She still didn't have access to the outside world, and it put her on edge.

'It's on my phone,' he said. He patted his pockets. 'I don't have it with me though. Sorry.'

'Don't worry,' Shilpa said. 'I'll get it from Millie when I next speak to her.'

Andreas busied himself in a store cupboard. 'You're here deciding which one of us killed Felicity Grave, aren't you? Is that why you were so interested in my relationship with Felicity when you came to my mother's café?'

'I'm interested in the case,' Shilpa said.

'Okay,' he said with a forced smile. 'Good luck.' The chef walked towards the door. As he left the kitchen, she heard a ringtone. In the distance, Andreas said hello.

Shilpa pushed her bowl of cereal away. She wasn't hungry anymore.

'There you are,' Millie said as she walked into the kitchen with purpose. 'Was Andreas telling you one of his tales?'

'Tales?' Shilpa enquired.

'He cooks the most amazing food *and* stories.' Millie laughed. 'Let me guess, he told you the one about Felicity getting him a job here when he was destitute.' Millie picked a shiny red apple from the fruit bowl and sat on the bar stool next to Shilpa.

Shilpa gave a slight nod.

Millie took a bite of the apple 'It could be true, I suppose Felicity did put in a good word for him, but no one really knows if they went to the same college or if he convinced her to lie for him. He's good at making people believe things. Felicity wasn't the altruist he would like you to believe though. He idolised her, and it wasn't healthy. I'm sure you know all this,' Millie said, giving Shilpa a sideways glance. 'He had to flee Romania, you know. Nearly killed a man.'

'I didn't know that,' Shilpa said. Andreas had referred to an incident in his past when she saw him in his mother's café. She eyed Millie, who held her gaze, suggesting she was telling the truth.

'You haven't been doing your job then,' Millie said.

'It isn't my job—' Shilpa started, but Millie cut her off.

'No, it isn't,' she said, 'and yet you're doing a lot of snooping around.'

Millie ate her apple without taking her eyes off Shilpa. The house manager had been so professional before, careful not to disclose anything about the family, so what had changed? And was there any truth in what she was saying about the chef?

Millie glanced at her watch. 'I have about ten minutes, so what else did you want to know? Your email said you had questions. I assume Andreas isn't your main suspect.'

'I'm not investigating in any kind of official capacity,' Shilpa said.

Millie threw her head back and laughed. 'Of course not, but you have a journalist for a boyfriend, and I know your type. I knew it the minute you set foot on the island. Once you get it in your head that something isn't right, you dig, dig, dig until you get it. I thought I'd make your life easier, God only knows why. This was all before the family decided to return.'

'Why are they all here?' Shilpa asked. If Millie was in a talkative mood, let her talk.

Millie held the half-eaten apple away from her mouth. 'It's a private matter,' she said. 'Something to do with Mr Grave's health if I'm not mistaken. The press have got hold of the story, and it's going to be in the papers tomorrow. Mr Grave thought it best to let his family know before they read about it.'

So the younger generation of Graves had been correct when Shilpa and Tanvi had overheard them talking on New Year's Eve.

'He's dying,' Shilpa said.

'I don't think he's just got a cold.'

'Jane called me,' Shilpa said.

Millie didn't respond.

'She comes here in the summer?' Shilpa asked.

'Used to,' Millie said. 'Not so much now. I've heard she does come this way though and stays somewhere in Parrot Bay. Maybe Mr Grave no longer wants her on the island. He would be well within his rights to insist.'

'Have you seen her today?' Shilpa asked. She knew it was a long shot, but it was worth a try.

'Not since that weekend.'

Millie wasn't stupid. She knew what Shilpa was up to. But Shilpa couldn't be sure if the house manager wanted to assist or if she was leading her down a rabbit hole away from what really happened that night. Shilpa doubted the woman wanted to help her, which left the other option. Millie was trying to distract Shilpa away from the truth. There were only two reasons why Millie would want to do that: she either knew who the killer was and was protecting them, or she was protecting herself.

The house manager was a good liar, and Shilpa knew that believable lies had an element of truth in them. She wondered what other information she could get from her host. Millie had already alluded to Andreas having a violent past and the mind of a fantasist. Who else was she ready to throw under the bus to protect the killer?

'Do you think anyone had reason to harm Felicity?' Shilpa asked.

Millie eyed Shilpa with a serious expression. 'Everyone,' she said. 'Felicity was Alan Grave's firstborn. She was set to inherit the lot. Someone wanted to kill her for the money. Either to get it, or because they just didn't want her to have it.'

'So you think money was the sole motivator?' Shilpa asked. 'Not jealousy?'

'They were all jealous of Felicity, weren't they? It goes without saying. We all saw the way her brother was around her. Watching him gawk at her was enough to make you ill. And he wasn't the only voyeur.'

'David?' Shilpa enquired.

'My, my,' Millie said. 'You have been busy. Then of course there was Gina. She would deny this, but she wanted to be Felicity in every way, and Andreas, well, I've told you about him. He idolised her, and she didn't want anything to do with him.'

'Because she was in love with Richard.'

'Yes,' Millie said quietly.

'Although, I don't think she was. That last night on the beach during the fireworks, Felicity told Richard that she no longer wanted to be with him,' Shilpa said. She had been going over various scenarios in her mind, and that was the only one that made sense. At his engagement party Albie had said Felicity had turned Richard's proposal down. It made sense as to why they had been arguing on the beach that evening.

'Very observant,' Millie said.

'So who was she in love with?' Shilpa asked.

'Herself?' Millie offered with a fake laugh. There was something else in Millie's eyes though. Fear, hatred; it was there. Millie abruptly stood up and adjusted her cape. Shilpa noticed it was the same cape Millie had been wearing the night Felicity's body had been found. Millie thrust her hand into her pocket and retrieved a small photograph, which she stared at like some kind of meditation. Shilpa caught sight of the upside-down image. She had seen it before.

Millie quickly placed it back in her pocket.

'Who is that?' Shilpa asked.

'Who? It's my insurance policy,' Millie said with a small smile. 'Now, I must go. Is there anything else I can help you with?' As Millie leaned towards her, Shilpa could smell alcohol on her breath. That explained why the house manager was so keen to talk to her. Shilpa glanced at her watch. It was only just past ten in the morning.

Shilpa asked Millie for the wifi code. Millie pulled out her phone from her other pocket and gave it to Shilpa. 'We change the code around here regularly,' she said. 'It's important for our security as well as that of the guests'.'

Shilpa thanked her. 'There just isn't any way of contacting the outside world from here without wifi.'

'No, there isn't,' Millie said as she walked towards the door.

# Chapter Forty-Five

**B**ack in her room, Shilpa quickly typed out messages to Tanvi and Robin and sent them. She immediately got a message back from Tanvi asking her if she had completely lost her mind. Shilpa ignored her friend's remark and asked if she had heard back from Jane's neighbour.

After waiting for Jane, they had knocked on the neighbour's door, and a tall woman had answered, two ginger-haired children hiding behind her legs. They had asked her to contact them if Jane reappeared, and of course, they had left a note for Jane in her apartment asking her to call them urgently on her return.

Shilpa found the message she had sent to Robin again and could tell from the moving ellipses that he was typing. She waited a moment, but nothing came, so she sent Brijesh an email asking him to check the Land Registry to find out who owned Dreamcatcher Island. There was a reason why David lived on the island untroubled by the Graves, and Shilpa was determined to find out what it was.

Only David wasn't untroubled, was he? Both her boat companion and Millie had accused him of observing Felicity from a distance. Shilpa couldn't reconcile this version of the man with the one she had met, but that's what made sociopaths so feared, that they were undetectable in society.

It was unlikely that she was going to get anything more out of Millie today, and tomorrow when the weather cleared, they would expect her to head back. She didn't have much time, and there was one more person on the island Shilpa wanted to speak to. She would have to brave the elements in order to do so.

Shilpa stepped out of the door and closed it firmly behind her. Her coat zipped up and her hood pulled tight around her face, she braved the rain that whipped up the dark blue water of the infinity pool. Beyond the pool, Shilpa could hear the roar of the waves crashing against the shore as she hurried towards the rear of the house. Hard pellets of rain drove into her back as she hunched over and quickly walked towards David's house.

When she got there, she rang the doorbell and waited. The covered porch provided some shelter, but not enough.

No one came to the door and she thumped her fist against the old wood. She peered through the window into David's little cottage as she waited. After a minute or so and another three thumps on the door, she saw him scurrying towards her from the depths of the house.

'What are you doing out here?' he asked as he opened the door, annoyed that his morning had been interrupted. 'This weather's dangerous. No one should be out in it, especially on this island now.' David ushered her inside and told her to stand by the roaring fire by the large leather settees.

'I'll get you a towel,' he said as he slowly made his way upstairs. Shilpa was standing in a pool of water on what appeared to be a beautiful rug. His dog lifted his head and then lowered it again, turning away from her. Shilpa didn't mean to cause such a mess in the old man's house, but she had needed to speak to him. She shouldn't feel sorry for David, she reminded herself, recalling what Clara had said to her on the journey to Dreamcatcher Island.

David handed her a bright blue towel, which she patted her face with. He found a clothes drier, and Shilpa hung her coat on it.

David busied himself in the kitchen and came back with a mug of tea, which he passed to her. Shilpa took a sip and settled into the sofa, only realising then that the drink could be spiked. She refrained from taking another sip, even though it was doing wonders to banish the chill. She placed the cup on a coaster on the mahogany table and watched as David stoked the fire.

'What couldn't wait?' he asked, returning to his seat.

Shilpa hadn't expected him to be so direct. His tone was sharp, and it didn't suit him. He was a different man to the one she had met the last time they had been on the island. She could tread lightly on what she wanted to ask him or she could come right out with it. The latter was a risk. She was alone with no mobile reception. If David chose to, he could imprison her. Felicity wasn't much younger than Shilpa when she died. The thought of it made her shudder.

'Have the tea,' David said. 'It'll warm you up.'

Shilpa picked up her mug and warmed her hands, but she didn't take another sip. 'Felicity was killed,' Shilpa said, waiting for David's reaction. She saw a flicker of something in his eyes; fear or even worry perhaps. No, not that. It was sadness; remorse, perhaps.

David blinked and the emotion was gone. 'We know that,' he said. 'It's been on the news.'

'Did you know Felicity well?' Shilpa asked.

'She came to the island often, and like her father, she wasn't just interested in wealth but people as well. She would often walk this way.'

'She came into your home?' Shilpa asked, wondering if David was referring to Alan's generosity of letting him stay on the island.

'Once or twice,' he said, a slow smile creeping onto his face.

'So you knew her well?'

'Unfortunately not,' David said.

'Why do you stay on this island?' Shilpa asked.

'I think I told you all this last time. It suits my way of life.'

'And the Graves haven't tried to make you leave?'

David smiled. He tapped a finger to his nose, telling her it was none of her business.

'Some of the staff on the island say you had a fascination with Felicity,' Shilpa said, trying to keep her tone even.

David turned away. 'Some of the staff like to create mischief,' he said. 'They think I'm curious because I live alone here. They're trying to label me, and that's upsetting, but understandable I suppose. We all like to pigeonhole people, make people fit into our way of thinking.' He turned back to Shilpa. The warm look in his eyes had been replaced by something else, something cold.

'Do you know if anyone wanted to hurt Felicity?' she asked.

'You're not a detective,' David said. 'I'm not sure what you're after.'

There was a thunderous clap in the sky and a flash of light which lit up the living room before the electronic gadgets around the house buzzed and went silent.

'Power cut,' David said, by way of explanation. Even though it was only lunchtime, it was dark, with thick clouds in the sky and heavy rain. David lit a candle. The sound of the howling wind and rain was even more noticeable now the whizzing of the household electronics had stopped.

A tree branch tapped against the window, making both of them start. There was a loud crash from upstairs and a small yelp that sounded human. David instantly put his hand to his chest and stood up. His sleepy dog woke from his slumber too.

'What was that?' Shilpa asked.

He turned to her as if he had forgotten she was in his home. 'The wind,' he said. 'You shouldn't be here, and now I can't let you go.'

Shilpa straightened.

David was angry at her for being in his home, witness to whatever was happening upstairs. Another sound came from above. This time it was the distinct padding of feet on the floorboards.

'Who's up there?' Shilpa asked, standing up. She wavered a little, realising how foolish she had been in coming here herself without having told anyone of her whereabouts.

'No one,' David said. 'Just stay here.' He walked towards the stairs.

Shilpa grabbed her coat, still damp from the rain, and put it on. She couldn't stay here. David could be holding someone prisoner upstairs for all she knew, and she could be next. She would need to leave the house and make her way to Dreamcatcher Mansion in the storm. Once she was there, she could raise the alarm.

*Don't be silly,* a voice inside her said. David could have easily had a friend or lover staying over. It could be innocent. But Shilpa couldn't risk it. She needed to get out of there. With David preoccupied with whoever it was upstairs, it was her chance to leave. She knew she should, but she couldn't help but have a snoop around while he was distracted.

Shilpa glanced around the living room for clues as to who David's guest was, but there was nothing, just a train ticket from London. On the kitchen windowsill was a black-and-white photograph of a man and baby. The man was familiar, but Shilpa couldn't place him. She momentarily picked the frame up, studied it and placed it back down again. She picked up the train ticket. David had been to London recently. It didn't tell her anything other than that. Next, Shilpa peered into the kitchen. On the kitchen top there was a tray with a half-eaten bowl of soup and a piece of toast. Shilpa studied the bowl. It could have been David's. It could have been his guest's.

Shilpa could hear raised voices coming from upstairs. She tried to identify a second voice, but she could only hear David.

'No,' he was saying. 'She mustn't know. I won't let her.' It was then that Shilpa remembered the day Alan was on the beach shouting into the wind about a wretched man soon after Felicity's death. She had assumed it was Julian or perhaps even Albie or Richard, but now some instinct inside her told her that the wretched man that Alan was shouting about was David. Was that why Alan had said the island was cursed? Perhaps it had nothing to do with the local legend like Shilpa had assumed. It was closer to home.

Shilpa took a breath and hurried towards the front door. She tried the handle, but it wouldn't budge. Had it been bolted? When had David locked the door? She thought back. When she was drying her face with the towel and had been distracted? It must have been then. She heard a soft growling behind her and turned to face the old grey dog, who was baring his teeth and pink gums.

Shilpa turned and put her hand on the door handle again. It wouldn't give.

'I told you not to leave,' a voice said from behind her.

## Chapter Forty-Six

'I told you not to leave,' David said again.

Shilpa spun around. David was standing on the stairs, staring at her like she was crazy. Behind him stood a woman, eyes red raw from crying.

Shilpa's hand flew to her mouth. 'Jane,' she said, staring at the woman incredulously.

David's eyes softened. 'It's dangerous out there. You could get hurt.'

'Come,' Jane said. 'Sit with us.'

Shilpa took off her damp coat and hung it on the clothes dryer. She sat on the chair closest to the door and asked why the door was locked.

'I always lock it with a key when there's a storm or it blows open,' David said.

Shilpa turned towards Jane, but she looked at her blankly.

'Here,' David said, fishing the key from his pocket and placing it on the coffee table in front of them.

'What are you doing here?' Shilpa asked Jane. 'You called me to your home in London, but when I got there, the place was abandoned. The fridge had been left open, there was a half-drunk mug of tea on the side and a packed bag by the door, containing your passport.'

Jane put the back of her hand to her forehead. 'I'm so heedless,' she said. 'And since Felicity died I'm even worse. I was expecting you, but I had also called for a taxi to take me to the train station before we spoke. I thought you'd be in Devon, you see. The taxi arrived, and I just left with my handbag. I had meant to go down to tell him to wait, but when I got there, I saw no reason not to just get in. I thought it safer to just come here, because I was in a bit of a state. Felicity's death has just… well, it has affected me.'

'Why had you packed your passport?' Shilpa asked.

'Because I'd had enough. I want to leave England and the Graves behind and just go someplace else.'

'Which won't work,' David said kindly. He put his hand on her knee. 'Her grief will just follow her around.'

'I never did right by my kids, and in the end, when I tried to put things right, it went wrong. Oh so wrong.'

'What did you do?' Shilpa asked.

Jane turned to David, and something passed between them. 'Nothing,' she mumbled. 'Nothing.'

Shilpa waited in the awkward silence. David moved his hand from Jane's knee and put his arm around her shoulders.

'Why are you here?' Shilpa asked.

Jane gazed at David. 'Because I love him,' she said.

Shilpa sank into a warm bath and closed her eyes. After Jane had explained their story she had excused herself. She claimed she was tired, but to Shilpa it was obvious that she just didn't want to talk anymore. Shilpa had decided to return to the house.

'I can't let you go out in this,' David had said, but Shilpa had explained that although she appreciated his concern, she was going back.

David eventually nodded and picked up the key from the coffee table. As he had walked over to the front door, he asked her why she was back on the island. 'You said it yourself,' he said in hushed tones. 'Felicity was killed here on the island. Someone on this island murdered her. You're running around playing detective and you aren't being very discreet. It could get you into trouble if you're not careful. They're all back, aren't they?'

Shilpa had nodded. David gazed towards the ceiling and opened his mouth as if to say something, but then he closed it again. 'Keep safe,' he had said. 'I said something similar to Felicity the last time I saw her and look what happened there.' Shilpa saw the sadness again in his eyes. She had waited while David opened the door. 'Godspeed,' he had said, and Shilpa stepped out into the elements.

Shilpa replayed her morning with David again. Something was troubling her. Eventually she realised what it was. It was the photo of the man and the baby she had found in David's house. The man was familiar, but where had she seen him before?

Then it came to her. Shilpa quickly stepped out of the bath and put on the complimentary robe. Padding over to the dresser, she opened the drawer. As expected, there was a folder of information about the house and the facilities. She flicked through the pages but couldn't find what she was searching for. She located her phone and found the website for Dreamcatcher Island.

It only took a few minutes to find it. It was all starting to make sense. She dialled Brijesh's number and asked if he had managed to locate the title and register like she had asked. When he told her he had, she immediately asked him to email it over.

'You should have checked your email before calling,' Brijesh said. 'Anyway, I already reviewed it, and there wasn't much in there.'

Shilpa's heart sank. Brijesh knew his stuff. If there was something to uncover, he would have found it. She thanked her friend for his time, told him not to say anything to Robin, who she knew he was in regular contact with, and disconnected.

Opening her email, she found what she was after. From the first page of the title register, she realised that Brijesh was right. It didn't tell her anything she didn't already know.

Shilpa put her phone down and got ready. She shifted her focus to the bay as she put her gold earrings in. The storm had subsided, and although it was still raining, it had eased. The body of water past the infinity pool was visible. For now, no boats would be on the water. The family were trapped on the island, as was she. They had nowhere to go, and she had questions. It was the perfect opportunity.

Shilpa had her suspicions as to what had happened to Felicity the day she died. She knew who the murderer was, but there was still a piece of the puzzle missing. Picking up her phone she scrolled through the Land Registry document again. There was definitely nothing on the first page, but as she examined the rest of the document, she caught her breath. With some conviction, she made her way downstairs.

## Chapter Forty-Seven

Shilpa gently opened the door to the drawing room. Instantly the family fell silent. All eyes were on her, and she in turn observed each one of them.

Alan Grave appeared to have been mid-conversation with Andreas, who had just served him a small plate of petit fours. Duncan was adjusting a stereo on the mahogany dresser that wasn't playing any music, and Julian was holding a cut-glass vessel of dark liquid, head drooped like a bored teenager at his parents' party.

Richard – Shilpa was surprised he had been invited to this gathering – appeared out of place standing by the bookshelf at the back of the room. Rashmi and Albie were sitting with their heads close together as if they had been deep in conversation, and Gina was standing at the window holding a half-empty glass of champagne. She was wearing a bright yellow sundress, completely out of keeping with the time of year. She picked up a white shawl that had been draped over the back of a chair and pursed her lips at the intruder.

'Sorry to interrupt,' Shilpa started. Ten minutes ago it had seemed like the perfect opportunity to speak to the family and reveal to them what she had only just uncovered, but now, with all eyes on her, it didn't seem right. She took a breath. She was here, and there was no going back. This was her one opportunity to get to the truth and confront a killer. She would be safe amongst all of them, she reasoned. She pushed away the idea that the Graves would stick together to protect their own.

'So why are you here?' Rashmi asked, as prickly as ever. She adjusted her black-and-white camellia brooch.

'I know what Felicity was going to announce the night she was murdered,' Shilpa said. She held her hands together to stop them from shaking.

'Have a seat,' Alan said. 'The others may not want to know. It may hurt them to know, but I don't have anything to lose anymore. So please, sit down and tell us what you know. Millie, can you make our guest comfortable?'

Shilpa turned. Millie was at the door, her face ashen. She pulled up a velvet chair, and Shilpa walked over to it. A minute later, Millie had handed her a glass of Bollinger.

'Go on then, if you know who killed my sister,' Julian said, his bored expression gone. He took a seat close to Shilpa, making her shift in her chair.

Shilpa pressed her lips together. She hadn't quite said that, but why else was she here, interrupting a personal family gathering like this if she hadn't some important news to divulge.

'This is ridiculous,' Millie said. 'I'm so sorry, Mr Grave. I'll have her removed from the premises right away.' Millie started towards her, but Alan held out a hand to stop her. 'Are you sure, Mr Grave? She has no authority here, and she's been digging around in all of our pasts. It's unethical.'

'Because I spoke to your previous work colleague?' Shilpa asked Millie.

Millie's face turned red, but she held Shilpa's gaze. 'You had no right to do that.'

'I was curious about your past,' Shilpa said. 'You were in Felicity's room so soon after her death. You were so quick to get rid of the cocaine.' There was a murmuring of acknowledgement around the room. 'And why do you keep a photo of your first victim in the pocket of your cape?' Shilpa had recognised the photo earlier when it had fallen out of Millie's pocket. The online article Shilpa had found about the housekeeper Millie had attacked at the Goldsmith Inn included a grainy picture of the victim. Shilpa was certain the picture was of the woman Millie had confronted.

Millie's jaw dropped open. It was the first time she was speechless.

'It's her insurance policy,' Duncan said from the other side of the room. 'Something to show me, to warn me of what she is capable of so that I don't betray her again.' Duncan turned to Alan. 'My wife roughed up a woman about fifteen years ago now. I cheated on her. Millie took it badly. It was why we moved away.'

'Twice,' Millie said. 'We moved away twice because you were cheating. In London I never did anything. I was disgusted with myself for what I did in Leicester. I wouldn't do anything like that again.'

Duncan shook his head, and Millie collapsed into a velvet chair. 'You were having an affair with Felicity. I'm not stupid,' she cried. 'I've seen the photos on your computer. Your password wasn't hard to guess. I know you were with her on New Year's Eve. You came back to the cottage stinking of alcohol and blamed the other guests for detaining you. I may have turned a blind eye before, Duncan, but I wasn't going to that night. I came to confront you, but as soon as I entered the house I heard the commotion. I waited in the study until Mr Grave called as I knew he would. I fix things for the guests of this house, and that was exactly what I was doing when I flushed away the cocaine. You wouldn't want a scandal like that getting into the papers.'

The group were silent. 'Duncan was in love with Felicity,' Shilpa said. 'But he wasn't the only one.'

'Come on,' Andreas said. 'This was why you were giving me the third degree at my mother's café, isn't it?'

'You've been on the run from the police before,' Millie said. 'In Romania. You told me once when you were drunk.'

Andreas scowled. 'I did nothing wrong. It was self-defence.'

'The police didn't see it that way. You loved Felicity and couldn't have her, so you didn't want anyone else to,' Millie said, giving Duncan a cold stare.

Andreas sighed. 'I may have been Felicity's lover, but I knew where I stood with her, always. I accepted my position for what it was.'

At Andreas's words, Duncan flew at the chef. He landed a blow just under his left eye. Andreas yelped in pain but didn't retaliate. Instead, he started to sob. 'I loved Felicity. I'd never have hurt her.'

'I wasn't talking about you,' Shilpa said. 'I was referring to Richard.'

Richard, who had been trying to disappear into the walls during this exchange, took a step forward. 'Of course I loved Felicity. We were going to get married. It was what Felicity was going to announce the night she died,' he said, his eyes shifting around the room.

'Is that how you weaselled your way here today?' Duncan said. 'She wasn't going to marry you, and she had told you as much during the fireworks. You never loved Felicity. You were just after her money. It's why you invented this cock-and-bull story about your impending engagement on the slim chance that you would get left something in the will,' Duncan turned to Alan. 'I hope you're smart enough not to leave him a penny.'

'He's right,' Albie said. 'Richard pretty much admitted that Felicity had rejected him.'

Alan coughed and wiped his mouth with a monogrammed handkerchief. 'Well, this certainly has been informative.' His eyes shifted from Shilpa to Duncan. 'As outsiders to this family, you won't know that my inheritance is already predetermined by a family tradition,' he said. He turned back to Shilpa. 'Or maybe you will know if you've been thorough.'

'But that's just a tradition,' Gina said. 'Traditions can be broken.'

'Is that what you were hoping for?' Shilpa asked. 'That the money would be left to you despite not being the firstborn?' Shilpa saw Gina lift her arm and quickly ducked, narrowly avoiding the champagne flute that Gina hurled at her. Alan's words came back to Shilpa from their first encounter in the kitchen of Dreamcatcher Mansion. His children were greedy and would do anything to get at his money.

'How dare you?' she asked as the glass smashed against the wall. 'Who are you? A nobody with nothing better to do than to get involved in another family's business. You want to know where everyone was when Felicity died, is that it? Will that make you walk away?

'I was in bed with Albie if you must know,' Gina continued. Albie gave his fiancée an uncertain look. 'Mum was with Dad, weren't you?'

Rashmi nodded.

'No,' Alan said. 'She wasn't.'

'Alan,' Rashmi said in a low voice.

'It seems everyone is getting things out in the open, so we may as well too,' Alan said. 'I woke and noticed you weren't there that night. You crept back into the room later. Where were you?'

Rashmi's eyes shifted from her daughter to Albie. 'I was just taking a walk,' she said.

Alan laughed. 'You hate walking at the best of times. You take a cab for a five-minute journey in Marylebone.'

'She was with me,' Albie said. Gina shot her fiancé a look. 'You were asleep,' said Albie, 'and I needed to speak to your mother.'

'About what?' Alan said.

'About the affair she's having with *my* mother,' Albie said.

# Chapter Forty-Eight

Rashmi turned away.

'Sorry,' Albie said, looking from mother to daughter. 'It's out now.'

'Because you know Alan is not long for this world and you have no need to blackmail me anymore,' Rashmi said. She stood up. 'I don't need to listen to any more of this.'

'Oh, I think you do. Sit back down,' Alan commanded his wife, and surprisingly she listened. 'I had a feeling something was amiss. It's why I visited my solicitor recently.'

'And Richard, where were you when my sister died?' Julian asked, breaking the tension in the room.

Richard stuttered before finding his words. 'I-I was taking a walk. I needed to clear my head.' He paused. 'And you, Julian? We all know your relationship with Felicity was less than perfect.'

'I was in my room, alone,' Julian said. 'I can't give you an alibi, but I certainly didn't kill my sister.'

'Is that all we have, your word?'

Julian shrugged. 'Believe what you will.'

'So,' Gina said, staring at Shilpa. 'Now that we've all told you what we were doing, will you leave us alone?'

Shilpa nodded. 'I will, but not before I tell you what I've discovered.'

'And what's that?'

'I know what Felicity wanted to disclose the night she was killed. Because on New Year's Eve, Felicity found out about her father, and she wanted to let everyone know,' Shilpa started tentatively.

'That Daddy's dying? What has that got to do with her death?' Gina turned towards Alan. 'Did Felicity know before all of us?' she asked, her voice laced with jealousy.

Alan shook his head. 'I only recently found out just what little time I have left...' He trailed off, his eyes glazed over. Then he turned back to Shilpa, focusing again. 'Felicity may have had a guess at what was happening with me. She was certainly perceptive like that, but she didn't know for certain. It's preposterous to say she did.'

Shilpa heard Rashmi laugh as she replied, 'I didn't mean that Felicity knew about your health, Mr Grave.'

'Then what did she know?' Gina challenged.

'The business?' Rashmi said. 'She was going to say something about our dealings in India. She didn't understand how things work over there. She had misunderstood, that was all.'

'Not about your business,' Shilpa said.

'Then what?' Rashmi asked.

'About her parentage,' Shilpa said.

'Meaning?' Gina said, taking a step towards Shilpa. Shilpa wished that she hadn't sat down. The Graves were closing in on her and she had nowhere to go.

'Meaning that Alan Grave wasn't her father. Felicity found out hours before she died. It was why she was arguing with her mother before the firework display.'

Gina was stunned into silence. Shilpa observed Alan. His face said it all. Her guess had been correct. It had all started to fall into place when Clara, her morning boat companion, had told her about David staring at Felicity.

At first she had assumed that David was a pervert, which was the same conclusion Clara and Millie had drawn. But then she started piecing it together. When she had spoken to Jane at Leoni's back in Otter's Reach, she had spoken of the party where Felicity was conceived and mentioned that she loved a man but hadn't realised until recently, and then she had trailed off.

Shilpa had assumed Jane had been talking about Alan, but it was only when she saw them together at David's cottage earlier that she realised that Jane had been talking about David.

That was why David would watch Felicity from afar: she was his daughter. He had mentioned that Felicity was just like her father in caring for other people. Shilpa assumed he was talking about Alan, but he had been talking about himself. Just hours ago, at David's cottage, before Shilpa had left, Jane had told her that she was in love with David, that they had been together the night Felicity had been conceived. It was the reason she returned to the island so often with her children.

'You knew who Felicity's real father was?' Shilpa said to Alan. 'That day you screamed about a wretched man on the beach not long after your daughter's death, you were referring to David. I thought you were referring to Richard for not keeping your daughter safe, but you were talking about David, your younger brother.'

Shilpa had done her research, and she explained what she had uncovered to the group. After realising the connection from the photo she had discovered in David's house and linking it to the one of Alan and his parents on the Dreamcatcher Island website, she realised there was a family connection. David was younger than Alan, or so his online professional profile told her, and by Shilpa's reckoning, it was likely that David was illegitimate.

Alan's father had purchased Dreamcatcher Island knowing full well that his illegitimate son had recently moved there on his coin. When Shilpa read through the title documents for the island, she clearly saw that no part of the island could be sold without permission from David Alexander. Shilpa presumed David used his mother's surname, and why not if his father wanted nothing to do with him, except to pay for his home.

In addition to that, Alan and David's father had given David a life interest in Dreamcatcher Island, therefore keeping the family tradition of leaving everything to Alan but still ensuring his other son had a place to live. David was the reason why Alan believed the island to be cursed.

There was an audible gasp from the group.

'He only found out the day Felicity died,' Jane said. Shilpa turned to see her standing in the doorway of the drawing room. 'I shouldn't have kept it a secret for so long, but I had little choice. Knowing I had slept with his brother the night we met would have killed Alan, and I loved him too much, or at least I thought I did back then. I was mistaken.

'I should have left you years ago for David,' Jane said, her eyes on Alan. 'David waited for me all this time, and even after our divorce I never let him love me. I punished myself because of the shame of what I did that night.' Jane shook her head. 'When I used to come here with the kids, I used to occasionally meet David at Rose Cottage when the children were asleep, but I put an end to it after a while. I couldn't continue that way. To this day, David still returns there to remember us and what we had. He never stopped loving me.'

Alan paced the room with his walking stick and then turned to each one of them. 'I wanted an island to host my thirtieth,' he said. 'I was the youngest person in our family to make the cover of *The Greats Magazine*. My father wasn't going to say no to me.' Alan puffed out his chest and smiled.

'I wanted somewhere in the Caribbean, naturally. Father convinced me otherwise, and I had to admit this place had a certain charm.'

'There's nowhere like it,' Jane said.

Alan ignored her. 'It was where my parents first met. Not here at Dreamcatcher but in Devon. I agreed and asked no questions when my father said there were a few staff living on the island. I took no notice of who was here. It didn't interest me. And then…' Alan gave an audible sigh. 'I saw him and I knew. Something inside me knew.

'My father had invited him to my party. There were hundreds of guests here that night. We had a band, free-flowing champagne, and the party planners went to town with the lighting. Amidst all that, despite all the alcohol I had consumed, I knew the moment my eyes met his.' Alan shook his head, recalling the painful memory.

'David held my gaze, and something inside me hardened. I couldn't believe the audacity of my father. My mother had been at the party too. She couldn't have noticed my brother because if she had, she would have known. He was the spit of my father.

'My father wasn't someone you could confront. I never said anything, but I vowed never to return. Only Jane was keen to come back. She pleaded with me every year.'

Jane said, 'And you let me because it gave you the freedom from me that you so craved. You didn't want to be tied down with a wife and child.'

'No, I didn't,' Alan said, staring at Jane. 'If I'd known of your deception then, I'd never have stayed.'

'Felicity wasn't your daughter?' Gina asked, her eyes boring into Alan, her voice two octaves higher.

'What difference does it make?' Rashmi asked. She was sitting on the edge of her chair.

'It makes all the difference,' Gina said, the colour draining from her face.

Rashmi was shaking her head in silent persuasion, trying to convince her daughter not to say anything further, but there was no stopping Gina now.

'It's all your fault, Mother. You and your pride. Does everyone know what you told me the weekend of Felicity's party?' There was an audible silence.

'Come on,' Albie said to Gina. 'Let's just leave it.'

Gina scanned the room. 'She told me in the cinema room, of all places, that Alan is my real dad. That I was conceived out of wedlock, but Mummy's family were too conservative to accept Daddy into the fold. Daddy was still married at the time, and so Mummy hid it from everyone, including me. Can you believe my whole life I thought I was adopted by Alan Grave when in fact I wasn't? I am his flesh and blood.'

'And by family tradition, the one to inherit his entire wealth,' Shilpa said. 'You believed that Felicity was his blood and his firstborn.'

'You had Gina before I was born,' Julian said, his eyes resting on his father. His jaw was set and his fists clenched. Alan gave a slow nod. 'You're pathetic.'

'I'm pathetic, yet you take my money every chance you get,' Alan sneered.

Julian took a step towards his father, but Jane was quick to intervene, putting a hand on Julian's chest.

Shilpa turned to Gina. 'When your mother told you that Alan was your biological father, you were angry that she had kept it from you, but at the same time this was good news. You were blood related to Alan. You would inherit the money you so badly wanted if only you were first in line. You knew Julian was younger than you, so you immediately discounted him, but Felicity stood in your way.'

Gina was shaking her head.

'You had to get rid of her, and the only way you knew how to do that was to murder her,' Shilpa said. 'You knew she favoured a Negroni. We all saw her knocking them back that night.'

'She liked her alcohol,' Julian said. 'She even took a stash down to the boathouse in her silver case for when she was playing dead.'

Shilpa kept her eyes on Gina. 'I noticed that all the rooms have a well-stocked minibar. You made up the drink in your room and added a splash of potassium cyanide. Easily obtainable when you're a jeweller,' Shilpa said, recalling her conversation with Brijesh. 'Then you paid her a visit, drinks in hand, for a sisterly chat. Is that right?'

Gina was staring at Shilpa. 'We talked about my engagement, the wedding,' she said.

'She was your stepsister,' Shilpa said. 'And still you–'

'She was set to get everything,' Gina said.

'You left her with the poisoned drink and then planted the drugs in her drawer. You waited for Felicity to fall, smeared cocaine around her nostrils to make it appear like an overdose, emptied the contents of the glass from her balcony and made your way back to your room, washing and returning the glass to your own minibar, while my friend and I were racing up the stairs,' Shilpa said.

'I didn't know she wasn't blood related–' Gina started.

'Stop,' Alan said. 'Just stop this. The tradition is nothing more than tradition. Everyone would have got their fair share. I was going to divide my wealth equally. This is ridiculous. I'm not even dead yet.'

All eyes were on Alan. Gina saw her opportunity. She made a dash for the door, and Albie followed. Duncan and Millie started after her. Shilpa knew exactly where they were headed. She ran towards the dining room and used the door that led to the swimming pool to leave. Shilpa made her way down the wet, slippery steps to the boathouse, but she was too late. In the distance Albie and Gina, in her bright yellow dress, were already on the water.

'We need to call the police,' Duncan said as he and Mille came up behind Shilpa.

Shilpa glanced towards Parrot Bay. A boat was heading towards them. She recognised the silhouette of one of the passengers instantly. 'They're already on their way,' she said.

## Chapter Forty-Nine

Shilpa stood on the beach with Robin's arms around her. He had arrived with DS Sharpe moments ago. Shilpa explained what had happened as the detective radioed the police boat that had been following them.

'You came,' Shilpa said, turning to Robin.

'I couldn't just leave you here with this lot,' Robin said. 'Not after receiving your message. Tanvi and Brijesh were worried too.'

'I thought you were still in London.'

'I came back early,' he said.

Two police boats caught up with Gina and Albie. The couple reluctantly climbed aboard one, and within ten minutes they were pulling up to the island.

The Grave family watched from the bay as Gina and Albie stepped onto the wet sand. Alan Grave was as frail as ever, standing with support from his stick while his daughter spoke to the police.

The heavy rain had ceased, but there was a light drizzle still, and it was bitterly cold. Only Rashmi appeared uncomfortable with the temperature. Her white rabbit fur gilet wasn't enough for Devon in January. The rest of the family were unfazed by the weather. The revelations of the afternoon had numbed them.

Shilpa heard soft voices behind her and turned. David had joined Jane on the beach with his dog. He put his arm around her, and she leaned into him. David turned towards Alan who stared at David for a moment before turning towards his daughter, who was being read her rights.

Alan had avoided his brother for thirty years, and it didn't seem like he wanted to make up for that lost time now, even though he was dying. His father's infidelity had nothing to do with David and still Alan couldn't cope with the deception, or like Gina, had he just been jealous of David? Like father, like daughter. The Graves were a strange bunch.

How terrible it must have been for David to be given such a small cottage when his brother had the right to live in the big mansion. Yet David didn't show any signs of resentment. He had been dealt his hand, and he had played accordingly. The Graves could learn a thing or two from him.

Shilpa turned from the brothers and noticed that Rashmi was staring at her husband, willing him to look at her. They were Gina's parents; they had to support their daughter through this, but it was unlikely that Alan was going to forgive his cheating wife anytime soon.

It had been curious and cruel to have kept Gina in the dark about her parentage, but Shilpa knew what it meant to save face in India. Keeping Gina's true father a secret must have been the price Rashmi was willing to pay to live the life she wanted with consent from her family. A high price, but perhaps Rashmi didn't believe it would cause any real damage given Alan was bringing Gina up as his own.

It wasn't the truth about Gina's biological father that had motivated Gina to kill. It was the inheritance. Gina knew Alan

Grave was her real dad when she killed Felicity; she just didn't realise that Felicity wasn't Alan's blood. Her fiancé had been ready to help her. Albie had told Shilpa that someone was going to get hurt on the island that weekend, and he had been right. If Gina hadn't already been thinking along the lines of murder, she would have been prompted by Albie. Shilpa was sure of it.

Julian walked up to his mother, hands in his pockets. 'Well, if this show is over, I need to be getting back.' He tilted his head to one side as he studied David, then he shrugged and turned towards his mother.

'Julian,' Jane said, her eyes pleading with him. 'Stay, just a little longer. We don't know yet what will happen to Gina.'

'You care about what is going to happen to her?'

Jane shook her head vehemently. 'I want to be sure that justice will be served.'

'I can tell you now, Mother, that they are not going to guarantee you that today. There will be lots of negotiation and countless legal fees for Dad before that happens.'

Jane bit her fingernails.

'You don't think that Father is just going to leave Gina to perish in a police cell, do you?'

Jane didn't say anything, but Shilpa could tell from her expression that she hadn't considered another option. Gina had killed her daughter, but Gina was very much Alan's blood. He would get her the best lawyer there was.

'I'm going,' Julian said. 'There's something I need to deal with sooner rather than later.' Julian's eyes shifted, and Jane turned away.

'What?' David asked what Jane was too afraid to. 'What is it that you need to deal with that can't wait?'

Julian looked David up and down. He sucked his teeth. 'A cat,' he said eventually. 'My neighbour's, if you must know. It was making a racket, and now it's dead on a rug on my sofa.

The whole place must be reeking by now, not to mention the maggots.'

Jane buried her face in David's chest. David gave Julian a tight smile and watched as the awkward brother of Felicity Grave walked away.

# Chapter Fifty

S hilpa sat on the floor of the bathroom and waited. When the three minutes were up, she looked at the stick and then opened the door.

'So?' Robin asked.

'Life is going to get a little crazy,' Shilpa said.

Robin pulled her towards him and held her close. Shilpa beamed. 'You are never going to scare me again like that,' he said. 'When I got your message, I was beside myself. I knew I had to call DS Sharpe and tell him what you were doing.'

'What do you think will happen to Gina?'

Robin shrugged. 'She should get life,' he said. 'Maybe she'll get out on good behaviour.'

'She has a good solicitor,' Shilpa said. 'A great one.'

'Speaking of solicitors, did you find out from Jane why she was visiting her solicitor that day in Otter's Reach?'

'Turns out she had found a purchaser for her family home here and she was signing the paperwork.'

'So nothing sinister,' Robin said.

'You can't blame me for thinking that. She had beautiful pieces of jewellery, and I was curious as to how she afforded it.

259

Alan gave Felicity money. Jane could have had a financial motive for visiting her solicitor so soon after her daughter's death. I didn't think for one minute that she was the killer, but she could have wanted to benefit from Felicity's death.'

'The jewellery was from David?'

Shilpa nodded.

Robin gave Shilpa a hug. 'Gina killed one of their own, and they're still supporting her. You were lucky you got off Dreamcatcher Island alive.'

'Millie and Duncan invited me back,' Shilpa said. 'They're working through things, apparently. They're staying on the island to run the mansion despite the change in ownership. Alan has gifted the island to his brother.'

'So there is a happy ending of sorts,' Robin said. 'I hope you have no plans to return to that place.'

Shilpa shook her head. 'I think I'll have other things keeping me busy,' she said, pulling away from Robin and putting a hand on her belly. Robin leaned forward and kissed her.

'It won't be just the baby keeping you busy,' he said. 'I may have done something a little drastic and out of character.'

'What?' Shilpa asked.

'Jacinta's.'

'My arch-rival.'

'Well, it turns out that her café was just a pop-up. Her well-to-do husband was only here on business, and now he's done she's going with him to Texas or somewhere like that and...'

'And?'

'The shop was fitted out and ready to let, and so I just thought... You've always wanted your own place, haven't you?' Robin pulled out a key from his pocket. 'It's yours if you want it? Do you want to go and take a peek?'

Shilpa didn't need to think twice. This was the push she needed. Jacinta had shown her that it was possible to be successful in the middle of a Devon winter. Shilpa would be there all year. She would make Sweet Treats more than a success. Shilpa grabbed the key from Robin and then picked up her coat and bag from the sofa.

'Come on,' she said, full of enthusiasm and hope.

'You ready?' he asked.

Shilpa smiled. 'Let's go.'

## THE END

# Acknowledgements

A massive thank you to all my friends and family. In particular Neha for her limitless knowledge on all things baking, Jigna for the great title and Subrina for her continual support. This book is dedicated to you. A thank you goes to Anna and Dad, Carl, Jan and Bruce for their encouragement and James, Nathan and Sophie who have to put up with the endless hours I spend tapping away.

A special thanks goes to Tony Prior who read and critiqued a first draft of this book; your comments were invaluable. Thanks to Emily Nemchick for your initial edit and a big thank you to the team at Bloodhound Books, in particular Clare Law for her insightful editing and Tara Lyons for keeping me on track.

Finally, a big thank you goes to the readers of my books. It's your support that keeps me going!

# A note from the publisher

**Thank you for reading this book**. If you enjoyed it please do consider leaving a review on Amazon to help others find it too.

**We hate typos.** All of our books have been rigorously edited and proofread, but sometimes mistakes do slip through. If you have spotted a typo, please do let us know and we can get it amended within hours.

**info@bloodhoundbooks.com**